JANE ISAAC

EVIL INTENT

Legend Press Ltd, 51 Gower Street, London, WC1E 6HJ
info@legendpress.co.uk | www.legendpress.co.uk

Contents © Jane Isaac 2022
The right of the above author to be identified as the author of this work has
been asserted in accordance with the Copyright, Designs and Patents Act
1988. British Library Cataloguing in Publication Data available.

Print ISBN 978-1-80031-0-100
Ebook ISBN 978-1-80031-0-117
Set in Times. Printing managed by Jellyfish Solutions Ltd
Cover Design by Rose Cooper | www.rosecooper.com

Jane Isaac studied creative writing with the Writers Bureau and the London School of Journalism. Jane's short stories have appeared in several crime fiction anthologies. Her debut novel, *An Unfamiliar Murder*, was published in the US in 2012, and was followed by five novels with Legend Press: *The Truth Will Out* in 2014, *Before It's Too Late* in 2015, *Beneath the Ashes* in 2016, *The Lies Within* in 2017, and *A Deathly Silence* in 2019.

Jane lives in rural Northamptonshire with her husband, daughter and dog, Bollo.

Visit Jane at
janeisaac.co.uk
or on Twitter
@JaneIsaacAuthor

In memory of the late Helen Sargeant, taken far too soon.

Also to Martin Sargeant – one of the most talented artists I know and a dear friend.

PROLOGUE

Across the dark fields, Shauna runs. Where stones in the soil pick at her stockinged feet and clods of earth conspire to throw her off balance.

Footfalls thud the ground behind her. He doesn't speak, doesn't call out. But she's already seen the hunger in his eyes, the visceral determination.

The tall firs of Blackwell Wood loom in the distance. It's her beacon, her chance for safety. Somewhere to think. Somewhere to hide.

She trips, hears the tear of her dress as she clambers back up and glances over her shoulder. The tunnel of light is blinding. She quickens to a sprint, tears streaking her face, lungs burning. Over the low fence and into the wood. Veering off at a side path, breaking through the bracken.

He's behind her, zigzagging through the undergrowth, his presence signalled by flickers of torchlight bouncing off the tree trunks. But not for long. Shauna knows this wood better than anyone. She grew up near here. Hacked her horse along its bridleways, explored the back paths and gullies with her brother, Tom.

She navigates east towards the river, away from the firs. To the broad-leafed trees with their wide protective branches and dark canopy. Tall, strong. Like Tom. Self-preservation numbing her torn, bleeding feet. Her toe catches a root, her ankle turns. She falls again. Splays her hands to gain purchase, staggers back up. He's so close now she can smell him: stale sweat, the thick nicotine in the folds of his clothes.

A bramble rips at her cheek as she lunges forward.

She needs to make it to the river. There's a recess there where the bank has eroded beneath an old willow; its overhanging branches providing a curtain of cover to a secret haven. She and Tom used it as a den when they were young. That's where Tom would go.

She's crossing the bridge when the beam touches her. She ignores it, scoots down the riverbank. Gnarly roots rip at her palms as she slides into the water, suppressing a gasp. It's icy cold. Shivers skitter through every fibre of her being.

The light weaves through the trees. Frantically, she stays beneath the beam and moves down the river, searching for the willow. It's further down than she remembered, around the bend. She almost gives up when she spots it, sinks into the recess behind, pulls the spindly branches across her front. And waits.

The torchlight fades. The air quietens.

She holds her breath, hardly daring to wonder if she's lost him. Sharp tears prick her eyes.

Seconds turn into minutes. An owl calls to its mate, who responds with a hoot. The wind rustles through the trees. Her shoulders slacken. She pushes her back against the riverbank, desperately trying to stop her teeth chattering. She needs to bide her time. Make sure he's far enough away before she climbs out and finds the path back to the road. Another shiver, stronger. She clamps her jaw shut.

The arm appears from nowhere.

She didn't hear him navigate the bank behind her. Didn't sense his presence nearby, the water smothering the stench of stale nicotine. He reaches through the willow, fingernails snagging at her skin. A hand grabs her hair. Pulling, dragging.

She screams now. Shrill and loud. Arms windmilling,

splashing through the water as she struggles for purchase on the riverbed.

Then he's gone. And the water stills.

Heart pounding her chest, her eyes dart in all directions, checking the area. She's about to move off when something is flung around her neck. Instinctively, her hands go to it. A thread. No, a wire. Pulling tighter and tighter. She panics, tries to grab at it, but it's too far embedded. Sinking into the skin. Tightening her throat. Constricting her airway. Her eyes bulge, her tongue fills her mouth.

A bat swoops in front. It's the last thing she sees before the river blurs and descends into darkness.

CHAPTER 1

Acting Detective Superintendent Helen Lavery squeezed through the bodies to reach the bar, supressing a chuckle as she watched a rather sheepish DC Steve Spencer step onto the stage in the corner, raise a microphone to his mouth and sing the opening lines to 'Livin' on a Prayer'. Colleagues rushed to the wooden dance floor, pressing themselves into the small area, jigging along to the tune.

A cheer rose from the back of the crowd, followed by a whoop. DC Rosa Dark's petite frame shimmied as she raised a glass to her colleague, her glittery dress swishing around her hips. It was Rosa's engagement party and Helen, sidling in late, found the celebrations already in full swing.

She slid onto a bar stool, ordered a large glass of Merlot and rested her elbow on the bar, her chin on her hand. Spencer was tapping his heel now, bobbing to the beat of the music, buoyed up by the bodies singing along at his feet.

'I didn't know he had it in him.'

Helen swivelled to face the broad Yorkshire accent and smiled at the bear of a man holding up a half-full pint of Guinness. 'I don't think he did,' she said and laughed. The disco strobe lighting flashed across DS Sean Pemberton's bald scalp. He looked well, the open-necked navy shirt and fitted beige slacks accentuating his recent weight loss.

'Perhaps we should introduce a karaoke machine to the team briefing,' he said.

Helen gave a wry smile. 'Is Jenny here?'

'No, Mrs P's taken a pass.'

'Ah.' Helen gave a backward nod of acknowledgement. Looking around, few of her colleagues had partners in tow. Not surprising really. Police had a habit of talking shop, even when they were supposed to be letting their hair down, celebrating.

'How was the dinner?' he asked.

'Fine.' When her mother had suggested a family meal out to celebrate Helen's eldest son, Matthew, finishing his last GCSE exam, she was pretty sure she'd imagined them spending an evening in a classy restaurant sipping wine rather than the local pizzeria with its bottomless, refillable soft drinks. But it was Matthew's choice, and everyone seemed to enjoy it in the end. 'I made the boys' night when I took them home,' she said. 'Let them have a half a lager shandy each.'

Pemberton snorted. 'Nothing like a bit of under-age drinking.'

A round of applause cut in. Having finished the song, Steve was taking a low bow, running a hand through his salt-and-pepper hair.

Helen scanned the room, past the friends and family, the cops dressed up for a night out. Rosa had moved to the entrance and was chatting to a new arrival. Helen watched her throw her head back and laugh, her engagement ring glittering under the lights as she adjusted the scarf at her neck. The bruises were barely visible now, though Rosa still felt the need to cover them.

The young woman caught Helen's eye and gave an excited wave, excusing herself and rushing over. 'I wasn't sure if you'd make it!' she said.

'Oh, you know me,' Helen said. 'Anything for a party.'

Rosa tittered at the sarcasm in her voice. *If only.* Helen

enjoyed a get-together as much as any of them but usually bailed out before the drunken dancers filled the floor.

'Tim, you remember the boss,' Rosa said as her fiancé arrived at her side.

'Helen,' Helen corrected.

'Sure.' He gave a thin smile that didn't reach his eyes and turned back to the stage. 'The karaoke's going down a storm,' he said.

His coolness wasn't surprising. Images of his bride-to-be's bruised and bound frame, teetering on the lip of a roof, flashed into Helen's mind. Helen wasn't to know the danger the young detective would face when she ordered Rosa to make a routine visit on their last case. It was a cop facing an unexpected dangerous situation in the course of duty. Even after assessing all the usual risks, it happened sometimes. Still, Tim felt the need to justify the incident by apportioning blame and he clearly wasn't about to forgive Helen, despite the senior detective saving his fiancée's life.

'Auntie Ellen's leaving,' he said to Rosa. 'We need to say goodbye.'

Rosa tore herself away and disappeared into the crowd.

Pemberton's thick frame moved into her place beside the bar. 'Can I get you another drink?' he said to Helen, motioning to a barman.

Helen swirled the wine in her glass. 'No. I'll stick with this one for the moment, thanks.'

A roar rippled around the pub. Another karaoke victim was making for the stage.

'Well, I guess you're a superintendent now,' Pemberton said, teasing. 'You have to watch your Ps and Qs.'

'Acting superintendent,' she corrected, her heart sinking at the reminder. 'It's only temporary.' She could hardly refuse Superintendent Jenkins's request to cover him while he took special leave to care for his sick partner. But a permanent senior rank, with the internal politics, endless stream of meetings, statistics and reports, wasn't a position she coveted.

She'd joined the police to be a murder detective, to keep her feet firmly on the streets, and she resisted anything that threatened a move away from front-line policing.

By the time Pemberton's drink arrived, the singer had climbed onto the stage and introduced himself. It was Graham, one of their analysts. He belted out the first line of 'I Will Survive', beckoning the crowd to join in.

'Someone's enjoying himself,' Pemberton said as Graham strutted across the stage like a rock star.

Helen laughed. 'Where's Newton?' she said, looking for their new DI.

'Haven't seen him.'

Strange. He'd joined them a few weeks ago from Leicester and if there was one thing Helen had discovered in their short acquaintance, it was that Newton liked nothing better than to play to an audience. She'd have thought karaoke would be right up his street.

Graham's voice warbled as he reached the chorus. Laughter rattled around the dance floor as his colleagues sang along.

'That's my cue to go outside for a smoke,' Pemberton said.

'Think I'll join you.'

The summer air was cool and fresh outside The Royal Oak, a welcome respite from the stuffiness inside. A faint spicy odour filled the air from the kebab takeaway next door. Pemberton pulled an Embassy from a packet, lit up and took a long drag.

A car passed, closely followed by another. Then silence. The top end of Hampton High Street was surprisingly quiet for this time on a Friday evening. Helen leaned up against the cold brickwork while they discussed their plans for the weekend – Pemberton preparing to decorate his back bedroom; Helen ferrying her children to friends' houses and cricket matches. Ruminating at how domestic their lives had become, how their respective university party-hearty days were a distant memory. Time passed easily until Graham appeared in the doorway.

'You're needed inside,' he said to Pemberton. 'Rosa's

organising two groups for a karaoke competition.' He looked across at Helen. 'She wants you to judge.'

Graham disappeared into the pub. Pemberton raised his eyes to the rooftops and stubbed out his cigarette. 'I guess I'd better go in and show willing. Are you coming?'

'I'll be there in a mo. Give you a couple of minutes to warm up.'

'I think we both know I'll need more than a couple of minutes.'

She laughed. Watched him wander into the pub, then took a deep breath and looked out into the street, enjoying the last few moments of the cool night air. A late jogger passed, breaths chugging. A taxi cruised along, its orange *For Hire* light lit. Her gaze rested on a couple on the other side of the road, sauntering along, her arm tucked into his. They were dressed for a night on the town – him in dark trousers and an open-necked white linen shirt, her in a navy maxi dress that swished around her ankles. The man leaned into the woman and said something into her hair. She nudged him, gave a sideways glance and giggled.

A distant longing tugged at Helen. There was a time when she'd walked these streets with someone by her side. So easy, so comfortable in their togetherness. She watched the couple until they were smudges in the distance, then finished her wine. She was about to go back into the pub when the rev of an engine filled the air. Helen turned on her heel and spotted a black BMW approaching. It slowed beside her, the driver turning to check her out for a split second. A squarish head, hair razored to number one. Dark, familiar eyes. Helen stepped back, her breath catching in her throat.

The car moved on, the moment gone. But Helen knew what she'd seen.

CHAPTER 2

Helen woke the next morning to the sound of her mobile phone buzzing. She opened half an eye, patted the bedside cabinet until she reached it and drew it to her ear.

'Morning, ma'am. It's Inspector Simon Carrington in the control room. Are you available today? The duty SIO's sick.'

Helen blinked at the clock – 7.50 am. Dull light seeped into the room through a gap at the top of the curtains, where they didn't quite meet. 'I can be. What have you got?' She kept her voice low, mindful of her boys sleeping in the next rooms. They wouldn't welcome being disturbed at this ungodly hour, especially on a Saturday.

'A woman's body was discovered at 7.20 am in Blackwell Wood.'

Helen knew the area well. It was on the edge of Hamptonshire – a working forest and local beauty spot, complete with a sawmill and farm shop on the western tip. The numerous tracks that snaked through the wood were frequented by dog walkers, cyclists, equestrians, families on an afternoon wander. She'd spent many a Sunday there with her boys when they were young, watching them make dens in the undergrowth.

'Whereabouts?'

'On the eastern side, near Cosford's Farm. Closest vehicular access is almost a kilometre away at Meadow Lane. The victim was stripped naked and left beside the river. From the marks on her neck, possible cause of death is strangulation. Uniform have cordoned off the area and called in a pathologist and crime scene investigation.'

'Any witnesses?'

'Just the informant. A Cecily Thomas. She was out jogging when she noticed the body.'

'Where is Ms Thomas now?' Helen asked.

'At Cross Keys Station, giving a statement. Pretty shaken up, by all accounts.'

'Okay, thanks.' Uniform would take a first account and retain her clothing for examination. Helen checked her watch. 'I'll be at the wood in thirty minutes. Could you call DS Pemberton and DI Newton and have them meet me there?'

'Sure.'

She was just about to end the call when he added, 'I've been asked to inform you that something's been cut into the dead woman's chest. Uniform at the scene described it as a star.'

Helen baulked. 'Are you saying the symbol of a star has been carved into the victim's skin?'

'That's what I've been told.'

* * *

Marnie O'Hennessey was brewing her first coffee of the day, about to collect the Saturday papers from the doormat and take them back to bed with her, when her mobile rang. She glanced at the phone screen, surprised to see *Aidan*, her daughter's ex-partner, flash up. They hadn't spoken for months, and their last conversation hadn't ended on a happy note.

'Morning, Aidan,' she said warily.

Aidan didn't bother with preamble. 'Where's Shauna? She hasn't arrived to collect the kids.'

Marnie bit back her anger at his clipped tone. She didn't like Aidan. She hadn't liked him from the first moment she'd met him, nine years ago. Oh, he was all charm and smiles in the early days, but as soon as his feet were under the table, he started on Shauna. 'Why does she need to wear make-up all the time?' he would say in company – not caring who heard. Encouraging her to dress down and wear frumpy clothes. And, 'Doesn't she have the love of her life at home?' when she made plans to go out with the girls. There was no reasoning with him. He moaned so much about Shauna going out with friends that eventually she stayed home. Even Marnie had to make an appointment to see her. Her own daughter! He was convincing too. Had Shauna defending him to the hilt until, four months ago, he dumped her. Walked out on her and the kids. She'd heard he was in a new relationship now. That didn't surprise Marnie either. She'd noticed his eye wandering on more than one occasion.

She watched the coffee dribble into the mug. Though she had to admit he was a good father. Her grandchildren, Charlotte and Ollie, spent every Friday night with him and came home on Saturday mornings with smiles on their faces and tales of cinema and theatre visits and dinner out.

'Have you phoned Shauna?' she asked wearily. The last thing she wanted was to get embroiled in another of their arguments.

'Several times. It just goes to voicemail.'

Odd. She distinctly recalled Shauna saying she was looking forward to a quiet night at home while the kids were with their dad. Having a soak in the bath, maybe catching up with her reading. Shauna loved to read. She could devour a book in an evening if she set her mind to it. That was probably it. She'd stayed up late finishing one of her beloved historical novels and slept through the alarm.

'I'll try her landline.' Perhaps she'd forgotten to plug in her mobile charger.

'I don't have time for this. She should have been here

twenty minutes ago. I'm going to be late for work if she doesn't come soon.'

Her mug was almost full now, the aroma of fresh coffee filling the kitchen. 'Okay, I'll come over myself and take the kids home. I'll see you in fifteen minutes.'

'Make it ten.'

The call cut. Marnie's heart sank as she turned off the machine, set the mug aside and trudged up the stairs.

By the time she was dressed and climbing into her car, it was 8 am. She tried Shauna's mobile again, then dialled the landline. What was the girl playing at? Admittedly, timekeeping wasn't her daughter's forte. She was often running late for appointments, but it was first thing in the morning, and she was never tardy where the children were concerned.

The traffic was busy through town. Cross Keys roundabout was closed for essential works and the back roads were at crawling pace. It was almost 8.20 when she arrived at the semi Aidan was renting in Broadmore Avenue to find him sitting on the doorstep with the kids, waiting. She'd barely climbed out of the car when he bolted down the short path and thrust their rucksacks into her chest.

'Traffic was a nightmare,' she said as he hugged the children.

Aidan didn't answer, pushing past her to get to his car. 'Tell Shauna from me, if they dock my pay for being late this morning, I'm taking it out of her maintenance.'

Marnie sighed, then plastered on her happy face, welcoming her grandchildren with big cuddles and herding them into her car. 'Come on, kids. Let's go and see what Mummy's been up to.'

CHAPTER 3

Helen turned off the main road and trundled down Meadow Lane, swerving her Volvo to avoid the potholes. A dead end, the road had once led to a hamlet of farm workers' cottages, long since gone. Apart from the odd canoodling couple on summer's evenings, and the occasional dog walker heading for the quiet end of the forest, it was mostly navigated by the local farmer these days, tending the nearby fields.

She parked behind the line of police and crime scene vehicles, cut the engine and glanced up at the slate-grey clouds thick with the promise of rain. Ironic, really – all week, she'd prayed for rain to end the sticky June heatwave being inflicted on them and the one morning she could do with a dry area, a dry crime scene without rainwater washing away potential evidence, it was set to arrive.

She climbed out of her car and turned on her heel, taking in the rolling countryside, the lush hedgerow, the surrounding fields rich with crops. Rural, remote, not a house in sight. She nodded at a group of suited CSIs returning to a nearby van and focused on the fir trees of Blackwell Wood in the distance.

'Odd place to dump a body,' a voice bellowed nearby. 'In the middle of a wood. So far from the road.'

'That's just what I was thinking,' Helen said. Pemberton's

face was almost as white as the Tyvek coveralls he wore. Thick dark circles hung beneath his eyes. She gave a sympathetic smile. 'What time did you get here?'

'About ten minutes ago. Mrs P dropped me off.'

'Ah. How's the head this morning?'

'Well enough to be here… just about. Thanks for asking.'

Helen grinned and looked back across the surrounding fields. The remoteness of the location bothered her – it was almost another half a kilometre to the edge of the forest and the narrow track down the side of the farmer's field that led to it was uneven and unkempt. 'Are there any footpaths or bridleways nearby?' she asked.

Pemberton shook his head, fished his phone out of his pocket and brought up a county map, stretching the screen to show Blackwell Wood's location. It spanned over two hundred acres, from Hampton Ring Road on one side to the county's boundary on the other. 'There's the main entrance on Blackwell Heath, about half a mile along the main road,' he said, 'and a couple of bridleways around the other side, not to mention broken hedges and unofficial openings. I'm told this is the closest route to the crime scene from a parked vehicle.'

'I take it uniform didn't notice any sign of a recent presence here when they arrived?' she asked.

'No.' She followed his eyeline to the sun-soaked, cracked earth. With the recent temperatures, there would be no record of tyre tracks or footprints.

Helen thanked him, opened the car boot and made a play of pulling on her coveralls. 'Where's the inspector?'

'No answer on his phone, ma'am. Control room have left him a message.'

He wasn't officially on call and none of them expected to be working today, but Helen struggled to bury her frustration. She was supposed to be mentoring him in the role of senior investigating officer and there was so much to learn from visiting the scene of a fresh murder – the views, the surrounding area, the smells, the environment.

'Any news on an ID for the victim?' she asked, leaning on the tailgate as she pulled on a fresh pair of sterile wellington boots.

'Not yet. Her clothes, mobile phone and any bag she might have been carrying are all missing. All we have is a description. I've called the team into the office and asked them to start going through missing persons.'

'Thanks, Sean.' She could always rely on Pemberton to get things organised.

'I'm told Charles arrived before me,' Pemberton continued. 'He's already made a start.'

Helen smiled to herself. At least they had bagged the most efficient pathologist in their area, a small mercy to be grateful for. 'What do we know about the informant?'

Pemberton checked his notebook. 'Cecily Thomas, twenty-nine, lives on the Trestle Lodge estate in Worthington, on the edge of town. Said she often jogs through the woods on a Saturday morning.'

'Alone?'

'She claims so.'

They moved past the vans and liveried police cars and climbed over a stile leading to a muddy path down a sloping field filled with maize. Silence fell upon them as they descended. The BMW outside The Royal Oak last night popped into Helen's mind. When she re-entered the pub, the karaoke competition was starting and the moment was forgotten, though now, in the cold light of day, uneasiness crept back in. She'd seen those dark eyes before...

Helen swallowed, picturing the hard face, the piercing stare of Chilli Franks. A local gang leader, Chilli was an adversary of her late father, also a detective. He'd hurled threats at the Lavery family when her father hunted him down and arrested him for throwing acid in a rival's face in the 1990s. Threats he reiterated when Helen's team charged him with abduction and drugs offences earlier this year. But Chilli was currently on remand awaiting trial...

'The resemblance was uncanny,' she said, sharing the exchange with Pemberton. 'I almost expected a phone call this morning to say he'd escaped.'

'It sounds like Davy Boyd,' Pemberton said. He placed his hands on his hips and paused to catch his breath. 'Chilli's half-brother. Same mother, different father. I'm told they look similar.'

Helen gaped at him. 'I didn't know Chilli had a half-brother.'

They moved off again. 'They're not close. Or they weren't. As far as I'm aware, Davy moved out to manage a bar in Spain in the 1980s and hasn't been back. Didn't even come over for his nephew's funeral in the spring.'

'What's he doing here now then?'

'There was talk in the pub last night that he's returned to resurrect some of Chilli's interests.'

Helen stopped and caught Pemberton's arm. They were almost at the wood now. 'What interests?'

'Apparently, he has a stake in some of Chilli's legitimate businesses – the nightclub, the nail bar. I doubt he'll give us any trouble though. Davy keeps his nose clean. Doesn't have a record here, apart from a few disposals for stealing cars in his teens.'

Helen was reminded of his heavy gaze. He certainly knew who she was. And the fact that Pemberton had taken the trouble to check his record did nothing to quell her disquiet.

'He's different from Chilli, from what I'm hearing,' Pemberton continued. 'He married late, is raising two kids. He's got a lot more to lose.'

Helen nodded, though his reassuring words failed to have the desired effect. She'd worked hard to shelve the ghost of Chilli Franks these past weeks and months, the grudge he'd held against her, the threats he'd made against her family. Now that he was in prison, awaiting trial, a trial she'd been assured would likely result in conviction, she'd resolved to put it all behind her, and the thought of him raising his ugly head again, albeit through his half-brother, filled her with a sense of foreboding.

They reached the wood, the sweet smell of pine pervading the air as they weaved through the tall firs, guided by yellow CSI markers. The air darkened as they moved into the denser broad-leafed area. It would take several days to comb this area, which meant long delays with forensics. Not a great start to an investigation.

They rounded a corner and reached a line of blue and white police tape – the inner cordon. A wider cordon would have been set up around a large part of the woods, with officers guarding the entrances and exits, but this was the initial area of focus – where the body was found. CSIs moved about like an army of white-clothed ants. Helen signed into the register, ducked beneath the tape and approached the riverbank where the body lay, beside the path. Glassy eyes staring up at the dappled sky. White porcelain skin. Dark hair fanned around her head. Arms folded in an X across her breasts. But it was what was above her arms that grabbed Helen's attention. The skin was torn, gaping open and ragged in places where the so-called star had been carved into it, surrounded by a messy circle.

'Helen!' It was the voice of Charles Burlington, the pathologist.

'Morning, Charles,' she said. 'Beat me to it again, I see.'

'It's becoming quite a habit.' He tugged back his hood and smiled warmly. 'How are you doing?'

'Fine, thank you. Sorry to pull you away from the family on a Saturday.'

'No worries. You got me out of a shopping trip with Sarah and the grandchildren.' He winked.

'Ah, a lucky escape then.' She looked past him at the body and flinched at the engraving. 'Can you say whether that was done pre- or post-mortem?' she asked.

Charles bent down and peered closer. 'Post, I reckon. I'd expect more leakage in someone living. I'd say the heart had stopped pumping the blood when the flesh was cut.'

One blessing, Helen thought.

Charles ran a gloved finger over a purplish line that had gathered along the bottom of the corpse. 'Lividity suggests she was killed here.' He leaned in closer. 'Cause of death...' He extended a hand towards the neck, nudged away some wisps of hair. A red line ran around the throat. A pink mark shaped like a teardrop sat below the ear lobe. 'See here?'

'Is that a birthmark?' Helen asked, pointing at the teardrop.

'Yes. But look at the wound next to it.' There was a tiny cut in the middle of the red line. 'With rope or other materials, I'd expect some chafing, abrasion. This appears to be a stronger and thinner weapon. I'd say she was garrotted by something sharp, possibly wire.'

'Interesting,' Helen said. A wire garrotte needed blocks tied at either end to protect the hands of the user. Either that or they wore tough gloves. It suggested preparation, planning.

'The thin lines cross over on the back of her neck,' Charles continued. 'I'd say our offender was behind her when they killed her.'

'Any defensive wounds?'

'Some bruising to the backs of her arms, but it's limited. Look at this.' He pointed out grazes on her elbows and knees, then moved to her feet. A road map of fresh cuts and scratches covered the filthy soles.

'She was barefoot.' Helen was incredulous. The thought of this young woman navigating the gnarled paths of the wood without shoes made her wince.

'Not only that. With uncovered feet, she would normally take the path gingerly. We might expect the odd snag or laceration. These are cut to ribbons. I'd say she was running, possibly trying to get away from someone. There are more cuts and grazes on the palms of her hands, indicating she fell several times. And scrapes on her back. There's knotweed in her hair too. I'd say whoever did this dragged her out of the river.'

Helen surveyed the thick forest surrounding them, intersected by narrow pathways. 'She was chased?'

'Possibly. The snags and abrasions suggest urgency. The location of her injuries, on her extremities and knees – her torso is relatively unscathed apart from the engraving – indicates she was probably dressed, albeit scantily. They probably killed her, then undressed her afterwards.'

Helen looked back at the young woman: her porcelain white skin, slight frame, the pillar-box red fingernails snagged and broken. She could only be in her twenties. So young. Her toenails were also painted a matching red, the neat straight edges hinting at a professional manicure. This was someone who took care of herself, was particular about her appearance.

Did she come here willingly, unaware of what she was about to face, or was she coerced? Was she restrained and broke free? She couldn't see any binding marks on the wrists or ankles. She imagined the woman charging through the woods, the uneven earth sending her off balance, the hawthorns, bushes and undergrowth picking at her skin. The visceral fear at being chased, running for her life.

Helen looked at the symbol on the woman's chest and suppressed a shudder. 'Can you get a photo of that emailed back to the team?' she asked Pemberton. CSIs would be photographing the victim from a variety of angles for the forensic file, but she wanted this shared urgently. 'See if anyone can find out what the symbol represents.' She left Pemberton to work his phone and turned to Charles. 'Do you know what sort of knife made those incisions?'

'Something with a short, straight blade,' he said.

'A scalpel?'

'Not necessarily. Could be a penknife or a craft knife. Anything with a sharp, thin blade.'

Either would fit easily into a pocket. 'What about time of death?'

'Rigor mortis is well advanced...' Charles paused a minute

and viewed the surroundings. 'In these conditions, best guess is between eight and twelve hours ago. A guess, mind you.'

'So, we are roughly looking at between 8.30 pm and 12.30 am,' Helen said. It would have been getting dark then. The killer possibly working by torchlight. Her gaze rested on the young woman. Whomever she came here with was armed with a wire garrotte and a weapon to carve the symbol into her chest and they either chased or dragged her here to this isolated spot with the sole intention of killing her, then laid her out beside the riverbank.

A flapping sound nearby made her turn. The CSIs were preparing the tent to cover the corpse.

Helen looked back at the body, close to the path. Whoever did this wanted her to be found.

CHAPTER 4

Back at headquarters, Helen entered the homicide and major incident suite to find a rather dishevelled-looking bunch of detectives and support staff – her team dragged in on their day off to start a new murder investigation, pale and weary from the party the night before. Not that they were letting aching heads stop them from throwing themselves into a new investigation: phones were glued to ears and fingers tapped keyboards as if it was a regular weekday. There were only a few members missing along with Rosa Dark, for whom Helen had left specific instructions not to contact under the pretence that she should be allowed the day off to relax after her party, and the DI. It was heart-warming to see so many make the effort. She nodded and called out greetings as she weaved through the desks to her office in the corner.

Pemberton was examining two boards at the front of the room when she emerged seconds later. The first with a photo of the body beside a close-up of the star symbol. The second displayed a map of Blackwell Wood, the crime scene highlighted with a yellow circle. A separate map of the wood's position in Hamptonshire county below.

'The ACC wants to see you,' Pemberton said as she joined him. He passed her a mug of steaming coffee.

I'm sure she does, Helen thought. Assistant Chief Constable

'Call Me Alison' Broadhurst was a tenacious boss. Militant, known for fighting for her staff, there was no pomp, no 'ma'am' or formal titles in her office. But she had high expectations and was crystal clear on how she wanted the force portrayed, and there was no way Helen was going to be grilled by her before briefing her team and making sure they had established a clear strategy forward. 'Thanks.' She held up the coffee in acknowledgement, cleared her throat and called out, 'Okay, everyone.' Pens dropped and conversations hushed. 'I'd like to thank you all for dragging your sorry arses in this morning, especially after what was undoubtedly a heavy night for some.' A low murmur and several sniggers passed through the room as her gaze rested on a few empty chairs at the back that likely belonged to officers still over the limit; they'd be joining them later when they were up to it. 'It's good to see the coffee's already flowing.' She glanced at the body on the board. 'Right. Gather around, let's see what we're dealing with.'

She waited for her staff to move forward and settle themselves in chairs and on the edges of desks nearby then talked them through the scene, step by step, as she'd seen it that morning, along with the pathologist's early deliberations. 'Okay, let's start with the symbol,' she said.

Spencer raised a hand. He looked surprisingly fresh in a crisp white shirt and grey tie. 'It's a pentacle,' he said, 'a pentagram inside a circle.' He clicked a button on his laptop and a similar star symbol with a circle around it appeared on the large screen beside Helen. 'The pentagram dates back to the ancient Greeks. The five points are supposed to symbolise the elements of earth, air, fire, water and spirit. It's also been used by Christians over the years to symbolise the five wounds of Jesus,' Spencer said.

Helen looked at the engraving across the victim's chest. 'You're suggesting this might be a religious killing?'

'Not necessarily. There have been lots of interpretations. More recently, the pentacle has been associated with paganistic practice and witchcraft. Many believe the inverted use, like this one,' he nudged his head towards the photo of the victim on the board, 'with the two points of the pentagram facing upwards, represents evil and darkness. The Church of Satan's emblem, the Sigil of Baphomet, is an inverted pentagram with a half man, half goat's head inside.'

'So, it could be connected to anything from spiritualism to witchcraft to devil worship,' Pemberton said.

'It seems so.'

'That's helpful.'

Helen ignored the sarcasm. 'Or it has some ritualistic meaning,' she said almost to herself. 'There are drag marks on the victim's back, indicating the killer deliberately moved her and left her beside a pathway.'

The room quietened, the only sound the rain which had now broken through the clouds and was hammering the windows.

'All right, let's look into local cults, religious groups, pagan societies, any gatherings that use or have used a pentagram or pentacle.' Helen stared at the photo, tapping her foot a couple of times in thought. 'I take it we've got no historic cases where a pentagram has featured before?'

Heads shook around her.

'Contact the National Crime Agency. See if they can tap into their register of experts – they might have an academic with experience on the occult or secret orders that can tell us more about it. In the meantime, check with other forces nationwide to see if the symbol or anything similar has featured in other investigations. Try engravings, particularly those that resemble stars and pentagrams – especially inverted ones.' She scanned the room. 'Where are we with identifying the victim?'

'We've been working our way through local missing person reports,' Spencer said. 'There's been a number of women in their mid-twenties recently. None with that birthmark.'

'What about fingerprints?'

'They were taken at the scene and put through the national database. She's not known to us.'

Helen's heart dipped. Without an ID, she couldn't step into the victim's shoes, learn about her social circle or build up a picture of her movements in the days and weeks leading up to the killing. 'Okay, search the national missing persons database – our Jane Doe might have travelled here from another area.' She looked back at the photo on the board. Something about the way the woman was laid out, almost ceremoniously, bothered her. 'Most perpetrators can't leave a scene quick enough, yet this offender took their time to strip her of clothing and jewellery. Why?'

Pemberton shoved his hands in his pockets. 'Perhaps they wanted to keep her possessions.'

It was common knowledge that some killers liked to keep a memento, or trophy, to remind them of their victims. A piece of jewellery, a lock of hair. But to take everything… 'Or maybe they don't want her to be easily identified,' Helen said. 'Lack of possessions prolongs the process. It must have taken a while to engrave the symbol on her chest.'

'That's a dense area of Blackwell Wood,' Pemberton said. 'It's pretty remote out there at night. I guess they weren't expecting to be disturbed.'

'We know the victim was killed last night,' Helen said, 'possibly between 8.30 pm and 12.30 am. Charles believed she died close to the scene, which is almost a kilometre from the nearest road.' She moved across to the board containing the maps and glanced at the larger county map. 'Let's look at all roads within a mile's radius of where the body was found. Check ANPR cameras, see what traffic was passing through. CSI are combing the area for forensics. The search teams are looking for her clothes and the murder weapon in case it was discarded nearby. We've called in the dog unit to try to track the route the victim took. Hopefully, we'll have something back from them soon.'

The door clicked open. Helen looked up, half-expecting to see her DI enter. Instead, the impish face of DC Rosa Dark appeared around the door frame.

'Rosa,' Helen said. She flicked a glance at Pemberton, who pulled a blank face. 'We weren't expecting to see you today.'

'I'm not letting you guys have all the fun,' she said, the hint of a smile tickling her lips. Her skin was pale, dark shadows hung beneath her eyes, but other than that, she seemed remarkably bright. 'I hear we've got an interesting one.'

'It's different, I'll grant you that,' Helen said. 'Shouldn't you be with your fiancé? Don't you have presents to open or something?'

'Tim's playing golf today. I'm sure you could use an extra pair of hands.'

Helen smiled. Her enthusiasm was encouraging. 'Okay, if you're sure?'

Rosa nodded.

'Thank you. There's a wealth of inquiries to follow up. We'll certainly appreciate your help.' A phone rang in the distance. Helen cast it an annoyed glance and turned back to the room. 'Right. I'll speak to the press office and suggest they issue a general statement reporting the discovery of a woman's body in Blackwell Wood, that we're treating it as suspicious, and appeal for any potential witnesses. Anyone who might have been in or near the wood last night. We won't mention a garrotte or the engraving at this stage. I want that kept inside this room until we know what we are dealing with. Charles is arranging to transport the body to the morgue and will let us know when he's ready to do the autopsy. We also need to go out and interview the farmer that works the land around Meadow Lane. It's possible he might have seen something.'

CHAPTER 5

The assistant chief constable's office was a large room on the top floor of headquarters.

'Helen. It's good to see you,' Alison said, beckoning her inside. She was a short, slim woman with cropped chestnut hair that accentuated wide owl-like eyes. She indicated for Helen to sit on one of the leather chairs opposite her desk. 'I hear we have something a bit different,' she said.

'You could say that.' Alison sat back and listened quietly while Helen talked her through their findings to date. 'Identifying the victim is our current priority. We can then work through victimology and look for any links.'

'Okay. What's your hypothesis?'

This was one of the things Helen liked most about working with the woman. A trained detective herself who'd served five years in CID, she cut to the chase.

'Without an ID on the victim, it's difficult to say.' She gazed past Alison and the jacket hanging on the back of her chair, out of the window and across the grassy field beyond. It was a beautiful vista, even in wet weather, a far cry from the dingy car park her little office overlooked. 'The engraving does give me cause for concern,' she said. 'We've applied for an expert from the National Crime Agency to find out more about it and what it might mean. In the interim, we're looking at local cults, religious groups – anyone that might have a connection with the symbol. We're not releasing the pentagram's existence to the public yet. I don't wish to scare people unduly.'

'I think that's wise. All right. What do you need?'

The offer almost knocked Helen sideways. With Jenkins, her superintendent, she was used to battling for more resources. Though she was dealing with the higher ranks now. The ACC was second in command to the chief constable, and she clearly had a lot more clout.

'Officers,' Helen said. 'We've appealed for witnesses for anyone in the area or driving close by last night – hopefully, that should drum up some calls. As soon as the victim is identified, there'll be bank statements and phone records to scrutinise, friends and family to interview. We also have camera footage from the surrounding area to examine. I've decided to cordon off the whole wood until we can be sure which access point the killer used.'

'The whole wood.' Alison raised a brow. 'That'll take a lot of resources to guard.'

'The killer could potentially have dumped her clothing anywhere in the vicinity. It's the only way to preserve evidence and keep the public away. The last thing we need is nosy journos sniffing around.'

'I'll see what I can do.' The ACC cleared her throat. 'There's something else.' She took a long breath, exhaled through the next sentence. 'DI Newton won't be joining us again.'

Helen baulked. 'I'm not with you.'

'It seems when he applied for the move here, he also applied for the Met. He had his Met interview last week and was successful.'

Helen felt her jaw drop. She'd spent the last few weeks teaching him the ropes of homicide, working through files with him, cold cases, and yet he hadn't mentioned he was progressing an application elsewhere.

Alison shook her head. 'I guess they pay more than we do. And he does have a family.' An imperceptible shrug. 'Anyway, his new superintendent phoned me this morning. They want him to start immediately. I've given permission. There's no point in investing any more in him here. It does leave us with a bit of a problem though.' She placed her hands on her desk and laced her fingers together. 'I'm going to be straight with you, Helen. We need a rapid resolution to this murder case.'

Helen's internal antennae twitched. She should have guessed the easy offer of help came at a cost.

'We've got the HMIC visit in four weeks,' Alison continued, 'and we need everything in order – every i dotted, every t crossed. I don't want another inadequate marking.'

Helen's heart dipped. HMIC, or Her Majesty's Inspectorate of Constabulary, was the regulatory body which independently assessed the effectiveness and efficiency of forces and ensured policing methods met the required standards. Their last inspection, just over a year ago, was during Helen's first week in homicide and they had criticised the force for poor accountability and efficiency.

'I realise their last report covered the period before you joined homicide,' Alison said. 'And I'm aware you've already made several changes in your department. The early signs are positive. But to quantify that, there is a lot I'm going to need from you. Files. Stats. Evidence. Plus, the feedback report from your last investigation.'

Helen's heart plummeted further. A young woman's body was barely cold, a killer on the loose, and here was her boss bleating on about a bloody feedback report for a solved crime.

Alison shifted, sensing her frustration. 'It is part of the superintendent's role to ensure everything is running efficiently,' she said. 'And that includes post-investigation.'

Frankly, Helen couldn't give a damn whose role it was. She bit back her irritation. 'The report isn't due until next month,' she said. 'We're working on it.'

'I'm going to need it early, I'm afraid. Look, the date of the visit is fixed. I appreciate you are only covering, and you've just lost another resource, but we're going to have to pull together to get it done. I'm happy to supply staff, or for you to move into the room next door if you feel the space would help.'

Helen had resisted the pressure to move into Jenkins's room when he started special leave, just as she had refused to take the purpose-built homicide and serious crime unit manager's room, located down the corridor from her staff, when they moved into this building. Admittedly, they were both larger and plusher, but space wasn't everything. She wanted to be in the incident suite, in the heart of the inquiry, with their murder wall – the noticeboards, the maps – and she wasn't about to abandon her team.

'I don't think that's necessary,' she said, fighting to keep her voice even. 'Superintendent Jenkins will be back in a few months. There's need to change things around.'

Alison lifted a perfectly manicured brow. 'As you wish. Okay, let's get this murder out of the public eye as quickly as possible, then concentrate on preparing for the audit. I'll need the feedback report on my desk in the usual format in three weeks.'

Helen resisted the urge to ask what 'the usual format' was – probably some kind of convoluted software package, something Jenkins usually dealt with.

She made to leave, was at the door, pulling down the handle, when Alison added, 'Keep me informed at every juncture of the investigation, will you? I'll need to brief the chief constable twice daily, particularly while it's fresh in everyone's minds. Call me if there is any news or an arrest, any time of the day or night. You have my number.' She smiled. 'And remember – whatever you need, I'm happy to throw resources at this one for a quick result.'

Helen nodded, closed the door behind her and wandered past the next office, glancing up at Jenkins's nameplate as she passed. A tough boss, Jenkins had surprised her after their last case by praising her efforts. She was beginning to think that they were finally reaching an understanding. Plus, he left her to focus on the investigation, instead of audits and statistics. 'Come back soon,' she said under her breath. She wasn't sure how much more of this she could bear.

CHAPTER 6

Pemberton was heading out as Helen returned to the incident room. 'Have you heard about the DI?' he said when they met in the corridor.

Helen rolled her eyes. Nothing like a bunch of coppers to get the rumour mill going. 'The ACC has just told me.'

'I can't believe it,' he said. 'You think he'd have said something.' He nodded at a passing officer, lowered his voice. 'Still, it explains why he wasn't there last night. Probably couldn't face any of us. Apparently, he accepted the position yesterday afternoon, sly fox.' He cleared his throat. 'Mind you, I think we dodged a bullet.'

Pemberton was probably right. Newton was a larger-than-life character; he'd already upset some of the support staff with his lewd jokes. She hadn't been thrilled about the prospect of mentoring another senior investigating officer on the team herself when he arrived, wary that it left her surplus to requirements. Though Newton did have a ton of experience and starting a new investigation with a senior detective down was the last thing she needed right now. Especially with the audit hanging over her.

'I do have some good news,' Pemberton said, changing the subject. 'Control room called while you were out. A Marnie O'Hennessey has reported her daughter missing.

Hasn't seen her since last night. Matches the description of our victim.'

A bolt of adrenalin. 'Excellent. What do we know?'

'Her daughter was alone last night. Her two children were spending the night with her ex-partner. Marnie last saw her at 4.40 pm. She became alarmed when Shauna didn't turn up to collect the children this morning and she couldn't reach her. She's now at Shauna's house looking after the kids.'

'Was Shauna planning to go out last night? To see anyone?'

'That's all the details we have at the moment,' he said. 'But she fits the description, and she mentioned the distinguishing feature, the birthmark beside her left ear. Spencer and Dark have just left Cosford's Farm, near the crime scene. I've asked them to head straight over and see her.'

'Great, thanks.' Helen's shoulders slackened, grateful for his efficiency, as ever. At least she could rely on the staff she had. 'Are the O'Hennesseys known to us?'

'No. None of them have a record. Interestingly, there is some intel on Shauna. Several 999 calls in the last six months by a neighbour alerting control room to nasty arguments between Shauna and her partner. Domestic incident reports were completed in some cases; no arrests made. The relationship has since broken down. The partner moved out a few months ago.'

'Can you get me copies of the domestic incident reports? I'd like to take a look at them.'

'Sure. Also, the press office released your approved statement thirty minutes ago. There's a copy on your desk. The phones have started, nothing of interest yet though. I've stood the team down on checking missing persons, pending the formal ID. We're concentrating on tracking possible sources for the pentagram.' He checked his watch. 'Won't be a sec. I'm just popping out for a smoke.'

* * *

Back in her office, Helen wrote *Shauna O'Hennessey* on her pad and circled it twice. This was the first positive piece of news they'd had all morning. If the ID was confirmed, they needed to look into Shauna's life: her friends, her family, her hobbies, her recent movements. And one of the quickest ways to learn about someone was through their devices. People often lived out their routine, their movements, through social media these days. She grabbed her mobile phone.

Dark answered on the second ring. 'Morning, ma'am. We're just leaving Cosford's Farm.'

'How did you get on?'

'Not much to report, I'm afraid. The fields that line the eastern end of the wood are arable – the farmer hasn't been down there in weeks. He was with his wife at home last night, didn't see anything.' The line crackled. 'I'm just on my way to see Mrs O'Hennessey.'

'Okay, thanks. You'll be seeing Mrs O'Hennessey at the victim's house. We'll need to tread carefully because her grandchildren are there with her.' She looked down at Pemberton's notes, checked they had the correct address, then swivelled in her chair to view the car park below. 'Can you pick up her devices? Laptop, phone, anything you can find. See if the mother knows the passwords. While you are there, check for any signs of a disturbance – we still don't know how Shauna got to the wood last night. It may be the killer visited her at home beforehand. We're going to need to move the victim's mother and children out while the property is searched. Let me know if you need me to arrange a hotel for the family.'

She finished the call and looked out into the incident room. It was time to make a formal announcement about the loss of their inspector.

CHAPTER 7

As soon as Marnie opened the door to the man and woman in raincoats, suits peeping from their collars, she knew something was deeply wrong.

'Detective Constable Rosa Dark,' the woman said, holding up an ID card. 'This is my colleague, Detective Constable Steve Spencer.' She, young and petite. He, old enough to be her father.

Detectives. She looked past them, through the rain, which was easing now to a fine flow, at Shauna's yellow Kia on the drive.

She'd been surprised to find the car parked there when she arrived with the kids that morning. Even more surprised when there was no answer at the door, and she'd had to access the house herself, courtesy of the spare key she kept for emergencies.

She could still see Charlotte and Ollie, dashing in, calling out, checking each room, racing upstairs. Charlotte clutching a special painting she'd made for Mummy at school yesterday, tears pricking her eyes when she couldn't find her. Ollie's befuddled face when he found the house empty.

'Are you Mrs O'Hennessey?' the female officer prompted. Marnie juddered a nod.

'We're here about your missing daughter.'

A dry swallow. She peeled the tongue from the top of her mouth. She'd called everyone she could think of before she rang the police earlier. The officer she had spoken to had said they would send someone out to take the details, but still… she hadn't been expecting detectives. Detectives sounded serious. Grave. 'Has something happened?'

'May we come in?'

Marnie's stomach twisted as she guided them down the hallway towards the kitchen. She paused briefly at the living room, where her grandchildren were huddled together in front of the television, and pulled the door to.

Darren, her husband, looked up from his bagel, mouth half-full, as they entered the kitchen. He was tired and drawn and still wearing his blue work overalls. Little wonder after arriving home from a long haul to Italy and back to a text message from her asking him to come straight to Shauna's. A missing daughter was the last thing he needed.

Darren's face tightened as the male detective closed the door behind them, introduced them both again and asked Marnie to sit.

'May we?' the female detective asked. She pointed at the chairs opposite them.

Marnie gave a silent nod and watched them settle. What were their names? She couldn't for the life of her remember, even though they'd introduced themselves twice, and so eloquently.

'Can you describe your daughter for us?' the female detective asked.

'I gave the officer a description on the phone.'

'It would be helpful if you could tell us again.'

Marnie took a breath. 'White, size ten-ish. Long dark hair. Five foot six.'

'Thank you. When you reported your daughter missing, you mentioned a birthmark.'

'Yes, beside her ear.' Marnie briefly touched the left side of her neck. 'Shaped like a teardrop.'

'I'm sorry to have to tell you that a young woman fitting Shauna's description was found dead in Blackwell Wood in the early hours of this morning.'

Marnie froze.

Darren gripped her elbow. 'It can't be,' he said. 'There must be some mistake.'

'I'm afraid the young woman bears the same birthmark. I'm so sorry.'

'Are you absolutely sure it's her?' Darren again, despair etched into every line of his face.

'We will ask you to do a formal identification, but we are as sure as we can be from what we've seen.'

The pain came from nowhere, like a surprise kick in the gut, doubling Marnie over. She dropped her head into her hands. No. Not her beautiful, kind, sensitive Shauna. The little girl with the tawny, teasing eyes. The young woman with the long, glossy mane. The notion was too agonising, too torturous to comprehend.

'I'm so very sorry,' the female detective said. 'We are treating Shauna's death as suspicious.'

'What do you mean?' Darren said, his mouth agape. 'What the hell happened?'

'She'd been strangled.'

'W-what?'

Another spasm of pain, fiercer this time. Marnie's breaths hitched as the tears came, bleeding through the gaps between her fingers. A thick arm stretched across her shoulders. The musty smell of Darren's work overalls cocooned her as she dug her head into his chest and wept. Time passed. She heard cupboard doors open and close around her. The whirr of the kettle as it boiled. Then a low mewling. A cat. Where was it? Shauna didn't have a pet; she was allergic to their fur. It wasn't until she opened her eyes and pulled back that she realised the mewling was actually coming from her. In her efforts to hush her cries, to keep them from her grandchildren, her sobs had turned into muffled whimpers.

She needed to pull herself together. They had the children to think of. Oh God, the children! What the hell were they to say to them? She couldn't begin to even consider how they'd find the words.

Marnie covered her face again and gulped deep breaths, in and out. Ignoring the movement around her. She didn't hear the kettle switch off. Didn't notice the detective making drinks. The slow rasps of her own breaths calmed her, settling her addled mind.

Two mugs of milky tea appeared in front of them, the china clinking against the coasters.

'When did you last see your daughter?' the female detective asked.

Darren scratched the side of his temple. 'A few days ago. I've been away with work. I did speak to her yesterday afternoon though. She sounded... happy.'

'I saw her yesterday evening,' Marnie interjected, her voice barely a whisper. She pictured Shauna's lithe frame in her black dress. The stockings covering her legs. She hardly ever wore stockings and she'd looked so fresh, so elegant. A knot formed in her chest. 'She'd been to a job interview. She called in to see me at my house afterwards.'

The male detective opened a notebook and took down her home address. 'What was the interview for?'

Marnie dabbed a soggy tissue to her eyes. 'A hairdressing position in a different salon. Longer hours. She separated from her partner a few months ago. They'd agreed on a settlement, were selling the house. She needed extra money to apply for a new mortgage. I was going to go part-time at my job to pick the kids up from school.' A tear dripped from her chin and plopped onto the table. She was vaguely aware of the male detective asking for details of the interview location and time, jotting them in his notebook.

'What time did she call in to see you?'

'Around 4.30-ish, I think. I hadn't been home from work long.' More writing. More recording. Hazy. Blurred. It was like an out-of-body experience. As if this was happening to someone else.

'How did she seem?'

'Um. Good. She said the interview went well. They were going to let her know today.' Another tear trickled down the side of her nose. She'd been so relieved when Shauna had reached out to her for help with childcare. The break-up, out of the blue as it was, had knocked her for six. It was good to see her rebuilding her life. *How could she be gone?*

'Was she intending to go straight home after visiting you?'

'No. The children were with Aidan, her ex-partner. They always go there on a Friday – he picks them up from school, they stay overnight – and Charlotte had forgotten her unicorn.' She waved her hand in the air as she explained. 'It's a soft toy. She still takes it with her on sleepovers, even though she's eight. She won't sleep without it. Aidan phoned Shauna while she was at mine and asked her to drop it by.' They checked the time she left – 4.40 pm.

'Do you know what her plans were afterwards?'

'She said she was looking forward to a rest, a quiet night in. She phoned me later – must have been about… quarter past seven – to tell me Tracey Ullman was on the telly. I used to love her years ago. I switched it on, and we chatted for a minute or so about how well she was ageing. That was the last time I spoke to her.' Darren reached across and grabbed her hand. Warm. Tight. She looked down at her whitening fingers.

'Does she go to Blackwell Wood often?'

Shauna had loved the woods as a child, hacking her horse through the narrow pathways. But recently… Marnie wracked her brains. They took the children there for a walk one Sunday afternoon, a month or so ago. Ollie stood in a deep puddle and soaked the bottom of his trainers and they had to leave early. As far as she was aware, Shauna hadn't been back, and she couldn't imagine her taking herself off there on a Friday evening. She passed the information over.

'And where were you last night?' the female detective asked.

'At home all evening.'

'Alone?'

'Yes. I got home from work just after half four.' She glanced at the photo of her children on the fridge – Tom and Shauna together, heads gently touching. The knot in her chest hardened.

They asked what her work was, and she told them about her job at the insurance company in town. She could hear herself speaking the words, the soft lilt of her voice, but they barely registered inside. So many questions. So much information. She wanted to lie down in a dark room, close her eyes, make it all go away.

The detective seemed to sense her discomfort. 'I'm sorry, I know this is difficult. We do need to ask for details of friends and family though. It'll help us track down her movements over the past week or so.'

Her final movements. Marnie pressed her eyelids together. They went on to talk about Shauna's hobbies. She could hear Darren saying Shauna didn't have any hobbies. Not really. What with work and the children and the separation, the poor girl barely had time to think for herself, let alone indulge in pastimes. When they asked if she was religious, Marnie was struggling to keep up. Murder. Inquiry. Investigation. It was surreal. Like something you watched on telly. This didn't happen to folks like them.

'I'm sorry, I have to ask you this,' the young detective said, sitting forward. 'Do you know of anyone who might want to hurt your daughter? Perhaps someone she might have upset recently?'

Darren's face hardened. 'Aidan.'

'You don't know that,' Marnie said.

The detectives exchanged a glance.

Darren ignored her. And when he started talking about his daughter's former partner, he couldn't stop. The words spewed out of his mouth like water from an overflowing drainage pipe. He talked about a nine-year relationship with a man two years'

Shauna's elder, a man who'd charmed her initially with fancy dinners and posh restaurants, then once he got his feet under the table and the children were born, he changed. He wore her down, controlled her movements – where she worked, when she went out, whom she saw. Then he'd dropped her like a skydiver in free fall, four months earlier.

'What makes you think he had reason to kill your daughter?' the young detective asked.

'Because he pushed her around.'

Marnie put out a shaky hand. 'We don't know that for sure.'

He shook her off. 'Their neighbour heard him going at her. Called the police several times. You need to check your records.'

Marnie recoiled. Shauna hadn't told them about the police visits at the time. She'd kept it to herself, just as she'd kept the arguments to herself. Shauna could be deep like that. Deep, headstrong and fiercely independent. Never one to confide or offload her problems, she preferred to deal with things herself.

They had found out about the rows from her elderly neighbour, Mary, one evening when they were babysitting, shortly after Aidan had left. Mary only too happy to chat to them over the fence and pass on the scandalous details. When they later confronted Shauna, she had played it down, said her neighbour was nosy, overzealous. Shauna maintained it was an amicable separation and, after the initial shock, the children did seem happy. It was difficult to know whom to believe.

'It was weird,' Darren continued. 'Even when Aidan started seeing someone else, Shauna refused to say or do anything to hurt him. The house sale was a prime example. She didn't need to move. It was unsettling for the children. We tried to talk her out of it, but she wouldn't listen. She offered Aidan ten thousand pounds from the equity. I'm convinced there was something else going on – he had such a hold over her.'

Marnie listened to her husband punch out the words, one

after the other, finishing up with: 'Aidan exploited her. He pushed her to the edge when they were together, and he's continued to push her afterwards.' He sat back in his chair and stared at the ceiling, spent. As if all the air had been sucked from his lungs.

The detective looked sceptical. 'I understand Shauna and Aidan have been separated for four months,' she said. 'What makes you think Aidan might attack Shauna now?'

'The house sale fell through last week,' Darren said. 'Aidan has been pushing for it since he left. Everything was in place. They were due to exchange last Monday, but the buyer was made redundant and pulled out at the last minute.'

The detectives traded another glance.

'The children were with Aidan last night,' Marnie said.

'Maybe he got a sitter, popped out…'

'No,' she said to Darren. As much as she loathed her daughter's ex-partner, she couldn't for the life of her believe he'd be capable of murder. Not the children's father… 'Charlotte had an asthma attack. She told me this morning. She got upset, needed to use her inhaler. They almost called Shauna. He let her stay up to watch telly.'

'Well, if he wasn't directly responsible, then he had something to do with this,' Darren said with conviction. 'Mark my words.'

CHAPTER 8

The woman's eyes widened on the screen as she gave her account. Dark curly hair swept away from a heart-shaped face. Cecily Thomas, the informant who found Shauna's body, looked like one of those svelte joggers who didn't have an ounce of spare body weight on her. Helen watched the recording of the interview play out as Cecily talked about setting her alarm to leave early that morning. An eight-mile run before the heat of the day kicked in – part of her training for a half-marathon next weekend. Tears rolled down her cheeks as she described finding the body beside the river. She'd seen no one.

Ms Thomas's route was recorded on the Strava app on her phone. Inquiries failed to show any connection with the victim. It was a pitiful account, probably the first dead body the poor woman had seen. A sight that would haunt her for weeks, months and probably years ahead, but there was no indication of any involvement.

The footage ended. Helen eased back into her chair. The body was back at the morgue. They were playing the waiting game. Waiting to hear from forensics, from the search team in the wood, a time for the autopsy. She looked up into the incident room. Officers tapped keyboards and spoke into phone receivers, dealing with the fallout from the public appeal, desperately hoping for some clue, some inkling of what had happened in those woods last night, to appear.

The pentagram was like a stone in her shoe. It was almost as if the killer was trying to draw their attention to something, maybe something in the victim's background. She clicked a key and brought up the Hampton Pagans' website – Spencer's passing shot before he left the office. A childlike drawing of Stonehenge sat above a message, actively welcoming new members. There was a section on the history of Druidism and Wicca. Another with a list of meeting dates in The Crown at Little Hampstead, just outside town. But the pentacle at the side wasn't inverted and the general message was a gentle one of appreciation of nature and the environment as an alternative force. Local satanic groups were proving more difficult to pin down. Though, even if they were involved, Helen couldn't imagine them drawing attention to themselves by using the emblem. The jangle of her phone broke her abstraction. *Dark* flashed up on the screen.

Helen grabbed the receiver and flicked a button on the phone. 'How are you doing, Rosa?' she asked.

'I'm with the victim's mother and father.'

Pemberton entered her office. She indicated for him to pull up a chair and switched the phone to conference call.

'How are the family holding up?' Helen asked.

'Shaken, understandably. They're getting ready to take the grandchildren back to their house.' Helen took down the address. It was in the suburb of Weston, not far from the southern tip of Blackwell Wood. She couldn't help wondering if this might be significant. 'No immediate signs of a struggle in the victim's house,' Dark continued. 'Shauna O'Hennessey's car is on the drive. Looks like she came home and left by some other means.'

'Okay, I'll get the CSIs out to do a thorough search of the house.' They couldn't rule out the fact that the killer might have met Shauna at home and shed some strands of hair or left bodily fluids or particles behind. 'We'll start a house-to-house in her road too, see if anyone saw somebody pick her up or noticed her coming and going yesterday evening. What could the family tell us about Shauna?'

Dark talked about a private woman, rebuilding her life after a relationship breakdown. Helen listened carefully as she relayed Darren's account of Shauna's relationship with Aidan Drinkwater. She'd read the domestic incident reports. All three of them – one six months ago, another a couple of weeks later. The final one completed a week before he left. On each occasion, police were called by the same concerned neighbour when they heard the couple fighting. The neighbour maintained the couple rowed a lot and were becoming more agitated, more aggressive. She was worried for their safety, concerned for the children. The officer's report showed no injuries to either party and noted that they were calm when the police arrived.

'Speak to the neighbour, will you? Find out when she last saw Shauna and whether she can add anything.'

'Will do.' Dark went on to talk about the house sale. 'I don't know, ma'am. The father seems convinced that if our victim is Shauna, Aidan had something to do with her death. He has a new partner, has been pushing for a quick house sale. Sounds like he needs the money. And with her out of the picture, he certainly stands to gain.'

'It looks like we need to pay him a visit. Leave that with me.'

'Okay. Is the victim back at the morgue? Mr O'Hennessey is struggling to accept it's his daughter. The sooner we can do the ID procedure, the better.'

Helen had delivered more than enough death messages to be familiar with the different reactions. The shock, the disbelief, the denial. It was a hopeless situation and a part of the job no copper relished. 'Yes, she's there. I'll make a call now, have them prepare her.'

Helen thanked Dark, ended the call and looked up at Pemberton. 'What do you think?' she asked.

He turned down the corners of his mouth. 'The ex was the last person to see her.'

'Hmm.' This wasn't the first time in Helen's experience as a murder detective that grieving families apportioned blame on someone nearby. It was natural for them to lash out, especially if they disapproved of Aidan's treatment of Shauna. And statistics indicated that most people were killed by someone they knew, someone close to them.

But they didn't know about the engraving on the body and the conditions in which she was left...

'Surely, if he was involved, he'd try to hide the body,' she said. 'Not take the trouble to carve a symbol on her chest and leave her close to a public pathway.'

Pemberton shrugged.

'As soon as the ID is confirmed, we need to start speaking with friends and family,' she said. 'We need to dig a bit deeper into Aidan Drinkwater's background too. See if there is any connection with the occult and whether he or Shauna has shown any tendencies to join cults or alternative religions. Let's check if Shauna's car pings on any of our cameras yesterday evening too. We could really do with bottoming out her movements.'

Pemberton nodded. 'I'll get that set up.'

'Okay, I'll meet you outside in ten minutes. I think we'll speak with Aidan Drinkwater now.'

Helen swivelled in her chair as he left the office. According to Mrs O'Hennessey, Shauna didn't have a best friend or confidante. Aidan Drinkwater had spent years living with Shauna. Sleeping in her bed, helping to raise their kids. If her parents' account was to be believed, they were still close. Perhaps they were involved in something together. Something that had got out of hand.

CHAPTER 9

Hampton Autocare was an old, prefabricated building situated on a side road off High Street, just around the corner from The Royal Oak. Helen and Pemberton parked on the tarmac out front, facing the peeling blue and yellow signage, in dire need of a paint job. A folding door was rolled back, a wide-open mouth, exposing a large workshop beyond. A small reception office sat at the far end.

The rain had abated, shards of sunshine breaking through the clouds as they exited the car. Helen moved to the side to allow a mechanic to reverse a Toyota and stepped over a puddle streaked with the rainbow colours of petrol. The pungent smell of oil and diesel pervaded the air.

Inside the workshop, a radio DJ was twittering about an upcoming band Helen didn't recognise. A silver Mondeo sat high on a rack at the far end. A bench stacked with tools ran along the back wall; a metal shelf filled with more tools lined the wall in front. A mechanic in blue coveralls was bent over the engine of a blue Mini. He looked up as they approached. Pale blue eyes staring out from a gaunt face. A vein protruded from his balding scalp.

Helen held up her badge and introduced them both. 'We're looking for Aidan Drinkwater.'

He pointed at a pair of black boots sticking out from

beneath an SUV in the centre of the floor and turned back to the Mini.

'Mr Drinkwater?' Pemberton called over. No answer. He moved in closer, bent down and tried again, louder this time.

'He won't hear you.' It was the balding colleague. 'He's got his earplugs in.' He crossed the floor and kicked the boots. The rumble of wheels on concrete followed as the mechanic rolled out and tugged at an earphone, bemused.

'Mr Drinkwater?' Helen said, flashing her badge.

Aidan nodded, slid off the trolley and stood. Military-short blond hair accentuated a blocky head, a square jaw. A line of swallows was tattooed on the side of his neck. Blue coveralls were tied at his waist, the edge of his pectoral muscles clear through the black T-shirt that covered his torso. He hovered over them, switching from one detective to another, alarm in his eyes. 'What's going on?' he said. 'Is it my kids?'

'No, sir. Your kids are fine,' Helen said. 'Is there somewhere we can talk?'

Perplexed tramlines gathered on Aidan's forehead. He nodded across to his colleague. 'I'm taking five. I'll be in the canteen.'

The canteen was a poky room behind the reception. Two Formica tables, littered with mugs and coffee stains and surrounded by orange plastic chairs, were scattered at angles. More coffee stains covered the empty work surface that lined the wall beneath the window. A couple of sandwich boxes were stacked beside a water heater at the far end.

The clasp on the door was broken and, as much as she tried, Helen couldn't make it engage. She pushed it to. At least it cut out some of the radio which was now playing a heavy metal beat at full volume. 'Is there somewhere more private?' she asked.

'Only the owner's office,' Aidan said. An ounce of exasperation crept into his voice as he slid into a chair. 'And he keeps that locked. Now what's this about?'

Helen lowered herself into a chair beside Pemberton and

delivered the news about Shauna's death as tactfully as she could, taking care to keep the finer details, including the engraving, to herself. As she spoke, she watched Aidan's reaction carefully, searching for any signs of latent guilt. An uneasy shift, a lack of eye contact. Any clues in his body language that indicated he knew more than he was letting on. Shauna was small and slender. Aidan almost twice her size. Helen was conscious of the alibi – he was with his kids all evening. Though experience had taught her that alibis weren't always as secure as they might initially seem. It wasn't out of the realms of possibility that the children had fallen asleep, and he'd slipped out and visited Shauna. Maybe they'd argued. It wouldn't have been difficult for him to overpower her.

But she couldn't reconcile the markings on Shauna's chest and the way she was laid out in the woods with what she saw now: a man built like an Olympic shot-putter who paled and shrunk before her eyes.

'I can't believe it,' he said, the calluses on his palms catching at his stubble as he swiped a hand down his face. 'I only saw her yesterday evening. She called by to drop off some of the kids' stuff.'

Helen checked the time – 5 pm. It concurred with Marnie's timeline. 'How did she seem?'

He gave an imperceptible shrug. 'Her normal self. She spoke to the kids, only stayed a few minutes.'

'I understand you were separated?'

'Yes, four months ago.' He narrowed his eyes. 'Why?'

'Are you still familiar with her friends, associates?'

He turned down the corners of his mouth. 'Some. She has her work colleagues. Her mother. Shauna doesn't go out much. Keeps herself to herself.'

Present tense. *Interesting*, Helen thought. 'Still, it would help if you could give us a list. We need to speak with everybody who has been in touch with her recently.'

He blinked widely and nodded. 'How are my kids taking it?'

'As well as can be expected. Shauna's parents have taken them to their house.' Pemberton opened a notebook and clicked the end of his pen. But Aidan stared into space, jaw hanging. Shock was setting in. She needed to find a way to keep him engaged, keep him talking. 'Can I get you a drink, a glass of water maybe?'

Aidan's Adam's apple wobbled as he swallowed. He shook his head.

She gave him a moment before she spoke again. 'Do you know of anyone who might want to hurt Shauna?'

'No. Shauna's a good person. A fabulous mother. We just got together too young. Grew apart.'

Again, spoken in the present tense. The news hadn't properly hit home yet. Though something about his words caught her. Mr O'Hennessey was convinced Aidan had something to do with his daughter's death, and yet it seemed he had only praise for his ex-partner.

'Can you tell me anything about Shauna's hobbies, her pastimes?'

He looked bewildered. 'She likes horses.'

'Is she a spiritual person? Perhaps she goes to church?'

'Shauna is the least spiritual person I know. Neither of us are. No, we don't go to church. Why do you need to know that?'

'We're just trying to get a feel for her life, her daily routine,' Helen said subtly. She tried to probe further. When Aidan wasn't forthcoming, she decided to change tack. 'I understand you have a new partner?'

'Jade.'

'How does she get along with Shauna?'

'They haven't met.'

'Does Jade live with you?'

'No. She has her own place near the pocket park in Weston. The children love her.'

'We'll need her details.'

'Why?'

'To check her movements yesterday. It's quite routine.'

His face clouded. 'She was at work. She works at a call centre out on Lamberton Industrial Park.'

'In the evening?'

'It's shift work.'

Pemberton's pen scratched the paper as he recorded the details in his spidery scrawl.

'I'll also need you to tell us your movements throughout yesterday evening,' she said.

'What?'

The drone of an engine filled the room as a lorry passed outside.

'Oh, I get it,' Aidan said, sitting back in his chair. 'It has to be something to do with Jade or me. This is Marnie, right? Or Darren?'

Helen stayed silent.

'Jesus, that family stops at nothing.' He huffed. 'Well, you can tell them from me, whatever happened to Shauna has nothing to do with me, and it has nothing to do with Jade.'

'If you could answer the question.'

'I was at home with my kids all evening. Alone. Just as I am every Friday. It's the only bloody time I have with them.' He snorted. 'Shauna's parents have never liked me. I was never good enough for their daughter before Tom died. No chance afterwards.'

Helen cut in. 'Tom?'

'Shauna's brother. He was killed in Helmand years ago. I guess Marnie didn't tell you that snippet of information. Not surprising. She talks about him as if he's still alive.' He raised his eyes, met Helen's gaze. 'They all do.'

56

CHAPTER 10

Helen glanced out at the line of cars in front of her, waiting at the traffic lights. Having read the domestic incident reports, she understood the family's concern: Shauna and Aidan appeared to have suffered a strained relationship before the separation. If his account was to be believed, they'd put their differences behind them. But before she could be convinced, she needed to confirm his movements last night.

Formally interviewing children involved in a major crime was a serious matter. They were treated as vulnerable witnesses, taken into a special suite with soft chairs and toys and interviewed by a specially trained detective; the whole event video recorded. It was a sober affair and not one Helen wanted to subject Shauna's children to on the day they'd lost their mother. But with the potential difficulties between the couple, she couldn't ignore the chance that Aidan could be involved and the only person that could verify his movements last night was his daughter. She needed to find a way around it.

The lights changed. Pemberton edged the car forward.

Helen pondered a second further, then checked the clock on the dashboard – 1.30 pm. Dark should be finished at the mortuary by now. She scrolled through her phone and dialled. The phone rang out several times before it was answered.

'Hi, ma'am,' Dark said. 'I was just going to call you.'

The enthusiasm in the young woman's voice, after everything she'd been through recently, continued to hearten Helen. She had taken some time off and only been back at work a week or so, yet nothing seemed to faze her.

'The ID is confirmed,' Dark said. 'We're back at the O'Hennesseys' house. I'm talking to you from their garden.'

'Thank you. How do they seem?'

'Calm. Numb. It's never easy.'

Helen related to that. Before they saw the body, many families held on to a tiny thread of hope that the police were mistaken and the victim wasn't their daughter, son, sister, brother, mother, father. Desperately wishing it was someone else laid on that gurney, and their loved one was still out there, heart beating. A positive ID shattered that hope in an instant and it never felt good.

'Spencer spoke with the immediate neighbours and then headed back to headquarters. He should be there now. Apparently, the neighbour who'd reported the rows before the separation last chatted with Shauna a few days ago. She didn't see or hear her yesterday. The neighbour on the other side was at home and didn't notice anything.'

'Thanks.' Another hope of a sighting of Shauna yesterday evening dashed. 'Do you think the family are up to more questions?' Helen asked. 'There's something I need you to do.'

Helen talked Dark through questioning the children and then passed on Aidan's comments about the O'Hennesseys' son. 'I'm not sure if there is any significance. Can you find out more about him?'

By the time Helen finished the call, she was confident the young woman would strike the balance needed to gain the information without unduly stressing the family further.

Pemberton pulled into headquarters and parked up. They were just climbing out of the car when Helen's mobile rang again with the *Dad's Army* theme tune: the ringtone assigned to her mother.

'You go on ahead,' she said to Pemberton, holding up her phone. 'I need to get this.'

She waited for him to cross the car park and disappear into the building before she answered.

'Hi,' her mother said.

She sounded breathless as if she'd been running. Jane Lavery was only in her early sixties and still super active, but she'd struggled to bat off a heavy bout of flu a few months earlier, a salient reminder that she wasn't getting any younger, and it had left her raspy and wheezy at times.

'Everything okay?' Helen asked.

'Yes. I'm just back from dropping off Robert. He's still looking after that new boy at school. He wanted to show him around town.'

Helen smiled to herself. Her fourteen-year-old was a kind, thoughtful soul. The perfect child to buddy someone new to the area.

'You got my text?' Helen checked.

'Yes.'

The fact that she didn't elaborate on Helen's message about the new case which would take up most, if not all, of the weekend wasn't lost on Helen. Her mother kept a close eye on the news. She knew her daughter was working on the murder of a young woman less than ten years Helen's junior, and she deliberately chose to skirt the issue.

'What's Matthew up to?' Helen asked, thoughts turning to her eldest son.

'Still asleep, I think. Hasn't left his bedroom yet anyway.'

'Post-exam stress.'

'Something like that.' The accompanying laughter dissolved some of the stilted tension. 'What time do you think you'll be back?'

'I'm not sure.' Helen glanced at her watch, an automatic gesture. It was 1.45. 'Could be late.'

The line went quiet. Helen's stomach dipped as she started across the car park. Until recently, Jane Lavery had championed Helen's police career, encouraging her to move through the ranks. But visiting her daughter in hospital with injuries sustained in the course of duty a few months earlier, injuries which took a spell of sick leave to heal, had shaken her to the core. When Helen returned to work afterwards, she had expressed concern. Concern for Helen, for the boys, for the impact of her daughter's job on their family. Concern that currently manifested itself in them both tiptoeing around the cases Helen managed.

'Okay, we'll bat on without you,' her mother said eventually. 'Take it easy.'

'Of course. See you soon.'

Helen ended the call, slipped her phone into her pocket and rounded the corner of the building, colliding with Pemberton, who had a smoking cigarette in one hand and a steaming styrofoam cup in the other. He immediately jumped back, the coffee in his cup spilling down his shirt.

'Sorry,' she said.

Pemberton stubbed out the cigarette and brushed himself down. 'At least it missed the trousers,' he said, scrunching his nose cheekily. 'Could have been embarrassing.'

Helen laughed.

'Actually, I was just coming to get you,' he said. 'We've just verified Jade, Aidan's girlfriend's, movements and confirmed she was at work yesterday, on the night shift.'

'Okay, thanks.' Another lead bottomed out.

'But that wasn't why I was coming to get you. The guys have been trawling through the camera footage from last night. There's something you need to see.'

CHAPTER 11

Helen walked back into the incident room to an array of new faces – the injection of staff Alison had promised. Two long desks had been dragged in and placed at the far end, beside the filing cabinets, and the new staff – at least twelve of them, she counted – had hit the ground running. Phones were glued to ears, pens scratched at paper as notes were recorded. She made a mental note to introduce herself to each of them later.

'There are plenty more,' Pemberton said, gesturing to the new bodies. 'They were here when I walked in. Just sent half of them out to interview the victim's work colleagues.' He rubbed his forehead, lowered his voice. 'Didn't recognise any of them. There's so many newcomers I've no idea who anyone is these days.'

Helen tipped her head in acknowledgement. There was a time when she couldn't step foot into a station without being greeted like an old friend. But things changed quickly in the police, and since the homicide team had moved into this new building on the county's periphery earlier this year, they were more detached.

He motioned for her to follow him to his desk and clicked a button on his laptop. A street scene filled the screen. Bushwell's Services on the opposite side of the road, flanked by a bank on one side, a boutique on the other. 'There was a mobile

ANPR van parked on High Street last night near Bushwell's Services,' he said. 'It picked up something interesting.' He pressed the start key. A car whizzed past. Then another. A Volkswagen Golf pulled onto the garage forecourt, a man climbed out and went into the shop. Helen passed Pemberton a quizzical glance. He held up a flat hand. She turned back to the screen just as a yellow Kia pulled into the garage.

'That's Shauna's car,' he said. 'Same registration number.'

Helen leaned in towards the screen. A young woman emerged and proceeded to unfasten the petrol cap and fill up the car. Shauna O'Hennessey wore a black knee-length dress and heels. Locks of dark hair hung freely down her back. It was like staring at a ghost. 'What time is this?' Helen asked.

Pemberton froze the screen. 'It's 5.14 pm.'

Shauna replaced the pump and entered the shop.

'That garage is on the route between Aidan's and hers,' Helen said. 'She must have been on her way home, stopped off to fill up.'

'Wait, there's more.'

They watched her slide her purse into her handbag as she left the shop. A figure in a black jacket, baggy jeans and beanie hat approached. It was a quick conversation, less than twenty seconds, Helen guessed, then the two parted and Shauna made for her car, glancing back fleetingly before she climbed in and drove off.

'Play it again,' Helen said. She squinted at the screen as they came to the part where Shauna left the shop. Pemberton slowed it down and they watched, frame by frame. When the figure entered the screen, he froze it, enlarging the image. But the face of the other person was angled away from the lens, their features hidden.

'Do they have CCTV at the garage?' she asked.

'They do. It was pointing across the forecourt, in the wrong direction.'

'Can we find out who was working there yesterday?'

Spencer wheeled his chair over to join them. 'I've checked

with the garage. The cashier working last night is off duty. I've left a voicemail. I'm waiting for him to call me back.'

'Good.' She tapped the screen. 'Whoever they are walked off in the opposite direction to Shauna's house, towards Roxten. See if there are any cameras that way that can give us a better image. We need to trace this person.'

The two men followed her as she crossed to the whiteboard at the front of the room.

'Let's work through our timeline,' she said. 'Shauna's mother says she called in to see her after her interview at 4.30 pm.' Helen wrote the details along with the time across the top of the board in red. 'Aidan stated she joined him at five-ish.' She made a note of this and turned to the map. 'Bushwell's Services is on High Street. She called in at 5.14 pm on her way home.' She noted the whiteboard and turned to the faces in front of her. 'Anything back from house-to-house in her road?'

'An elderly gentleman who lives two doors down spotted her returning home,' Spencer said. He pulled out his notebook, flipped a few pages. 'Thinks it was about half five. Nothing afterwards.'

Helen pushed her tongue against the side of her teeth. 'Marnie O'Hennessey claims her daughter called her at 7.15.'

Spencer nodded. 'That concurs with her phone records. There were only a few phone calls yesterday – one from her dad at 2.18 pm – I presume him wishing her luck for the interview. We'll check that. One from Aidan at 4.39 pm. Then the final one to her mother at 7.15 pm.'

'No texts?'

'Not that I can see. It might be she uses other messaging apps – Snapchat or WhatsApp. We're checking with friends and colleagues, but without having her phone, we can't be sure at present. Her last entry on Facebook was a photo before her interview.' He pointed at the board beside him, to an image of Shauna in the same black dress she'd been wearing on the garage forecourt. It was a more detailed shot showing off the fitted dress, the plunging neckline, the tiny frill that laced the bottom, just above her knees. She was holding up her phone, photographing herself in the mirror. The caption *Wish me luck* ran beneath it.

'No sightings after she arrived home at 5.30?' she checked. Heads shook.

Helen scanned the map. Shauna lived in Worthington, a suburb on the periphery of Hampton, at least three miles from where she was found. 'Why did she go to the woods and how did she get there?'

The room quietened. Heads looked up, a knot of minds mulling over the question. A phone rang. Spencer moved away to take the call.

'Have we sited the phone during the call to her mum?' Helen asked.

Pemberton nodded. 'It's not completely accurate. It puts her within a couple of hundred yards of her home. Her phone was last sited in the woods at 11 pm last night. It's been switched off ever since.'

Helen could see where he was coming from. If the killer had taken the phone and left it on, it may have led them broadly to his location. 'So, we know nothing more about the victim, apart from she was a mother of two who worked as a hairdresser,' Helen checked. 'What about computers?'

'Her laptop is password-protected. The techies are trying to get into it.'

'Bank records?'

'Still waiting for them. We've just chased.'

There were no reports of similar cases in other forces either.

Helen's cheeks billowed as she let out a long breath. They were no closer to catching the killer than when she'd visited the crime scene that morning.

The sound of a phone receiver crashing into its cradle caught her attention. Spencer jumped up. 'That was the cashier at the petrol station. He doesn't remember the incident specifically, but he does remember Shauna.' He grabbed his jacket off the back of his chair. 'I'll head out, see if I can jog his memory.'

CHAPTER 12

Marnie stroked Ollie's crown and watched him fix another piece of Lego to the green base. He hadn't left her side since she'd delivered the news earlier, telling the children their mother had gone to heaven. Charlotte had asked if she'd be back to take them to school on Monday and when Marnie said no, she'd burst into tears. Then Ollie had cried too, and they'd all sat on the floor, heads buried in each other while Marnie tried to comfort and console them.

It was a miracle they were both too young for mobile phones. At least she could keep them from the news and the gruesome details of her daughter's death. One tiny blessing. But for how long? And what was she to tell them? She'd have to say something before they returned to school and heard about the murder elsewhere. Though she had no idea how to find the words. How to tell her beautiful, bright, happy-go-lucky grandchildren that their mother had not only been taken from them, but she'd also been killed, murdered in cold blood. And they didn't even know by whom, or why.

She looked across at Darren, sitting in the armchair, skin paper-thin and tinged with grey, eyes fixed on nothingness. The poor man who'd returned from a routine forty-eight-hour drop and trundled over to his daughter's house to find his worst nightmare realised. He hadn't wanted to believe the detectives. He'd only spoken to Shauna yesterday, to wish her luck for the job interview, and she'd seemed optimistic, upbeat. She couldn't possibly be dead.

The trip to the morgue had silenced him. Marnie had wanted to accompany him, but she couldn't leave the children with anyone else – not after the news they'd received today. She could only imagine how awful it must have been. Watching the broken body of his precious daughter being wheeled in on a gurney. She'd seen family identifications on dramas on television. The clinician folding back the sheet.

What would Shauna look like? Would they cover her neck? Marnie shuddered. The thought of her beautiful daughter, with the porcelain complexion, the mane of glossy hair, dead, sent a fresh rush of bile to her throat. How could someone do that to her?

Darren hadn't said a word when he returned. Breaking his silence only briefly to help her deliver the news to their grandchildren. Soothing, cuddling, mopping up tears on automatic pilot. And now he sat in the chair, zombie-like, the very life sucked out of him.

Poor Darren. He was bereft. He'd never recovered from losing his son. Now he'd lost his daughter too, and in the worst possible circumstances.

Charlotte tipped a fresh Tupperware box of Lego onto the laminated flooring, the blocks rattling across the floor. She hadn't flinched when the detective had walked in with Darren. She was making a sunflower for Mummy. Sunflowers were Mummy's favourite flower. She wanted it to be perfect, she had said, and she made a play of selecting the right coloured pieces and arranging them carefully on her base.

'That's a lovely watch,' the detective said to the child.

A tear pricked Marnie's eye as she watched the detective slide onto the floor beside Charlotte. The woman had been a godsend this morning. Answering their questions. Guiding Darren through the process at the morgue. Coming back to the house and making them all tea and sandwiches. Another tear welled in her eye. She fought it back as she remembered choosing the child's first watch with Shauna. 'I want her to have one with an old-fashioned clock face,' her daughter had said. 'There'll be plenty of time for digitals in the future.' And they'd found the perfect one in Lewis's with a pink strap and a silver face, adorned with tiny black numbers; the face circled in sparkly crystals. Charlotte had loved it the minute she opened it. She only took it off to go to bed or have a bath.

'She got it for her birthday last month, didn't you, darling?' Marnie said to her granddaughter. 'A special present because she'd learned to tell the time.'

The little girl didn't look up.

'That's very impressive,' the detective said. 'And it's such a pretty one too. What time is it now?'

Marnie's stomach clenched. Charlotte's face was still red, her neck blotchy from crying.

The child twisted her wrist, viewed her watch and turned to the detective. 'Quarter to three.' The words were spoken slowly and with authority.

'Well done. You are clever,' the detective said. 'That's not what the clock up there says.' She pointed at the mantel.

Charlotte followed her eyeline. 'That's wrong. It's five minutes fast. It's always like that because Grandma doesn't like to be late.' Marnie fought back fresh tears. Charlotte loved to impart knowledge, especially when she was showing off a new skill, and now was no exception.

'Did you wear your watch last night when you were poorly?'
The child nodded.

'Can you remember what time you were poorly?'

A headshake. 'It was just before Ollie went to bed.'

'What happened?'

'I had an asthma attack. Daddy gave me my inhaler and we waited for it to pass.'

'How long did it last?'

She shrugged a single shoulder, rolling a yellow piece of Lego between her thumb and forefinger.

'Did you go to bed afterwards?'

'No, Daddy let me stay up late with him. Sometimes, I get another one soon after. He wanted to make sure I was all better.'

'What time did you go to bed?'

A wary look. 'Daddy said I shouldn't tell anyone.'

The detective sat forward. 'It's all right. You're not in any trouble.'

'Twelve o'clock.' Wide eyes gazed up at the detective. 'And I slept in Daddy's bed.'

'No, it wasn't!' Ollie said. 'You're telling lies.'

'I'm not,' she said. 'I know because I checked my watch.'

68

CHAPTER 13

Later that afternoon, Helen emerged from the toilet cubicle, fastened the buttons on her clean shirt, smoothed her trousers and pulled a suit jacket on – the spare outfit she always kept at the office. The victim's identification confirmed, it was now time to face the press, release the victim's name and appeal for anyone who might have seen Shauna yesterday evening. She placed her phone on the surface beside the sink and brought up the Facebook photo of Shauna – the image the parents were content for them to share. She looked vibrant, happy, alive. Blooming with optimism of what the afternoon might bring. No idea that her life would be over in a matter of hours.

A stark difference to the greying lifeless corpse she'd seen on the mortuary slab that afternoon. Helen sighed as the image on her screen faded. They'd had little back from this morning's appeal. They still needed to fill the gap between 7.15 and 12.30 am and photographs, especially in the same attire, concentrated the mind. Hopefully, this picture of Shauna would jog someone's memory.

She ran a brush through her hair and glanced down at the sheet of paper in front of her – the list Spencer had thrust into her hand as she left the office. Disappointingly, the National Crime Agency had no experts on the occult or devil worship on their database, which meant pursuing an expert internationally. In the meantime, Spencer had researched and put together a list of active movements using inverted pentagram emblems in the UK. It filled an A4 page.

Children of Satan in Birmingham. Something else near Nottingham. Others in Derbyshire, Cambridgeshire, West Yorkshire, Northumberland. They'd start by examining the closest, scrutinising their membership. But what concerned Helen was that while some of them were relatively nearby, they were still an hour or so away by car. There was no mention of anything in or around Hamptonshire, and the way Shauna was left, in the quiet part of Blackwell Wood, almost a kilometre from the road, suggested local knowledge.

The door flapped open and Dark entered.

'Ah, they said you were in here, ma'am.' She leaned her shoulder against the wall beside the dryer, her face sombre.

'How are the O'Hennesseys holding up?' Helen asked.

'Okay in the circumstances. Aidan has just taken the children to his house.' Dark stared into space. 'Those poor little mites. I don't think they've really grasped what's going on.' She passed on the confirmation of the alibi.

Helen listened carefully as she brushed her hair. That ruled out Aidan as the killer. He could still be involved in some way, but they'd found nothing in his background, or his girlfriend's, to link him to pentagrams or sects or alternative religions. Plus, numerous friends and colleagues of Shauna's had now been interviewed and none of them had mentioned anything to suggest the couple were interested in either devil worship, witchcraft or the occult. Something about the killing, the way it was executed, made her think they needed to branch out, look further afield.

She retrieved a hair tie from the bag and viewed Dark through the mirror as she gathered her hair and fastened it at the nape of her neck. 'Did you speak to the family about Tom?'

'Yes. He was in the army, deployed in Afghanistan. Blown up by an IED, an improvised explosive device, four years ago. Nothing left of him, by all accounts. All they've got are his medals.'

'That poor family.' Helen thought of her own boys. Losing one child would be heart-wrenching; she couldn't imagine how anyone would recover. To lose two was tragic. 'Let's hope the public can give us something,' she said, tightening the tie in her hair and tucking her hairbrush into her bag. She updated Dark on Spencer's visit to the petrol station. 'Spencer talked to the cashier. He didn't see much of the other person, sadly. They only walked across the forecourt, didn't enter the shop.'

Helen gathered her belongings, about to make her way out when her mobile rang. *Alison* flashed up. 'Sorry,' she said. 'Better take this.' She moved out to the corridor. 'I'm just on my way up,' she said to Alison.

Alison sounded harried. 'No need. *I'm* going to be handling the media on this one.'

Helen almost dropped her phone. She didn't relish press conferences, far happier keeping the public informed and appealing for witnesses via statements, which were often more fruitful in the long run. In the past, Jenkins had taken the lead with the media. Occasionally, she'd appeared on the periphery: appealing for witnesses, or for the public to respect the privacy of a victim's family. But being senior investigating officer and covering the superintendent role, she'd assumed she would take centre stage here. It was unusual for those heading the case to be excluded.

'I'm not with you,' Helen said.

'It's the chief's new policy. One point of contact.'

'Surely that should be me since I'm leading the inquiry.'

'The chief thinks not. This isn't personal, Helen. You're covering for the super and you're an inspector down. You concentrate on the investigation. I'll handle the press.'

The call cut. Helen pressed her back against the cold plaster of the corridor wall. It was a kind offer. Though if experience had taught her anything, senior officers rarely offered their services without an ulterior motive.

CHAPTER 14

Helen woke early the following morning, her mind immediately turning to the case. She checked her phone and frowned. No overnight messages. No pressing news then. By 6.05 am, she was dressed and downstairs.

In the kitchen, the French doors were already flung open, the sweet scent of honeysuckle wafting in from the garden. She flicked the switch on the kettle and squinted out of the window, just about making out the silhouette of her mother sitting on the patio at the end, reading a book, taking advantage of the clear morning.

She made the drinks and carried two steaming mugs of coffee down the garden under a blue sky dotted with puffy white clouds, the freshly washed borders and hedgerows the only sign of yesterday's rainfall.

'Morning,' Helen said. 'You're up early.'

'I could say the same.' Jane placed her book face down on the table beside her and thanked her daughter for the coffee. 'How are you?'

'Good, thanks. Busy day ahead.'

'Ah.' She placed the coffee on the table.

Helen shuffled into a seat beside her. It was blissfully quiet. The only sound, the odd bird chirping. 'How were the boys yesterday?' she asked.

'Fine. The newsagent's around the corner are looking for help. Sorting out the papers, filling in with deliveries, a bit of counter work. I've put Matthew's name forward.'

Helen stretched her eyelids back at the prospect of her eldest being up at dawn to sort newspapers. 'Does he know?'

'I told him last night. He pulled a face, but it brightened when I told him what they were paying.' She sported a manipulative smile. 'Robert brought his new friend home for dinner. Zac, I think they call him. We had home-made burgers. You missed out.'

Helen laughed. 'You okay with Robert's cricket practice this morning?'

'Sure.'

Helen stared down the garden to the house. She had been apprehensive when they'd decided to pool resources, buy this new build and move in together. In the end, the situation suited them both. Jane Lavery was a hands-on grandmother who enjoyed spending time with her family and watching her grandsons grow, while retaining her independence in the granny flat attached. After losing their father in a helicopter accident when they were young, Helen was mother and father to her boys and, if it wasn't for her own mother running the boys to their clubs and keeping a watchful eye, she couldn't work the unsociable hours the police demanded. Inevitably, it meant the two women's lives were entwined. Jane was Helen's confidante, the person she shared her life with. Although, as grateful as she was, there were occasions when Helen hankered after her freedom – a normal life, shared with a partner of a similar age. Somebody other than her mother. Especially when uncomfortable situations arose and aspects of her work affected her family, like now.

Davy Boyd's hooded dark gaze, as he slowed to pass her the other evening, flashed into her mind. Did her mother know Chilli had a half-brother? The fact that her mother's concern over Helen's job stemmed from the injuries she sustained on the case that brought down Chilli Franks left her uneasy. Should she tell her Davy was back? According to Pemberton, Davy Boyd was a married man with a family, a different character to Chilli. And if Davy had invested in Chilli's businesses, why shouldn't he come back and run them? It would be natural to show an interest in the person who had brought his half-brother down too. There was nothing to suggest her family were at risk and certainly no point in having a conversation that raked up old wounds. The last thing she needed was to highlight the potential dangers of her job at the moment.

She glanced across at her mother, sipping her coffee, watching the flower head of a fuchsia gently sway in the soft breeze. Enjoying the quiet, a clear sky blooming with the promise of a balmy day. No. Her family had lived under the ghost of Chilli Franks's threats for long enough. It was time to move on. Hampton wasn't a huge town, but big enough for her family and the Boyds to avoid each other. Perhaps it was time to let sleeping dogs lie.

* * *

At 6.30 on a Sunday morning, Hampton town centre was unsurprisingly quiet. Helen navigated the empty roads, ruminating on the press conference she'd live-streamed in her office last night. The seminar suite at headquarters had been packed to the rafters; cordoning off the whole of Blackwell Wood attracted widespread attention.

The buttons on Alison's jacket had glistened under the bright lighting as she stood on the stage and reassured members of the press that her officers were 'working around the clock to unearth the offender' and were pursuing 'a number of inquiries'. Police bullshit for they didn't have anything yet. Cameras flashed as she released the victim's identity. An enlarged photograph of Shauna in her dress alongside the grainy image of the figure she met at the garage had filled the wall behind her as she appealed for anyone who had seen either of them on Friday evening, or with information about the incident, to come forward. No questions were invited. She finished up with a warning for the public to adhere to the cordons and avoid flying drones or other devices over the area until their search was complete.

Succinct, clear. The message imparted in less than five minutes. It still seemed odd to be excluded, but she shrugged it off. Alison was clearly adept at dealing with the press and if that's what the chief wanted, then so be it. At least she could focus on the investigation.

Helen continued up High Street, her gaze falling on the peaked building of Bushwell's Services ahead. She glanced at the dash, then indicated and pulled onto the forecourt, lining her Volvo up beside pump number three. The pump Shauna O'Hennessey had used on Friday evening.

The forecourt was empty. A single cashier behind the desk in the shop eyed her as she unfolded herself from her car. Helen pulled out the pump and refuelled, listening to the drone of the electrics as she imagined Shauna standing in the same spot, less than forty-eight hours earlier. She'd watched the footage of Shauna over and over, and Spencer had been out and spoken to the cashier working on Friday evening, but she wanted to see it for herself. This was the last spot Shauna was seen alive and she wanted to get a feel for the place.

There was no pay-at-pump facility. Bushwell's was old-fashioned, the only independently owned station in the area. All customers were required to pay at the shop or kiosk. It was extraordinary how it kept going with two supermarket garages within half a mile offering fuel at least two pence cheaper and several petrol stations on the nearby ring road.

She tried to imagine the scene on Friday. The footage showed Shauna alone with her car on the forecourt – the only customer. At 5.14 pm, rush hour would have been in full swing. People passing, either on foot or in cars, all potential witnesses.

Helen finished up and entered the shop, passing the rack

of magazines along the end wall, the aisles of 'essentials', the fridges filled with milks and other drinks. No one at the petrol station could identify the person who spoke to Shauna. Perhaps the press appeal would come up with something. She hoped so.

She ordered a round of fresh takeaway coffees, paid up and carried them out to her car in a cardboard tray to find a battered old Audi had pulled in front of her. The sun was rising in the sky now, bouncing off the boot. While she loaded the coffees into the back of her car, the Audi driver moved off to the shop.

Helen wasn't sure what made her look over the car. It was nothing more than a fleeting glance, until a line of stickers across the bottom of the Audi's back window caught her eye. Sun-dried and peeled, barely readable. Something in the one on the end, a faded sky-blue sticker, curled at the edges, made her peer closer. It looked like an upturned star symbol. A website beneath. She squinted to read the address; it wasn't clear.

'Can I help you?'

Helen spun round.

The Audi driver was back at his car now and viewing her suspiciously. He was dressed in gym bottoms and a T-shirt that accentuated bulbous biceps.

'Do you own this car?' she asked.

The Audi driver narrowed his eyes and nodded.

Helen flashed her badge, then pointed at the sticker. 'Can you tell me where this came from?'

He looked at the sticker, then back at her. 'Why?'

'You're not in any trouble. It just might be helpful in an investigation I'm working on.'

He raised a single brow, said nothing.

'Did you place the sticker there?' Helen asked.

'No. I've only had the car a few months. That's been on there donkey's years. Must have been a previous owner. My wife's always moaning at me to clean the windows and scrub those off properly.'

'Do you mind if I take a picture?'

'Be my guest.'

Helen took a photo, made a note of the registration number and the man's name and address and thanked him.

Back in her car, she checked the clock again – 6.40 am – and dialled the incident room, expecting to catch one of the night shift, and was surprised to find Pemberton answer. 'Sean, you're in early.'

'Couldn't sleep.'

'Ah…' She passed on the details of the sticker. 'It could be something or nothing, but we haven't found anything local using that symbol yet. I'll text you a photo. See if you can enlarge it and decipher the website.'

CHAPTER 15

'Morning, guys,' Helen said to a rather weary-looking desk of night staff as she entered the incident room that morning. She brandished the tray of coffees. 'I've brought you a little pick-me-up.'

A cheer rolled around the desk. 'This isn't the shit we get from the machine,' Eric, one of the support staff, said, a grin stretching from ear to ear.

Helen smiled. 'Thought they'd keep you awake on your journey home. Which is,' she placed down the tray and glanced at her watch, 'in just over an hour.' Another cheer.

She leaned over Eric's shoulder, peered at his screen. 'Any leads from the appeal last night?'

Heads shook. 'We've logged every call,' Eric said. 'No new sightings of the victim, and nothing on the person who spoke to her at the petrol station.'

Helen did her best to hide her disappointment. 'Oh, well. Thanks, anyway. Perhaps the day staff will get a better response.'

She crossed to Pemberton's desk and placed another coffee down. He looked up and nodded appreciatively.

'How long have you been here?' she asked.

'I arrived just before you called,' he said, taking a sip of coffee then turning back to his screen. 'I've done some digging, found a website. It's pretty primitive.' A blue background with yellow writing so bright it blurred slightly filled the screen. 'Doesn't say much. Their mantra is all about opportunities and exceeding expectations – looks more like a business networking group.'

'Do we think it's the group from the sticker?'

'I wasn't sure at first. They are called The Alternatives, which fits with the parts we can read on the sticker. And when you go back through their old blog posts, there is a tribute to a man called Lacey who died a couple of years ago. Looks like he used to run the group and used a white inverted pentagram on a blue background as their symbol, just like the sticker. They've dropped it since.'

Helen scrunched her eyes and scanned the screen. No pictures. No images. Just lots of text about exploiting life chances and reaching potential – like some sort of corporate training programme – although they did call it an 'alternative belief system'. How long had that car been travelling about with the aged sticker on? How many more were out there? The problems with finding information on the use of the inverted pentagram and what it meant was bothering her. She'd spent an hour scouring the internet last night and, like Spencer, had received mixed messages. Some said the inverted pentagram represented evil. Others disputed it. It was all very frustrating. 'See if you can get hold of someone from The Alternatives,' Helen said. 'Might be worth speaking to them. At the very least, they might be able to enlighten us on what the use of the symbol actually means. And contact the DVLA, will you? See if you can trace previous owners of the vehicle sporting it.'

* * *

An hour later, Helen stood in front of her team at morning briefing.

'The autopsy report is through,' Pemberton said. 'Nothing new in there.'

'What about forensics?'

'They're hoping to get a preliminary report to us by tomorrow morning. No sign of her clothes and no luck with the dog unit. I guess it was always a stretch.'

She moved around the room, checking on interviews with the victim's work colleagues and her phone records. Building up a profile of Shauna O'Hennessey and finding out more about the woman behind the mother, the hairdresser, the daughter, was proving surprisingly problematic, especially for someone in such a sociable profession. Friends and colleagues corroborated her parents' statement, saying she was outwardly friendly but reticent to discuss her personal life. She had no social media apart from Facebook. It seemed peculiar she hadn't confided in a particular friend or some other outlet. It didn't help that the techies hadn't yet been able to crack the password on her iPad.

Spencer talked about the farmer, Dark about the family, each revealing nothing new.

They'd obtained a list of previous owners of the Audi and started working their way through.

Helen stared at the photo on the board, of Shauna dressed up for her interview. *Why her?* A regular working mum with no skeletons in the closet, no hidden secrets in her background – at least none they'd found so far.

The autopsy showed no sexual interference. Another motive stifled.

She switched to the image of the corpse and the split skin where the pentacle was engraved. Was Shauna a member of some mysterious society? Was this where she shared her secrets?

'Ma'am?'

She suddenly became aware that Dark had finished speaking and all eyes were on her.

'Do you have anything to add?' she said.

'Yes.' Helen pushed herself off the edge of the table and turned back to the room, sharing the chipped, sun-bleached sticker she'd seen that morning and Pemberton's findings.

'We've got an address for the leader, or convenor as he calls himself, a Mr Guy Thorne. The sergeant and I will head out to see him this morning. See what they represent.'

Spencer scratched his head. 'Is it worth it? You said yourself, the old man is dead. They don't use the symbol any more, and they didn't come up when I was looking at active groups.'

Helen understood his concern. The investigation was stretching resources to the limit, even with the injection of additional staff, and inquiries into other spiritual organisations thus far had been less than fruitful. 'They're local, and if their website is anything to go by, they're an alternative belief system. We need to understand more about their ethos, and we need to find out why they don't use the symbol any more. We can't rule out the possibility that our killer is connected in some way, either to them or a former member.'

CHAPTER 16

Marnie accelerated through the empty streets. Rows of terraces, bungalows with cars parked outside, detached houses with sweeping driveways – many with curtains tightly drawn. It was barely 9 am, and the residents of Hampton were taking advantage of a Sunday morning lie-in.

A metallic taste filled her mouth as she passed the green lawns of Oakwall Park. Her gums were bleeding again. They always did that when she was stressed, a legacy of a restless night, clenching her teeth, grinding them against each other until her head ached and her gums bled. The bedroom silence had been punctuated by the ebb and flow of Darren's breaths. She envied his ability to sleep. She wished she could. If nothing else, it would provide a welcome respite from the waterfall of gruesome thoughts cascading through her mind and the image of Shauna's limp, translucent body laid beside a river.

Tears pricked her eyes as she imagined her daughter's tiny frame, waves of dark hair, her dainty little hands in the mud. She'd been such a perfect baby: large tawny eyes, an infectious chuckle. People used to stop them in the street, in the supermarket, in the park and comment on her spidery lashes, her mop of rich curls. Such a pretty child, a prettiness that blossomed in adulthood.

A tear escaped, slipping down Marnie's cheek, dropping off the edge of her chin.

What was Shauna doing in Blackwell Wood on a Friday evening? Her car was still at home. How had she got there?

Shauna didn't have enemies. She hated discord, did anything to keep the peace. Even with Aidan. Despite him leaving her alone with the kids, talking her into selling their home, she'd found a way for them to get along. It didn't make sense. And she needed sense. She needed an explanation, because right now the question marks surrounding her daughter's death were driving a molten rod through her insides. Finding the culprit wouldn't bring Shauna back; she knew that. But she needed to know who did this, and why.

She'd turned Friday evening over and over in her mind. Those last precious moments they shared together. Shauna had been so upbeat when she'd called in. Standing in the kitchen doorway in her black dress, dolled up as if she was ready for a night out. Eyes shining as she told her mum about the interview. She was pleased with how it went, optimistic about the possibility of a job offer. After the struggles of the last few months, facing the prospect of building a new life for her and the children, finally things seemed to be picking up. She'd looked brighter. Taller, somehow. When they'd spoken on the phone later, she'd sounded relaxed. Said she'd opened a bottle of wine. Chatted about the celebrities on television, the vagaries of the ageing process, how actors worked hard to maintain their youthful looks. Superficial, everyday conversation. She was having a restful evening. *Chillin'*, she called it. About to have a bath.

You couldn't fake that kind of breeziness, could you? What the hell had happened?

Marnie squinted through the morning sunshine. The road widened into open countryside, the houses of Hampton's border little boxes behind. She drove through a tunnel of trees, the branches leaning across the road, intertwining with each other, and slowed to navigate a sharp bend. And then she saw it. Blackwell Wood, reaching to the horizon. She shouldn't have come here; she knew that. Darren would say it wasn't good for her. Though the pressing need to visit the place her daughter took her last breath was like a magnetic draw.

Liveried police cars were parked across the main entrance, blocking access to the car park and the road through the woods to the sawmill. An officer standing sentry at the gate watched as she crawled past. Marnie's chest knotted. She wasn't sure what she expected. She knew the police had closed off the woods and advised people not to attend. But the woods spanned over two hundred acres. They couldn't guard all of it, could they?

Fifty yards or so up the road was a long lay-by, the overspill parking area. Marnie steered in, cut the engine and stared across at the trees. Branches of aged oaks and sycamores reached out, beckoning her in. A quick check in the rear-view mirror. The road was empty behind her. This area was sparse. A canopy of broad leaves shaded the earth beneath from vegetation. The hawthorn hedging was thin and broken in places. Just enough to wriggle through.

The cool morning rushed to meet Marnie as she climbed out of the car. She inhaled, long and deep, taking the fresh air down into the pit of her lungs. The lay-by was littered with rubbish: crisp packets, cans, takeaway cartons. A supermarket carrier bag wafted about in the wind. She peered through the gaps between the leaves to the darkness punctuated by dappled sunshine. And suddenly, the ground shifted beneath her. She reached out, pressed a hand on the car door to steady herself. The jagged lines were coming back on the edge of her vision. Her head was throbbing. Perhaps this wasn't such a good idea.

'Hey!' A voice behind. She turned. It was one of the uniformed officers from the entrance, jogging down to meet her. She froze, watched him a second, gulped another breath, then climbed into the car and turned over the engine. The sudden need to get as far away as possible pressed down on her.

She could see the officer in her mirror as she sped off. He jogged to a stop, placed his hands behind his head. She was just turning the bend when she saw him speak into his radio.

Marnie's mouth was dry. Her heart thumping. Sick rushed into her mouth. Coming here was supposed to help and it was only making her feel worse. All she could think about was Shauna, in the middle of the woods, screaming for help. Help that was never to arrive.

Her lifeless body laid on the muddy ground.

Shauna hated bugs. Ants, beetles, spiders. Many a time when she was a kid, Marnie was called to her bedroom to rescue one, put it outside. She made such a fuss when a fly landed on her. And yet she'd been left there, free for the critters of the woods to crawl over her.

A shiver skittered down Marnie's spine. She wiped the tears from her face with the back of her hand, only to make way for more. The journey home was a blur. She didn't remember driving around the back of the woods. Open fields changing to lines of houses marking the edge of town. Stopping for the lights in Hampton High Street. Crawling towards the roundabout at Cross Keys. Before she knew it, she was back in her road, pulling into her driveway.

The front door opened as she cut the engine. Darren appeared in the doorway. Tired and pale. He'd always been a big man, a heavy build, always battled with his weight. Yet today he looked gaunt, ill.

He shook his head as she climbed out of the car. 'I woke up and you'd gone,' he said. 'You left your phone on the bedside table. I've been worried sick.'

'I'm sorry. I just needed to get out.'

He shuffled aside for her to enter, closed the door and pulled her close.

His embrace was long and tight. Marnie buried her head into his shoulder. She could still smell yesterday's work clothes where he hadn't washed. Usually she'd moan, usher him into the shower. But none of that mattered now. Nothing mattered, their world hollow and empty without their girl.

She wasn't sure how long they stood there, holding on to each other.

Eventually, Darren released her. He looked spent, as if every ounce of energy had been squeezed out of him. 'Thank God you're okay,' he said. 'I was afraid you'd—' He broke off, swallowing. A tear glistened on his eyelash.

Marnie didn't answer. She had considered walking away, ending it all. Anything to extinguish the pain, the agony scouring her insides. But she had a husband, grandchildren. People who needed her. She needed to keep a grip on life for their sakes.

Darren's face turned grave. 'There's something you should see.' He grabbed her hand, led her through to the kitchen. It had been years since they'd walked hand in hand and it felt strange, out of kilter somehow. He sat her down and gestured to the open laptop on the table.

'What is it?'

'Wait.' He sat beside her and brought up a news article – *Police appeal in the wake of body found in the woods.*

Marnie's mouth dried again. The articles, the news pieces had started yesterday morning. She knew that because her phone had pinged at a rate of knots until she turned the notifications off. She didn't want to read reports about her daughter's death. And she didn't want to think of others doing the same. Shauna loathed being the centre of attention. She'd have hated her photo being plastered everywhere. Marnie passed Darren a quizzical look. What was he trying to show her?

He held up a single finger, pointed at the screen. *Have you seen this person? Police appeal for someone they believe to be the last person seen talking to the victim at Bushwell's Services on Friday evening*, the article read. He scrolled down, paused when he reached a photograph of a character on a petrol station forecourt.

Marnie gasped. The face was pointing away, a hat obscuring the hair. She pressed a hand to her mouth. But the familiarity in the stance was unmistakable.

CHAPTER 17

Pemberton navigated the windy lanes of Bossington on the south-west border of Hampton. Once a village, before the town expanded and swallowed it up in the 1980s, it still held a rural appeal with quaint cottages at its centre, a stone church and graveyard overlooking open fields.

He continued out of the village, crossed the bridge over the river, then checked his satnav. 'It's a turn down here off to the left,' he said.

They continued down the road for another hundred metres, slowed for a sharp bend and almost missed the turn – the satnav directing them at the last minute into a single track flanked by lines of trees on either side, leading to a thicket in the distance. No houses or dwellings in sight.

'Are you sure this is right?' Helen asked.

'This is the address he gave me on the phone.' *He* was Guy Thorne, the leader or convenor of The Alternatives.

The Ford Focus rocked over the uneven ground. Helen clung on to the grab rail. 'Wouldn't fancy this track in winter,' she said. 'Not without a four-by-four.'

'Me neither.' Pemberton cast a fleeting glance at the clock on the dash. It was 10.08 am. 'When I called, I told him we'd be there about ten.'

'What have you told him about our visit?' They had to be

careful. The last thing they needed was for any information on the murder and the possible ritual surrounding it to be leaked to the press.

He swerved to avoid a pothole. 'That one of our inquiries suggests a possible interest in alternative religions. I didn't give specifics.'

They were nearing the end of the thicket, gnarly branches of elms reaching over the track, when she spotted an old brick-built cottage, set back from the road by a long driveway. A separate double garage stood beside it. Nestled in the pit of the valley, the thicket of elms on one side, a line of tall firs marking the edge of the garden and rising fields on the other, it couldn't have been more obscured.

Chickens clucked around their feet as they climbed out of the car.

Pemberton looked at them and pulled a face at Helen. 'Let's hope he's not rearing those for some ritual or other.'

A sign above the door read *Partridge Cottage*. It was quaint, if a little neglected, with an arched wooden door, the white paint blistered and peeling, a cracked stone doorstep, latticed windows that needed a good clean. Not at all what she had expected from the corporate nature of the website.

A short, thin man opened the door as they approached, running a hand through a thatch of dark hair streaked with grey. He wore a navy waistcoat over dark denims, a checked shirt beneath.

'Mr Guy Thorne?' Helen asked.

He nodded, taking his time to examine their badges as they introduced themselves. His face was angular, his eyes dark and inquisitive, and, when he spoke, his tone was rich and mellow. Almost musical.

'Well, this is all very intriguing,' he said, looking from one to another.

A high-pitched bark sounded from out the back. He ignored it and led them into a dimly lit hallway, their shoes clattering the quarry tiles, and through to a living room that ran the length of the house. A colourful Turkish rug covered the wooden floor. A stuffed fox's head glared at them from above the wood burner.

They declined drinks, the thick film of dust covering the sills and surfaces making the offer rather less appealing than it sounded. Guy invited them to sit on a leather sofa opposite the fireplace. Settling himself into a low-slung armchair in the corner, he looked across at them enquiringly.

Between the two seats ran a long vivarium that appeared to be empty, apart from a layer of substrate along the bottom. Pemberton frowned uncomfortably at it. 'Do you live here alone?' he asked.

'That depends on what you mean by alone,' Guy said, a glint of amusement in his eyes.

'I'm not with you.'

'Well, I have my chickens. And my Collie, Nigel, in the kennel out the back. And of course, Cyril.'

'Cyril?'

'Yes.' He swept a hand down to the vivarium. 'My python.'

Pemberton's face paled.

'Ah,' Helen said. 'That's what you keep in the tank.'

'Yes. He's upstairs at the moment. Taking his exercise.' Guy cast a teasing eye at Pemberton. 'It's okay. I've closed the door.'

'Good,' Helen said, resisting the temptation to roll her eyes. 'We're working on a case where a pentagram has cropped up,' she said. 'I understand it used to be the emblem for your group, The Alternatives.'

'A case?' he angled his head curiously. When Helen didn't elaborate, he said, 'The recent murder, I presume?'

'What makes you say that?' Pemberton asked.

'Acting superintendents and sergeants don't come out for a burglary, and certainly not at this time on a Sunday morning.'

'Yes,' Helen said, cutting in. 'Yes, but this is just a part of our inquiry, and we'd ask you to keep anything we discuss to yourself at present. We're not sure how relevant it is.'

'Of course.' He bowed his head as he spoke. 'Happy to assist.'

Helen shifted in her seat. His clownish, almost mocking manner was beginning to grind. She was in no mood to be played with. 'Tell me about The Alternatives,' she said.

'What do you want to know?'

'How many members you have, how long you've been going, what you stand for... I understand the group was started by a Gareth Lacey.'

'Yes, twelve years ago. I've been with them eight years. I took over when Gareth passed away two years ago. Membership is pretty fluid.' He waved a bony hand and Helen caught his fingernails. Long and yellowing.

'What does that mean?' she asked.

'People come, people go. We have about twenty-six active members at present and meet bi-monthly.'

'What do you stand for?'

He looked up at the ceiling as if he was trying to find the right words. 'We're a group of like-minded individuals focused on pride and liberty.'

Helen let the ensuing silence linger and when he didn't expand, she asked, 'What do you do at your meetings?'

'What do we do?' He raised a brow. 'We talk about our ethos. Celebrate achievements. Explore carnal desires.' He stretched out the last sentence, hooking Helen's gaze. 'Consensually, of course.'

Helen stared back at him. If he thought a bunch of old cronies having an orgy was going to embarrass her, he had another think coming. 'How did The Alternatives come about?'

'Gareth, the founder, and a group of associates used to meet regularly and chew the fat. It became apparent they were disillusioned with the way things were and wanted to explore different routes to fulfilment.' He held out both hands. 'Hence the title, The Alternatives.'

'And you used the inverted pentagram as your emblem,' Pemberton said.

'That's right. Lacey himself was enamoured with the

Church of Satan and Anton LaVey's work. I guess it seemed the obvious choice at the time.'

'Would you call yourselves devil worshippers?'

Guy's face scrunched as he sniggered. 'Satanism has nothing to do with devil worship. We don't worship anyone. We're individualists.'

'But you are a Satanist?'

'I identify with the movement, yes. I'm an atheist. Put generally, I see "Satan" as a symbol of personal passion and pride. Which means I feel free to explore my needs without the guilt or hang-ups modern society imposes.' He sniffed. 'But that's really just my interpretation.'

'What about others in the group?' Helen asked.

'Well, that's the thing.' He sat back in his chair, arched his forehead. 'They might infer something slightly different. Doesn't mean they are breaking the law.'

Helen pressed her teeth together. They were getting nowhere fast.

'What about rituals?' Pemberton asked. 'Ceremonies.'

A derisory smile played on Guy's lips. 'We don't go in for those much.'

Pemberton shot him a stony stare.

'Look, it's a flexible club. People participate as much or as little as they wish. We meet, we chat. Sometimes we organise outings. But Satanism, or our general interpretation of it, isn't what people generally think. We don't go in for any supernatural nonsense, have nothing to do with the occult. Some Satanists believe in witchcraft and black magic, but that's not something we explore.'

'What does the inverted pentagram mean to you?' Helen asked.

'It can mean any number of things. Some say it's evil, others, the more broad-minded, shall we say, understand there's more to it. I dropped the symbol when I took over. There are far too many misconceptions about Satanism. I think the inverted pentagram gives the wrong impression.

We're more of a networking group these days. It's all about reaching your potential, both in business and individually. Alleviating life's stresses.'

'Where were you last Friday evening?' Pemberton asked.

'The day of the murder.' Guy paused before he answered. 'Why, that's easy. It was our group outing to the Ashmolean. We spent the day in the museum, stayed overnight in Oxford afterwards.'

'We?'

'About twenty of us from the group.'

'So, not all your members?'

'No, not all of us. Some couldn't take the time away from work.' He turned down the corners of his mouth. 'Thankfully, I work as a gamekeeper. As long as the work is done, my hours are flexible.'

Helen sat forward. 'Had you heard the name Shauna O'Hennessey before the news on Friday?'

'No.'

She asked about Aidan, Jade. Marnie and Darren. To no avail.

'Do you keep membership details?' Pemberton asked.

'Yes. People come along for a trial session. If they enjoy it, they fill in a form, pay a monthly sub. Just like any other group, really. We're no different.'

'What about short-term members?' Pemberton said. 'People that have attended once or twice and decided it's not for them.'

Helen could see what he was getting at here. A disgruntled member, someone dipping their toe into the dark side.

Guy's eyes widened. 'Oh, we get plenty of those. I'm sure you'll appreciate, our movement attracts all sorts. If they attend more than once, we keep their contact details on file.'

'Right,' Pemberton said. 'We'll need details of all members, past and present, and everyone who attended your outing on Friday.'

'I couldn't possibly do that. Membership is confidential. I mean—'

'We can get a warrant,' Helen interjected.

He gave Helen a long, hard stare. 'You're not suggesting one of us is responsible for killing that young woman.'

'We're not suggesting anything,' Helen said. 'We just need to eliminate each and every one of you from our inquiry.'

CHAPTER 18

The clouds conjoined as they drove back to headquarters, blocking out the sun and making for a grey day. After an annoying hour with Guy Thorne, they were no closer to pinning down the relevance or the interpretation of the pentagram, and his flippant manner and attempts at humour had riled Helen. At least they weren't coming back empty-handed. After much persuasion and the threat of a warrant, he'd agreed to part with a list of their members, past and present. Though she found it hard to believe an active member would draw attention to themselves by using their old emblem.

'He was an oddball,' Pemberton said. He pulled out to overtake a cyclist. 'Do you think he feeds the chickens' eggs to the snake?'

Helen recalled Pemberton opening the sitting room door gingerly when they left, peering up the stairs before making a dash for the front door, and stifled a laugh. There was no way he was coming face to face with Cyril, the python. It reminded her of another case they'd worked on when he'd been spooked by a rat and fallen out of a loft space onto the landing below. She wasn't keen on rats, something about the tail made her shudder, and she didn't fancy meeting Cyril, but she wasn't frightened of a house snake slithering around. If it didn't fancy eating its owner, it was hardly going to show any interest in them.

The traffic thickened as they reached Roxten, another village that had been swallowed up by the town, this time in the early 1970s when Hampton had expanded to accommodate London's overspill. She glanced absently at passing signs for The Queen Victoria and The Royal Albert. Housing estates that had shown so much promise when they'd been built and later became generically known as 'the rabbit warren' when austerity dragged them into the gutter and the design, incorporating numerous alleyways and back entrances, made them particularly difficult to police. Many a time she'd raced through those alleys, chasing a shoplifter or car thief on the run.

They continued up the road, past a high fence – the peaked roofs of industrial units beyond. Pemberton slowed at the lights and Helen's gaze turned to an imposing Victorian building straddling the corner, painted in black, a green pair of cat's eyes at the top. The nightclub had been closed, Sitex covering the windows since Chilli Franks's arrest, but the neon *Black Cats* sign was still in situ, an indelible reminder of his presence. This building had been the centre of Chilli's operation during his heyday, fronting as a nightclub, yet behind the scenes a hub for his illicit interests in drugs and vice. Helen glanced idly at the car park. And her throat tightened. There it was: the black BMW she'd seen last Friday evening. The BMW belonging to Chilli's half-brother. She tugged at her shirt collar. Pemberton was looking ahead at the junction, oblivious to her discomfort.

Whether Davy Boyd was thinking of reopening or selling the place, his presence solidified his interest in Chilli's businesses and something about it made her uncomfortable.

A ringing pulled her back to the present. Her mobile. She fished it out of her pocket. It was Spencer.

'How did you get on?' he asked.

Helen passed on a quick summary of their visit. When she mentioned the snake, Spencer snorted. 'I bet that pleased the sergeant.'

Pemberton turned his eyes skyward.

'You could say that. How are things there?'

'I was calling because I've just had an interesting call with the O'Hennesseys,' he said. 'You're not going to believe it. They recognised the person on the petrol station forecourt – the one we were appealing for.'

'Really?'

'Yes. They reckon it's a family member. And Marnie O'Hennessey's car was seen at the crime scene this morning. There's something not quite right there.'

Helen's pulse quickened. 'Where are they now?'

'At home in Weston.'

The lights had changed. She motioned for Pemberton to take a left. 'We'll head straight out there.'

CHAPTER 19

'Can we get you a tea or coffee?' Darren asked, indicating for Helen and Pemberton to take a seat on the sofa.

'No, thank you,' Helen said.

Marnie's throat tightened to a raw channel.

'Come on, love. Sit down,' Darren urged.

She eased herself into the chair beside him, the heat of the detectives' gazes burning her cheeks.

'How are you holding up?' the acting superintendent asked.

She didn't look much like a senior officer to Marnie. She was small, petite, with dark hair tied back into a half-ponytail and a clear complexion. Pretty much how she imagined Shauna would have looked in eight or nine years.

'We're doing our best,' Darren said. 'Thank you for coming, Superintendent.'

'Helen,' Helen corrected.

'Helen,' he repeated. 'I know you must be...' He turned to her colleague beside her and back to her. 'You both must be really busy.'

'That's okay. It's a difficult time.' She turned to Marnie. 'I understand you were at the woods this morning.'

Creases formed across Darren's brow. 'What the—'

Marnie touched his forearm to silence him. She hadn't told him about her trip to the woods. She didn't want to pile any more heartache onto him. 'I-I just wanted to see where…' Her throat constricted further. She cast her eyes to the floor. Was it so wrong to want to visit her daughter's resting place? 'I just wanted to be close to her.'

Darren's face pained. He took an awkward breath. 'Something has happened,' he said, changing the subject. 'Something has come to our attention…' Now it was his turn to lose his tongue.

Marnie cleared her throat. 'We saw the press appeal. The person Shauna met at Bushwell's Services – we know who it was.'

The male detective pulled a notebook and pen from his pocket, unspeaking.

'And?' Helen asked.

Marnie flinched as her colleague clicked the end of his ballpoint pen. 'It's Darren's sister, Kerry.' The detective's face scrunched. 'I hadn't mentioned her before because we don't see her. We're not in touch. In fact, Darren and I haven't spoken to her in…' She looked across at Darren. He was facing away, fixed on the white wall beside him. 'About twelve months. And before that, we hadn't seen her for around thirty years.'

The detective was quiet a moment as though gathering her thoughts. 'What about Shauna?' she asked.

Marnie's heart shrank. 'We didn't think Shauna was in contact with her either. Until we saw that photo.'

A heavy silence hung in the room.

'May I ask what happened between you?' Helen asked.

Marnie blew out a breath, long and hard, until her lungs were empty and raw. 'It's complicated.' She didn't want to talk about Kerry. She didn't want to rake it all up. The sofa displaced as Darren shuffled back and folded his arms across his chest. He refused to have her name mentioned in the house at the best of times.

'Please…' The detective edged forward. 'Start at the beginning.'

'It's a long story.'

'The more we find out about Shauna, the closer we are to finding out what happened.'

Silence lingered in the room until Marnie could bear it no more. She closed her eyes, rubbed her forehead, delving into the depths of her mind. 'We had a son,' she said eventually. 'Tom.' She pointed at the photo of a young soldier in dress uniform on the mantel in a silver frame, her heart contracting at his youthful face.

'Yes, I heard about your loss,' Helen said. 'That must have been tough.'

'It was.' Fresh tears burned the backs of Marnie's eyes. But she couldn't afford to stop now. 'He's not actually our son though. Or he wasn't.'

The air in the room thickened.

'He was Darren's nephew,' she continued. 'His sister, Kerry's, boy. We were living in Leicestershire, newly married when he was born. It was a bit of a surprise.' She closed her eyes a second, the words paining her. 'Maybe I need to go back further.'

The detectives said nothing.

'Kerry is two years older than us. Darren's family and mine, we grew up in the same road, went to the same school, used to play out in the street together. She was really into swimming. Swam for the county when she was ten.' She could see Kerry now, her long blonde hair, her wicked smile. Riding up and down the road on her bike. It hadn't all been bad. There was a time when Marnie had looked up to her as a sister figure and she wanted the detectives to see that. 'Kerry was twelve when their father ran off,' Marnie said. 'Their mother always said that was what changed her. She took it badly, went off the rails, got in with the wrong crowd. By the time she was fourteen, she didn't want to know us any more. She was hanging round with the big kids outside the shops. Smoking weed. She ran away a few times. The police brought her back.' Marnie looked across at Darren for moral support, but he stayed as still as stone, puce face staring at the carpet. As if at any minute he might explode.

'Anyway, she left home a month after she finished school. Jess, their mother, got up one morning to find a note beside the kettle to say she was going to live with friends in London. No address, no forwarding details.'

Helen glanced at Darren. 'That must have been difficult for you all.'

If he heard her, he didn't acknowledge it.

'We were just kids,' Marnie said. 'The hardest thing was watching Darren's mum. She checked the letter box every morning after Kerry left. Jumped at every ring of the phone. Right up until her last days, she still hoped Kerry would reach out, let her know she was okay.' Marnie pictured Darren's mum. The short Brummie woman with the crop of dark hair and the razor-sharp wit. 'Darren's mum died of a heart attack five years after Kerry left.' Marnie shook her head. 'I'm sure it was the stress.'

The air in the room stilled.

'Anyway, time passed. We left school, started work, got married. Then, out of the blue, social services got in touch. Kerry had moved to London and had a baby there. She was a heroin addict, couldn't take care of him. There was talk of him being placed in care. We couldn't bear to see our blood, Darren's blood, taken away, so... we took him in. Kerry phoned a few times, promised to visit. There was talk about her coming back to Leicester to live. Eventually, the calls stopped, and she vanished. We didn't hear any more from her. Tom was six months old then.

'When he was eighteen months, we put in for adoption – it seemed like the natural thing to do. Then Shauna came along, and our family was complete.' She shook her head again as the memories flooded back. 'We moved to Hampton, and they were inseparable in their younger years. So close. And then. I don't know... Tom entered his teenage years. Started smoking. Staying out late at night. Got into the company of a gang of older kids. Played hookey from school. We were worried he'd follow in his mother's footsteps.'

Darren placed a hand over hers. Warm, solid.

Marnie looked across at the detective. 'We moved him to a different school to give him a fresh start, a clean break. And things improved. He made new friends. There was always an edge to him though. He wasn't academic. He hated school, was easily distracted. We worried for his future. When he expressed an interest in joining the army, we were thrilled. Sixteen was such a young age to leave home, but we thought it would give him a focus, some discipline. And it did. He blossomed into a lovely young man.' A tear leaked out of her eye and trickled down her face.

'I understand you lost him in Helmand.'

'Yes, he was doing well. Served his first term and had just signed up again when it happened.' She swiped the tear from her chin. 'We couldn't believe it when we got the news about him...' Her words splintered. 'Still can't.'

Quiet fell upon them.

'We tried to contact Kerry to let her know about his passing,' Marnie said eventually. 'Even reached out to the Samaritans to help find her. To no avail. She didn't come to his funeral. I even wondered if maybe she'd passed away herself. Then, just over a year ago, she turned up on the doorstep. Out of the blue.' Kerry's tall frame crept into Marnie's mind. The sunken cheeks, the yellowing teeth, the thin, lank hair. She looked more like sixty than fifty. 'I barely recognised her, she'd aged so much. She told me she'd been working for a homeless charity in London, cleaned herself up. Decided to move to Hampton to build a new life. She had a job, was living in town. And she wanted to see her son.' Marnie took a breath. She could still see Kerry on the doorstep. The faded sweatshirt she wore over jeans, even though it was the middle of winter. 'She took the news about Tom's death badly. Blamed us for pushing him into the army, said it was our fault he was killed. We should have kept him safe.' A stone filled her chest as she relived the moment. 'It was dreadful.'

'Did you see her again afterwards?' Helen asked gently.

'Twice—'

'She came by here asking for money.' It was Darren. He moved his hand back to his lap. 'All she ever wanted was money. Money for drugs. I sent her packing.'

The room was quiet a moment. 'What about Shauna?' Helen asked.

'Shauna never met her,' Marnie said. 'Oh, she knew Kerry was back. We talked about it. She never expressed an interest in meeting her. But…' Marnie felt a cold sensation on the back of her neck. 'I wouldn't put it past our Shauna to reach out to Kerry.'

'No!' Darren said.

'She was a bleeding heart, love,' she said to her husband. 'Would do anything to help anyone. If she thought she was helping Kerry…' Marnie stopped at the sight of her husband's rigid face. It pained her to see him look so distraught. 'I'm sorry. She'd do anything to get close to Tom. You know how much she missed him.'

'Did Shauna know Tom's parentage?' Helen asked.

'Of course. We didn't have any secrets. Shauna knew Tom was her cousin, but she always referred to him as her brother. Like he called us his parents. I guess we were the closest thing he'd had to parents anyway.'

The detective moved to the edge of the sofa. 'Are you certain it was Kerry with Shauna?' she said. 'The face in the photo is well covered.'

'The jacket she's wearing,' Marnie said. 'It's Superdry, a special edition. I bought it as a Christmas present for Darren and he never wore it. I gave it to Kerry last time she was here. She always came without a coat. I worried she'd be cold.'

CHAPTER 20

Helen climbed into the car, fastened her seat belt and called the office. Her mind was racing, trying to compute the relevance of the information she'd heard. She passed on their findings and ordered an immediate trace on Kerry O'Hennessey. Whatever significance this woman held in Shauna's life, or death, she was the last person who spoke to the young woman, and they needed to track her down.

As she ended the call and looked out at the passing houses, something about the story niggled her. 'What do you think?' she said to Pemberton.

Pemberton slowed as a set of traffic lights turned red and gave a long sigh, eyes fixed on the road ahead. 'Kerry believed they were responsible for sending her son into the army, into a war zone where he lost his life. It's a stretch, but it could give her a potential motive,' he said. 'Especially if she's not of sound mind.'

'She hadn't seen or bothered with him in years.'

'He was her only son. If, as they say, she was rebuilding her life, turning things around, perhaps she was finally looking to establish a relationship with him.'

'Why target Shauna?' Helen was playing devil's advocate, she knew that, but she couldn't ignore the doubts drilling into her mind.

The lights changed. Pemberton accelerated up the road. 'She was their only child,' he said. 'Well, only child by blood. Perhaps Kerry wanted them to experience the loss she felt.'

Helen churned this over. Murderers didn't always act rationally. Maybe this made sense to a deranged mind. 'And why now?' she said. 'Why not twelve months ago when she found out? Why approach her that particular evening? You heard the O'Hennesseys: they didn't think Shauna and Kerry had ever met.'

He paused to change gear. 'We can't be sure of that. Maybe Kerry has been meeting Shauna in secret. Building a relationship. One thing's for sure. If she knew Shauna, it would be easier for her to entice her out to the woods. Perhaps Kerry lured her out there under the pretence of a walk, a chance to catch up, redeem herself. When Shauna realised her true intention, she ran for her life.'

Helen pulled up the footage from the petrol station on her phone and watched it through again. It was quick, barely a few seconds, as if Kerry was asking Shauna for something. What struck her was the deadpan expression on Shauna's face. Almost as if Kerry was a stranger asking for directions. There was no familiarity, no indication they knew each other. And they parted there: Shauna climbed into her car alone; Kerry made off down the street. They hadn't picked her up on other cameras. *Where did you go?* Helen said to herself.

If Kerry was involved, she must have met up with Shauna again later. But something about the scenario felt wrong.

* * *

A plethora of questions were still circling Helen's head like a song on replay as they climbed the stairs back at headquarters. Pieces of the story didn't quite fit together.

The incident room was humming when they entered, the news of a possible suspect instantly lifting spirits. Helen greeted everyone, poured herself a water from the dispenser and approached Spencer standing beside the noticeboard at the front.

'Any news?' she asked.

'No previous record. It seems Kerry O'Hennessey keeps her nose clean.'

That seemed strange for a woman who lived a life dominated by illegal drugs. 'What about an address?'

'The address the O'Hennesseys gave is the same as the one on the voters register – the terraces on Combi Gardens in town. They were bought up by a developer and gutted last month with a view to converting them to flats. There's no one there now.'

'Okay,' Helen said. 'Check with the developer. See if he has a forwarding address for any of the residents.'

'There's some old intel on file linking her to drugs gangs,' Spencer said. 'A few sources reckon she was pushing for Chilli Franks in her teens, but she was never caught. Nothing recent. It seems she's been living under the radar recently.'

Helen gritted her teeth. There it was again, the mention of Chilli Franks. He was tucked away in a prison cell, yet his legacy followed her around like a bad smell. 'She can't be living on fresh air,' she said.

Spencer passed her a knowing look. 'Exactly. I've requested a trace through the DWP.' He viewed the clock on the wall. It was almost 4 pm. 'Though, at this time on a Sunday, I doubt we'll hear much before the morning. In the meantime, I've circulated the still from the garage internally and marked Kerry as a person of interest.'

Marking her as a person of interest meant every officer, every patrol car, would be looking out for her. 'Excellent. Let's find out when she last used her credit card or bank account. Might give us an indication of where she is.'

He nodded. 'I've also reached out to source intelligence and asked them to dispatch their handlers out to speak with contacts in the field. Someone must know where she is staying.'

'Well done.' She turned to the room. 'Right. Our priority is to locate Kerry O'Hennessey.'

* * *

Marnie rested back on the sofa and stared at the blank television screen. Darren was lying on the other sofa, a cushion covering his face. He wasn't asleep – she knew that from the shortness of his breaths. He just didn't want to be there, so he lay still and hid his face.

Is this what they'd become? A couple so bereft they were speechless. And the shocks kept on coming.

What was Kerry doing with Shauna on the night she died? How long had they been seeing each other? The detective said they had no reason to suggest Kerry was responsible for Shauna's murder, but the very notion, the very idea that she might be involved, brought sickly acid to Marnie's throat.

She could still see Kerry's contorted face a year earlier. Hear the shrillness of her voice as she hurled abuse. She'd left her son with them for safekeeping, and they'd led him down a path which had caused his death. She was demented, keening like a screaming banshee. And she wouldn't listen to any reason.

Darren had forced her out of the house that night. Refused to speak of her afterwards, just like he didn't want to talk about her today.

Thoughts whizzed around Marnie's mind like a car on a Formula One track. She had no idea what this meant, but of one thing, she was sure. If past experience was anything to go by, nothing good could have come out of a relationship between Kerry and Shauna.

CHAPTER 21

Helen tapped the end of a pen against her chin as she stared up at the wide smile of Shauna O'Hennessey on their murder wall. They had a name, a description, a potential suspect. Someone with motive and opportunity. She switched to the enlarged still of the hazy character on the petrol station forecourt.

It was Monday morning, 7.15 am. After a late night preparing an update for the ACC, she'd arrived in at the crack of dawn to review the intelligence and arrests overnight, hoping for news. And she hadn't been the only one to dash in early. Already the office was full to bursting, the tension palpable. Detectives and support staff shuffling papers, tapping into computers. All on hyper-alert, anxiously awaiting the next ingredient in their search for their suspect: a valid address.

The victim's clothes still hadn't been recovered. Preliminary forensics found nothing of interest on the victim or close to the scene. No scraps of clothing, hairs or particles. It was a clean kill, almost clinical. Well planned to ensure nothing was left behind. And the question of transport tugged at Helen. How did the murderer get the victim to the woods? Shauna's car was at home. Checks with DVLA revealed Kerry didn't have a driving licence.

She turned to the room. 'Any news on Kerry's bank checks?'

'I chased yesterday,' Spencer said. 'Looks like our request got lost in their system. They're dealing with it.'

Helen rolled her eyes. The odds seemed to be set against them at every stage of this inquiry. 'Where are we with checking cameras near the scene?'

Dark raised a hand from the corner of the room. 'The nearest cameras to the woods are Cross Keys roundabout at the end of High Street. We're working our way through the vehicles that passed through on Friday evening, heading out in the direction of Blackwell Wood. Tracing and interviewing the owners. It's a mammoth task.'

Helen thanked her. Cross Keys was Hampton's biggest and busiest roundabout, a direct route to the motorway from the trading estate nearby, but it was a long shot. The killer had timed their kill well to avoid witnesses and, looking at the map, there were several alternative routes they could have taken. Back routes with no cameras to record their movements.

The sound of a phone crashing into its holder turned her attention back to the room. Spencer clambered up from the corner, waving a scrap of paper, triumphant. 'Someone's in early at the DWP, and they've come up trumps. She's been living at 46 Beaumont Street in the town centre for the last ten months.'

The mood in the room instantly lifted.

'Excellent,' Helen said. 'Does she live alone?'

Pemberton was already tapping at his keyboard. 'The property is rented by a Bradley Jones.' He spoke slowly as he read the words from the screen, then clicked a few more buttons. 'Nothing on PNC,' he said. 'He's not known to us. No flags or markers on the property either.'

Helen's shoulders eased. Dangerous flags or markers meant previous violent activity, or threats to officers' safety. If it was clear, she wouldn't be obliged to engage firearms backup, which would delay them going out there, picking Kerry up. Still, they were dealing with a potential killer, and she wasn't about to take any chances. 'Okay, let's organise an urgent warrant.' Groans filled the room. Warrants demanded paperwork. Paperwork that needed to be signed off by a magistrate. 'Look, we have the element of surprise on our side,' she said, lifting her hands to quieten the room. 'Let's do this by the book. If this is her correct address, I want to make sure that, whatever happens, we have the power to search the property when we get there.' She turned to Pemberton. 'Get uniform organised with the battering ram, will you? We may need to break the door down to gain access.'

CHAPTER 22

Beaumont Street was located off Hampton High Street, a row of three-storey terraced houses facing each other across a narrow road. Parked in adjacent Charente Street, in an unmarked car, Helen pulled on a stab vest while uniformed officers spilled out of a white van behind.

A light rain had started to fall, spotting the pavement. A woman cast them a lingering gaze as she dashed from her door to her car, shielding her forehead with her bag. A net curtain at the house beside them fluttered. They might be out of sight of their suspect's address, but they were already attracting attention. They needed to move fast.

'Right,' Helen said as everyone gathered around, thankful they'd obtained maps and taken a few minutes to study the house layout. It was a late nineteenth-century terrace build with front access directly onto the pavement and rear access through a garden that ran to a channel that separated it from the back gardens of the street behind and led to the main road. Which meant they needed to cover front and back. 'You've got your positions.' She turned to Spencer. 'Have you tested your video?'

Sported mostly by uniformed officers, body-worn videos had proved their worth in recent years. Victims' memories could be hazy. Witnesses might miss something, which later could be questioned or denied in court. A video was like a third eye, a recording that couldn't be disputed, and Helen was keen to utilise the technology. If nothing else, it recorded the suspect or witness's initial reaction. And there was a lot to be gleaned from body language, especially when it was recorded in real time.

Spencer patted the camera on his chest and nodded.

'Great, let's get started.' She pressed the microphone to the top of her ear. 'Let me know when you are all in position.'

The rain picked up as they turned the corner into Beaumont Street, spattering the cars lining the kerb. Arriving at number 46, Helen knocked hard. No reply. She glanced over her shoulder, tried again. A curtain twitched at the house next door. She flicked open the letter box. The hallway was lined with shoes, trainers. A pile of junk mail sat neatly on the bottom stair.

'Kerry O'Hennessey. It's the police. Please open up!'

When there was no answer, she moved aside for the officer carrying the red battering ram.

He swung it back, bashed the door. Once, twice. On the third hit, the door flew open, thudding against the wall and flitting back.

Officers rushed in. Feet thundered the stairs. Within thirty seconds, they were out.

'Empty,' the officer that had wielded the battering ram said.

'Okay, check the loft space, will you?' Helen said. It wouldn't be the first time a suspect had hidden in the attic to avoid capture. She turned to Spencer. 'Try the neighbours. See if they've seen Kerry or Bradley recently.'

She pulled on a Tyvek suit and stepped inside, scanning the shoes along the hallway. Trainers. Converse. Boots. All at least a size eleven.

In the living room, a glass ashtray sparkled on the coffee table. She looked at the unburned candle beside the clock on the mantel. The landscape print on the far wall. The room was sparsely furnished with one sofa, a sideboard and the coffee table. But what struck her was the lack of photos or memorabilia. Was that because it was rented accommodation and temporary, or was there another reason?

The kitchen smelled of tomato ketchup, but the surfaces were clean and tidy. An upturned mug sat on the drainer. She pulled open a drawer, the handle cold through her rubber gloves, and sifted through a tangle of old wires and phone chargers. The next drawer housed instructions for various appliances. A tray of cutlery in the next. The fridge was bare, apart from a half-pint of milk, a carton of margarine, a couple of cans of Carlsberg lager and a jar of pickles that looked past its best. Nothing personal...

She was just mulling this over when Spencer wandered in. 'I've spoken to both neighbours,' he said. 'Guy on the left is as deaf as a post. Hasn't seen anything. Woman on the right knows Kerry to say hello to and hasn't seen her in a couple of weeks.'

Helen narrowed her eyes. 'What about Bradley?'

'She said he'll be at work. A warehouse on Higham Industrial Estate around the corner called Cleavers. He left at 7.30 this morning.'

'Very precise.'

'That's what I said. Apparently, she's an early riser and was just back from walking her dog when she saw him leave.'

'Okay, get over to Bradley's work. See what you can find out.'

An officer was levering himself out of the loft space when Helen reached the top of the stairs.

'All clear,' he said. 'There's nothing much up there. Christmas tree decorations. An old stool.'

Helen thanked him and wandered into the bedroom. The wardrobe was a mishmash of men's shirts, jackets, trousers. A coat on the end. Footwear filled a rack at the bottom. Nothing remotely feminine. It was the same story in the chest of drawers. She moved into the bathroom. Shower gel and a bottle of shampoo on the side of the bath. A bar of soap beside the sink. One toothbrush…

Pemberton joined her in the bathroom. 'Are you thinking what I'm thinking?' he said.

Helen frowned up at him. 'She doesn't live here.'

* * *

They were back in the car, battling their way through the morning traffic when Spencer rang.

'You're on speaker,' Helen said. 'Any news?'

'Not much. Kerry had been living with him for about eight months. They met at The Red Lion in town where she was working in the kitchens and moved in together after a whirlwind romance. Two weeks ago, he came home from work, and she announced she was leaving. Said the relationship had gone stale.'

'Out of the blue?'

'Not completely. Things had been strained for a while. She left her job at the pub last month, was supposed to be looking for another. They'd been arguing. But he wasn't expecting her to leave. He went out to The Royal Oak to give her time to think. When he got back, she'd packed and gone. No forwarding address. He hasn't heard from her since.'

That explained the lack of her presence in the house. 'What does he know of her background?'

'Very little. She told him she'd had a difficult upbringing, wasn't in touch with her family. She'd been working for a charity in London – something to do with the homeless, he said – before she met him. London became too busy for her. She came to Hampton to make a new start.'

What was it about this woman? Wherever they looked, she was shrouded in mystery.

'Poor chap,' Spencer added. 'Seemed really cut up. Said he didn't even know she was related to Shauna O'Hennessey.

He was gobsmacked when I asked about her. He went pale when I said we were searching his house.'

'Where was he on Friday evening?'

'Tried that one. In The Red Lion on Bridge Street.'

* * *

It was a solemn crew that traipsed back into headquarters later, the burden of the morning's disappointment weighing heavily.

Helen was in her office, removing her stab vest, when she heard a cry in the incident room. She rushed into the main room to find Pemberton grabbing hold of a nearby desk to steady himself, his drawer hanging open. He held up a rubber snake and cursed.

The room erupted in laughter.

Another toy snake sat along the top of his computer screen. Pemberton's shoulders juddered as he sank to his seat and guffawed.

Helen couldn't help but chuckle, grateful for the easy release, the humour dissolving some of the tension and frustration of their wasted morning.

She moved back into her office, still laughing as she grabbed her phone receiver. They needed to repeat the public appeal on Kerry O'Hennessey. She made a mental note to chase the bank checks too. If she was in Bushwell's Services last Friday evening, she couldn't be far away.

CHAPTER 23

The house was quiet when Helen heeled the door closed that evening. It had been another disappointing afternoon. Kerry's phone hadn't been used in two weeks. The landlord of the pub where she'd worked called her elusive; she didn't socialise with the staff there and had left suddenly. No explanation. Her bank card was last used at an ATM on Hagley Road in Birmingham last Wednesday where she'd withdrawn her last two hundred pounds. If she was doing a vanishing act, she was making a good job of it. Though, if the O'Hennesseys' story was to be believed, it wasn't the first time she'd disappeared...

A faint cheer filtered down the stairs as Helen slipped off her jacket. She followed the voice to Robert's room where the door sat ajar and pushed it open to find her two boys sat beside each other on Robert's bed, leaning their backs against the bedroom wall, staring at the screen of the games console on the dressing table opposite.

'Hey,' she said.

Matthew passed her a cursory glance, then clicked his handset.

'All right, Mum,' Robert said, eyes glued to the screen.

She stood watching them a moment. Robert was still in his school uniform, the collar tucked in on one side. His hair had grown over the tops of his ears and needed a cut. Matthew was wearing a navy hoody and jeans that looked short on the leg. Her boys were growing up fast. It was hard to believe Matthew would be starting sixth form in September, let alone be taking driving lessons next year.

A crash filled the room.

'Yes!' Robert said, bouncing up and down. The whole bed rocked under his weight. 'You're dead!' He elbowed his brother, triumphant.

Matthew groaned and pressed play again.

Helen smiled to herself and left them to it. At least they weren't arguing.

Downstairs, the kitchen was empty. She sauntered into the front room to find her mother on the sofa, head lolling to the side, eyes closed. An open book resting on her lap. She was just steeling herself for a quiet retreat when Jane Lavery jumped and opened her eyes.

'Oh! Hello, darling.' She sat forward and glanced at the clock on the mantel. It was almost 7 pm. 'What time did you get back?'

'Just now. Are you okay?'

'Yes. Dropped off for a minute there.' She blinked, placed the book on the sofa beside her and stretched her arms back.

'Have you had dinner?' Helen asked, her stomach kicking out. She hadn't eaten anything since breakfast and suddenly she felt ravenous.

'I made lasagne. There are some leftovers in the fridge.'

'You're a star. Fancy a tea?' she called over her shoulder as she moved into the kitchen.

'If you're making.'

Helen busied herself with plating up a generous portion of lasagne and placing it in the microwave, then flicked the switch on the kettle. The smell of cheesy pasta quickly pervaded the kitchen. By the time her mother joined her, Helen had made tea for them both and was sitting at the table, tucking into her dinner.

'Actually, there was something I wanted to talk to you

about,' Jane said. She grabbed her tea off the side and settled herself into the chair opposite her daughter, wrapping her hands around the mug. A sleep crease had formed beneath her cheekbone, but her pale blue eyes were bright, and her white-grey hair was still neatly tucked into a bun at the back of her head.

'Okay.' Helen flinched as a chunk of pasta burned her lip.

'I thought I saw a ghost today.'

She'd been expecting her to say something about the boys – maybe Matthew was finally looking for a summer job or had an interview with the newsagent, or Robert had an extra cricket match scheduled. She jerked back. 'What?'

'I was in High Street, having a coffee with Gill in Hayes, when a figure walked by.'

Helen stared at her mother.

'A very familiar figure.' Tramlines formed across Jane's forehead as her face tightened. 'Why didn't you tell me Chilli Franks was out of prison?'

Helen sat back in her chair, her appetite suddenly waning. The cat was out of the bag. Out of the bag and crawling all over the kitchen. 'He's not.'

'What do you mean he's not? I saw him with my own eyes.'

'It wasn't Chilli. It was his half-brother, Davy.'

'What half-brother?'

Helen took a breath. She had hoped to avoid this conversation. For the two to have avoided each other. Though it seemed Davy Boyd was intent on making himself known in the town. 'I didn't know he had a half-brother either, not until recently. Davy moved out to Spain in the 1990s and has lived there ever since.'

'What's he doing back here now?' Her mother looked afraid.

Helen explained how he'd come over to support Chilli's business interests.

'Should we be worried?'

'No. Not at all. I'm reliably informed he doesn't have a record. He's a family man, married, raising children, a very different kettle of fish to Chilli. Honestly, I don't think we have anything to worry about, Mum.' As she formed the words, memories of what they'd found in Chilli's premises, months earlier, wriggled into her mind. The guns, the drugs. How could she be sure? For all she knew, Davy Boyd was Chilli's equivalent in Spain – or even part of his wider operation.

Jane Lavery closed her eyes and pressed a hand to her forehead. 'How long have you known he was back?'

'I found out by chance at the weekend.'

'And you didn't think to say anything?'

Helen placed her fork down. 'I didn't want to upset you.'

'Well, it's too late for that now, isn't it?'

'Mum, please. We've no reason to suspect—'

'Is there a date for Chilli's trial yet?'

The interruption stung. 'We're still waiting to hear. It's likely to be late summer.'

'Right.' Jane stood.

'Look, Mum, if I believed there was cause for concern, I would have told you. You know that. Try not to worry.'

Her mother's voice lifted an octave. 'Men like Chilli hold a grudge.'

'Please!' Helen whispered. 'Calm down. The children will hear.'

'Maybe we should tell them.'

'No.' Helen shook her head emphatically. When Chilli Franks threw acid into an assailant's face back in the 1990s, it became one of the biggest investigations of her father's career. Her parents had tried to keep the details away from Helen. But, during the trial, night after night, she'd snuck down, sat on the stairs, peered through the bannisters and eavesdropped on their conversations. And when she heard her father mention Chilli's personal threats against her family, she was petrified. Her father called them 'the shallow threats of a condemned man'. Though it didn't stop the fright, the terror, the fear gripping her. Fear that leached into her tender sleep, morphing her dreams to nightmares.

There was no way she was going to subject her boys to that same fear. Especially when the prospect of any potential danger had diminished.

'They're not little any more,' her mother continued.

'I said no.'

'I'm only saying, perhaps you should consider telling them. The trial will be up in a few months. It's bound to be in the news.' Her chair scraped the floor as she stood. 'Think about it.'

Helen watched her walk through the door at the side of the kitchen that led to the adjoining granny flat. She thought about the day of Chilli's previous conviction in the 1990s. Her father had taken them all out to Theo's, a posh Greek restaurant in town, to celebrate. Long gone, a bakery now, but Helen could still picture the lines of manicured tables. The rows of sparkling cutlery. The elegant portions of food presented like a colourful painting – her first experience of fine dining.

She pushed the plate of lasagne aside. As a child, she'd grown up living and breathing her father's cases: celebrating his successes, commiserating his defeats. It was infectious. One of the reasons she'd joined the police was to follow in his footsteps, become a murder detective herself, rid the streets of danger. Her father had passed away by the time she joined the force. Chilli served his time, was released and appeared to keep his head down. The years folded past and the danger, the knot of fear inside her, galvanised to anger. She was ready for him. But their paths didn't cross. Until she had joined homicide.

Helen pushed the thoughts aside, retrieved her laptop from the hallway and snapped it open. A new email graced her inbox, sent via the National Crime Agency. An expert on the occult and Satanism.

The text was long and academic, written by a Dr Arch Swindon. *Doctor of what*, she wondered. She imagined a small man in glasses, a mouse-like face. He talked about links with the inverted pentagram and Satanism. The misinterpretation of both. As much as she hated to admit it, his opinions concurred with those of Guy Thorne from The Alternatives. *The inverted pentagram is incorrectly considered evil by many... No known rituals of figures laid out the same way as your victim. Crime related to Satanism tends to be based on a misguided perception.* At the bottom of the email, he'd included links to other cases, mainly outside the UK, of sexually abusive groups linked to the occult. She read through them. None of them appeared to have any similarities with her murder.

Helen sighed and rested back in her chair. The numerous scratches and bruises on Shauna's back came to mind. She'd been dragged up the riverbank, laid by the path. Admittedly, Kerry was tall with broad swimmer's shoulders. But her shoulders had shrunk, atrophied over the years, and it would have been a struggle to single-handedly drag Shauna's lifeless body along the ground.

Unless, of course, she had help.

CHAPTER 24

Helen completed her daily update for the assistant chief constable, closed her laptop and looked out into the incident room. A rubber snake, hanging from the ceiling above Pemberton's desk, the legacy of Monday's practical joke, swayed wearily in the light breeze: short, languid movements mirrored by her team as they moved about the office. It was 5 pm on Wednesday and everyone was jaded – the long hours demanded by a new case coupled with leads drying up starting to take their toll.

Despite their best efforts, they hadn't been able to trace Kerry O'Hennessey.

She looked down at the membership list of The Alternatives. They were working their way through, tracking down and interviewing each one, but it had proved a fruitless task so far. Everyone seemed to have an alibi for Shauna's murder, and they couldn't find any links with the victim.

They'd worked through all the owners of the Audi that sported the old sticker and discovered that the sticker had been placed there by the son of a previous owner who was now living in Canada – another lead bottomed out.

She glanced at the file on the edge of her desk that had arrived from the ACC this morning: her demands for the upcoming HMIC visit. A list covering two A4 sheets, plus a renewed request for the feedback report on their last investigation. How she was supposed to prepare the details with a live investigation running was anyone's guess.

The wheels of her chair squeaked as she rolled back, hauled herself up and wandered into the incident room. 'Listen up, everyone.' Voices hushed, heads turned. 'You've all put in more than enough hours these past few days. Let's call it a day now, eh?'

A low-bellied roar gathered momentum as it rattled around the room.

Helen smiled. 'Spend the evening with your families. Have an early night. We'll come to this again tomorrow with fresh eyes. 8 am sharp.'

The room's mood instantly loosened. Officers shuffled about, shutting down computers, gathering their belongings. Helen made her way back into the office, her gaze resting on the pile of papers from the ACC. Perhaps it was time to make a start.

* * *

Superintendent Jenkins lived at Elmtrees, an old shoe factory recently converted into exclusive apartments that overlooked the River Weir on the southern edge of Hampton. A gust of wind sent a shiver down Helen's shirtsleeves as she pressed the keypad. After several hours staring at a computer screen, working through lists of figures, it was getting late, the balmy air of the day beginning to cool.

'Helen, come on up,' a voice called through the intercom. 'Floor five.'

The foyer was an open space edged with wood-panelled walls. Rows of locked letter boxes, European style, lined the far wall. Winding staircases with brass balustrades rose from either end of the floor. A glass chandelier hung from the ceiling. *Very plush*, Helen thought, the heels of her boots tapping the marble flooring as she approached the lift. She pressed the button, then checked her watch. 9.05 pm. It was Wednesday – Robert's cricket practice night. Her mother and the boys would be home now, settling down for the night after a late dinner. She pictured them earlier, sitting around the table together. It had been days since they'd eaten together and she missed their anecdotes, their easy chatter. Plus, she'd been home late for the last couple of nights and only seen her mother in passing. Nothing unusual. Long hours were expected with a new case; her family understood that. But she hadn't had a chance to talk to her mother, not properly, since their discussion about Davy Boyd on Sunday evening and the undercurrent made her uncomfortable.

She pulled out her phone to call home and sighed at the faded signal bars.

The lift doors cranked open. Helen stepped inside. When she reached floor five, she tried her phone again, to no avail. She was still fiddling with it when she arrived at number 19.

'No signal?'

Helen jumped. She was still staring at her phone screen; she hadn't noticed the door open. 'Oh, sorry,' she said, gazing up at Chris Jenkins. He was dressed in a plaid shirt and a pair of beige trousers, his grey hair neatly combed back.

'Don't be. There are only a couple of networks that get a reasonable signal here. David and I had to switch when we moved in.' He stepped aside for her to enter. 'It's good to see you, Helen.'

Helen smiled. She'd phoned ahead, of course. Superintendent Jenkins wasn't the kind of colleague you called on unannounced, especially at this late hour. 'How are you?'

'Doing okay in the circumstances.'

'And David?'

'Chemo's wiping him out. He wanted to meet you...' He looked over his shoulder and pressed his lips together apologetically. 'Well, maybe another time.'

'Of course.'

Jenkins's cream moccasins squeaked on the tiled floor. The hallway was bright and airy, courtesy of an atrium window above.

'This is nice,' Helen found herself saying, feeling a pinch of guilt. She'd considered visiting on several occasions during the few weeks he'd been off, but it never seemed like the right time.

He showed her into a large sitting room. Net curtains fluttered in the light evening breeze beside open French doors at the end, leading to a balcony. Furniture was sparse and looked expensive: an oversized sofa with matching cushions, an ornate oak coffee table, a matching dresser. Everything placed at angles across polished oak flooring that gleamed against the white walls.

Jenkins hovered in the hallway. 'Tea, coffee?'

'Coffee would be lovely, thank you.'

She stared at a large painting above the fireplace, tilting her head to take in the swirls of colours. Jenkins had a similar abstract painting in his office back at headquarters. She'd studied it many a time, never been able to work it out, and she couldn't decipher this one either. A bit like Jenkins himself, really. He wasn't one of those people with whom you talked about your weekend or shared an anecdote. Even now, standing here in his living room, she felt like she was gearing up for a job interview rather than visiting a colleague on a career break.

She moved out to the balcony, savouring the fresh evening air. The River Weir gushed below against a backdrop of arable fields reaching to the horizon. She looked down at the river, sparkling in the waning evening sunshine. Last time she'd been this close to a water source, she'd been staring at a dead body laid out beside it. The significance jabbed at her. Was Shauna's body laid out beside water deliberately?

'There you go,' Jenkins said, handing her a coffee. 'It's a nice evening, isn't it?'

'It is.' The coffee smelled strong and mellow, not the

instant variety she was accustomed to from the machine at work that tasted like woodsmoke. It was just like Jenkins to make real coffee. She noticed a row of steps at the side. 'Where do they go?'

'To the roof terrace.'

'Nice!'

'It is. We don't use it as often as we should. David's afraid of heights.'

'Maybe you should have bought an apartment on the ground floor.'

'And lose this view. I don't think so.'

She tittered at his attempt at humour and followed him back inside.

'So, how are you coping?' he asked. 'I hear you have a new murder.' He indicated for her to sit at one end of the sofa while he took the other and crossed his legs. He seemed instantly more comfortable raising the issue of work. 'I also hear you lost your inspector.'

'Sounds like you're keeping up to date.'

He laughed. 'I try. Any news on the case?'

'It's early days.' Helen glanced towards the window, her thoughts fleetingly returning to the water below. She made a mental note to check on connections with the pentagram and water.

'How are you getting along with Alison?'

Helen pictured the additional staff, the ACC taking over liaison with the press. 'The ACC's been quite supportive actually.'

'Good, as long as she hasn't written me off.'

It was Helen's turn to laugh. 'I don't think there's much chance of that. Actually,' she paused, took another sip of coffee, 'there is something you might be able to help me with.'

Jenkins narrowed his eyes as she told him about the HMIC visit. 'They're not wasting any time,' he said. 'We weren't expecting them back until later in the year. I was hoping I'd be back to get everything set up.'

'No such luck.'

'That's okay. Let me give you some pointers.'

'I confess, that is exactly what I was hoping for.'

By the time he'd gone through various reports and software packages, Helen had written two pages of notes and was beginning to feel weary.

'Don't look so forlorn,' he said. 'Tim in technical will help. Failing that, Britt Evans in organised crime is a whizz with the software. You can always tap her up.'

'Thanks. I really appreciate it.' She tucked her notebook back into her bag.

'Another coffee?'

Helen stared down at her empty mug. The offer was tempting; it had tasted delicious. But… 'No, thanks. I'd better get going.' She held up her phone. 'Can't be AWOL for long.'

* * *

As soon as Helen crossed the apartment car park, her mobile bleeped and buzzed.

Two messages: one from Pemberton, another from the control room. And a missed call from Robert.

She stopped in her tracks. Robert rarely phoned. She hoped there wasn't a problem. She clicked to call him back, crossing her fingers he was still awake.

'Hi, Mum.' He sounded chirpy, upbeat. *Thank goodness.*

'Hi, darling. Just got your missed call. Everything okay?'

'Sure. I've got some news. I've been picked to play cricket for the school on Saturday.'

While he struggled academically, Robert excelled at sports. Already in the school football team, he'd only taken up cricket last year, which made this selection all the sweeter. 'That's brilliant,' she said. 'Well done! Who are you up against?'

'Ryland,' he said. 'They usually pan us. Can't wait to beat them.'

The excitement in his voice was infectious. 'I'm so pleased for you.'

'Will you come and watch?'

Helen's heart swelled. 'Of course. Wouldn't miss it.'

She found herself grinning from ear to ear as she ended the call. She shouldn't have agreed so easily. She had no idea where they'd be with the case on Saturday, but it was so rare her boys asked her to attend anything these days, and it obviously meant a lot to Robert. She'd make sure she got there, somehow.

She climbed into her car and opened Pemberton's message. *Can you call me back when you get this, please? Soon as?* She clicked the control room message: *We are trying to locate you as a matter of urgency.* It was just after ten. She'd only been out of signal an hour. Good job she hadn't had that second coffee.

Pemberton answered on the second ring as if he was waiting for her call.

'Sean, I just got your message. What is it?'

'There's been another murder. A fisherman found a woman's body beside the lake at Henderson Ley. Victim bears the same engraving on her chest as Shauna O'Hennessey. I'm at the scene now.'

'I'm on my way.'

Helen ended the call and turned over the engine. Henderson Ley was a nature reserve and lake on the western side of town. Private property, the lake licensed for fishing. Her father took her down there when she was young, harbouring some ill-conceived idea that she might be interested in fishing. It didn't last; she only went half a dozen times. But something about the location caught her now – once again the body was left beside water.

CHAPTER 25

Crime scenes were different at night. The weather cooled, the area hushed; day animals retreating, making way for their quieter nocturnal neighbours. Even with a full moon bestowing a milky light, darkness cast shadows, blind spots across the landscape.

Torchlights flashed up and down the dirt track leading to the entrance of Henderson Ley, highlighting the white Tyvek suits of the CSIs, as Helen parked up behind a stream of other vehicles.

Temporary forensic lamps were lit like beacons in the distance, marking the scene. Helen nodded to a couple of CSIs, made her way through a tunnel of trees and signed into the crime scene log, her overshoes crunching the packed earth as she continued towards the lamps. She could see the water in the distance now, dark ripples glimmering in the moonlight.

Another line of police tape ran just before the water's edge. The lamps coalesced, blinding her as she approached. She raised her hands to shield her eyes. The body was fifty yards or so up the shore, away from the entrance. The ground was soft and uneven. It took her a good couple of minutes to reach it.

'Helen!' A voice called as she approached. A figure in blue stood, pulling back his hood.

Helen nodded at Charles Burlington, the pathologist.

'Out on the town, were we?' he said.

Helen chuckled. 'I wish.' She lowered her gaze to the corpse. The woman was naked. Dark hair fanned in a halo around her head. Arms folded across her chest. Glassy eyes staring upwards. Young, slim, pretty. But what struck Helen was the resemblance to Shauna O'Hennessey. They could have been sisters.

'How long do you think she's been here?' Helen asked.

'Not long,' Charles said. 'Rigor is only just starting to set in. She was killed in the past four hours.'

'As recent as that?'

He nodded.

She turned slowly, taking in as much of the surrounding area as she could. It wasn't far from the spot where she'd fished with her father all those years ago. In front of her, the lake spread into the distance. Behind was a field, a copse, then more fields rolling back into the valley. One access point: the track she'd taken.

'Looks like our killer has developed a taste.'

Helen turned and greeted Pemberton. They both took a moment to examine the inverted pentagram carved on the victim's chest.

'I've done a preliminary examination,' Charles said. 'A knife with a shallow blade, just like last time. Marks on the neck indicate a wire garrotte.'

Helen glanced at the victim's knees, her feet. They were clean. At least this poor girl hadn't run for her life. 'Any defensive wounds?'

He lifted a bagged hand to reveal several nails, split and torn. Scratches and abrasions on her fingers.

Helen imagined the wire flung around her neck, the poor girl grappling with it. The panic. The tension. The pain.

'Injuries apart from those to the throat are localised to the hands and fingers,' Charles said. 'I'd say she came here consensually.'

The thought made Helen shudder. What kind of hold

did the killer have over her to draw her out here at this time of night?

'What kind of barbaric mind are we dealing with?' Pemberton said.

Helen took another look at her surroundings, then checked her watch. It was almost 10.45 pm. It had been dark less than an hour. 'One that isn't afraid to work in daylight,' she said.

* * *

The moon slipped behind a cloud, darkening the track as they made their way back to their vehicles.

'I take it her belongings haven't been found nearby?' Helen asked.

Pemberton shook his head. 'Nothing yet.'

'What about the informant?'

'A man named Clive Hardcastle. Retired. Came down to do some night fishing. Quite shaken, by all accounts. Uniform have taken him to the station to get a first account.'

Another innocent victim. Another informant mentally scarred by what they'd seen.

They reached their cars and unzipped their Tyvek suits. Pemberton's phone rang.

Helen opened her boot and leaned on the tailgate of her Volvo to remove her overshoes. Her suit crackled in the night air as she took it off and folded it away. She couldn't help but think of Kerry O'Hennessey, Shauna's aunt. The woman whose presence still eluded them. If the cases were linked, as they appeared to be, did she play a role in all of this?

Pemberton ended his call. 'Looks like we might have an ID. A woman reported her sister missing earlier this evening. Description matches our victim.'

CHAPTER 26

The silhouette of a woman was visible through a window of number 17 Parkfield Close, a modern estate on the eastern fringe of town. Helen watched her silently as she parked behind Pemberton and cut the engine. By the time they were walking up the driveway, the woman was at the door.

Helen lifted her badge and introduced them both. 'Miss Jasmine Carnwell?' she said.

The woman nodded. Several hours had passed since she'd phoned control room and she looked relieved at their presence.

'Is there some news?' she asked, combing swathes of dark hair away from her face with her fingers. She wore a loose pink T-shirt and black leggings. Her feet were bare.

'Can we come inside?' Helen said.

They were interrupted by a voice from the hallway. 'I want Mummy.'

Helen angled her head past Jasmine to view a little girl in a yellow nightie on the stairs. She could only have been about five. 'Hello!' she said.

The child stared back at her, wide-eyed. Dark curls edging her shiny red cheeks.

'What are you doing awake?' Jasmine said softly. She picked up the child and rested her on her hip.

'Where's Mummy?'

'She's been held up, darling. Which means you get an extra night with Auntie Jas. Isn't that nice?' The child didn't return her smile. 'I tell you what, why don't I tuck you up in my bed? We can pretend we're on holiday.'

The child looked doleful but nodded.

'Sorry,' Jasmine said to the detectives. She pointed to a door on their right. 'Go on through and take a seat. I'll be down in a minute. Just get this munchkin settled.' She leaned in, nuzzled her nose into the child's face as she spoke.

It was a tender moment. Touching. A salient reminder to Helen of how the fallout from murder reached far and wide. A woman losing her sister. Children losing their mother. Friends, family, acquaintances.

Helen followed Pemberton into the front room and exhaled long and hard at the photos of children lining the mantel, the box of toys in the corner. The portrait of two women grinning on the wall behind the sofa, arms hooked around each other. One of them Jasmine, the other, very definitely as she peered closer, their victim. They weren't fixed smiles posed for a portrait. Faces creased, eyes shining, heads almost touching, the lens had caught them in a genuine moment of laughter. It was a beautiful shot and it made Helen sad. Because she wondered if Jasmine would ever laugh freely like that again.

The clock on the mantel struck 11.30 pm. Another sitting room; another family life shattered.

'Sorry about that,' Jasmine said, rejoining them. 'Please sit down.'

Helen lowered herself onto the sofa, searching for the right words. Before she could speak, Jasmine launched in.

'It was good of you to come so late. Did the officer tell you all the details? Oh, but I was in a stress. I forgot a few things on the phone.' She shook her head. 'Lou dropped the kids off with me after school. It was... just after five. She said she'd be back by half six. I didn't have anything in for their tea – we had to have fish and chips. And then when she didn't answer her phone. Oh God, that's what worried me.' Her eyes darted from side to side. 'I mean, it's not like her. And that bloody car she drives – it's a liability. I'm sure she must have broken down somewhere and her phone battery has run low.' She paused to take a breath, her face freezing as she looked from one detective to another. 'Something's happened, hasn't it?'

'Miss Carnwell, please sit down,' Helen said.

'No, I don't want to.'

Helen swallowed. 'I'm very sorry to tell you that the body of a woman was discovered at 9.03 pm this evening at Henderson Ley. We have reason to believe it's Louise.'

A hand flew to her chest. 'No. It can't be.'

Her face paled. Helen and Pemberton jumped up, just in time to catch an elbow each as Jasmine's legs buckled. They guided her to an armchair in the corner. Pemberton disappeared into the kitchen. Helen encouraged her to put her head between her knees.

'Breathe,' Helen said. 'Slowly.'

Seconds flitted past. Pemberton returned with a glass of water.

'I think I'm going to be sick.'

Pemberton shot back out to the kitchen. The sound of cupboard doors opening and closing filled the room. He returned with a mixing bowl.

Jasmine's hand trembled as she took it from him, her eyes glacial. 'I don't believe it.'

'Please take a sip of water,' Helen said.

She did as she was told, hand juddering to her mouth. 'What happened?'

Helen waited for her to place the glass down. 'It appears she had been strangled. I'm so sorry.'

Jasmine's jaw dropped. 'She was supposed to be back by half six. I called everyone. She's never late, not for the kids.'

Helen's stomach clenched. It hadn't sunk in. 'I'm so sorry,' she repeated. Instinctively, she reached out and pulled the woman close as Jasmine's shoulders racked and the tears came. She wasn't sure how long they remained there. Time stood still as the woman's tears descended into sobs. Eventually, Jasmine's breathing evened. She lifted her head, dabbed a tissue to her cheeks and stared into space.

Helen moved across to the sofa and gave her a minute before she asked, 'Do you know what Louise was doing at Henderson Ley?'

'No.' A single headshake. She met Helen's gaze. 'She wasn't dressed for it. She had her nice red jacket on. Not the sort of thing you wear to go walking.' Pemberton asked for a description of what she was wearing and scribbled down the details.

'She told me she had errands to run,' Jasmine said. 'I was annoyed with her. We quarrelled. I babysat last night too and thought she was taking liberties. I don't mind looking after the kids, I love having them, but asking me two nights in a row – especially on my only days off this week.' She sniffed, pressed a tissue to her nose. 'Our last words we had were an argument.' Her voice splintered.

'I really am sorry,' Helen said. She gave her another moment before she asked, 'Where do you work?'

'Wilson's care home around the corner. I do shift work.'

'What about Louise?'

'She worked part-time in the offices at Nields, the builder's merchant on Cross Keys.'

'So, you don't know exactly where she went this evening?'

'Not really. She said there were a few things. A dress she had to return to Bants on High Street. A jacket she'd left at a friend's house in town she needed to collect. She gave me the impression none of it would take long.'

Helen double-checked the times and waited while Pemberton jotted the details down.

'The friend she collected the jacket from. Do you remember their name, or address?'

'No. It's a guy she met off one of those dating apps. She went out with him last night. The kids slept over here.'

Helen exchanged a glance with Pemberton. 'Which dating app?' she asked.

'I don't know. She's got several on her phone. This was her fourth, or maybe fifth date with him. They went to The Royal Oak, I believe.'

Helen asked for her phone number and Pemberton scratched it down. She could request billing, have the phone sited, but it was such a loss not to have the device. People stored their lives on their phones these days – their diary, their music, their contacts, their apps. A wealth of information missing.

'Have you met her new friend?' she asked.

'No. Lou wouldn't even show me a photo. She's secretive about men. Likes to get to know them before she introduces them to anyone.' She reached down for the glass and took a sip of water. 'Why? You don't think it was him, do you?'

'I have no reason to believe so. We will need to question Louise's friends and acquaintances though. Do you feel up to giving us a list?'

Another sip of water. Her hand was trembling now. 'I'll try.'

Helen thanked her. 'Do you have a spare key to Louise's house?'

'Yeah, in my bag. Why?'

'We'll need to search it. It's quite routine.'

Jasmine looked down, forlorn.

'Do you have anyone nearby that could come and sit with you?' Helen asked. 'Some family maybe?'

'No. Mum died last year. It's just the two of us now.' A sob escaped. 'Or it was.' She pressed her hand to her mouth, dropped her head and wept again.

CHAPTER 27

Assistant Chief Constable Alison Broadhurst looked impressively fresh as she bustled through the incident room to meet Helen, given it wasn't yet 5.30 am.

'Is it true?' she said to Helen, closing the door. 'Are the murders linked?'

Helen glanced at the ream of notes before her. It had been a long night – securing the scene, interviewing the sister, accompanying her to confirm the ID.

'We believe so.' She gave Alison a summary of their findings at Henderson Ley. 'The victim bears the same marking on her chest.'

The CSI photos squeaked between Alison's fingers as she leafed through them. 'So, we have a serial killer on our hands?'

'The MO certainly looks the same.'

'What about the suspect on the first murder?'

Helen sighed inwardly and shook her head. She wasn't even sure if Kerry was a suspect. 'No sign.'

'I mean where does she fit into things, in light of this new development?'

'If it was Kerry at the petrol station, she was the last person to see Shauna. We still need to trace her. The second murder does muddy the waters somewhat. We need to find the connection between the two victims and work out why they were chosen.'

'What else do we have?'

'We're checking cameras on the approach to the Ley, and we'll start interviewing everyone associated with Louise to build up a picture of her last movements when people rise this morning. We've got a description of what she was wearing last night. We also need to get a statement out to the press and appeal for public sightings of her. Louise's sister has supplied a photo. And we need to trace her car – a white Volkswagen Polo.'

'What about forensics?'

'Nothing immediately obvious. Once again, her clothes and possessions are missing. Charles will do the autopsy first thing.' She paused a second, met Alison's gaze. 'I'd like to bring in a profiler.'

'Now?' Alison tipped her head back and frowned.

'The victims look similar. The MO is the same. If the second scene is anything like the first, it's unlikely to give us anything and, if my instincts are right, the second family won't be able to help much either.' She cleared her throat. 'I think we might be looking at stranger attacks. If so, we need to step into the killer's shoes, work out their pattern.'

Alison's face hardened. 'You sound pretty certain they are going to kill again.'

'Whoever did this is sending a message. We'll work through the usual background checks, appeal for sightings of Louise and her car. But our best chance of catching them comes from working out what that message is.'

Helen combed her fingers through her hair. 'I met a contact when I was at the College of Policing in May. He gave a talk at one of the seminars about the benefits of criminal profiling, especially in serial cases. He's worked on some big investigations, written for *UK Policing Today*. He might be able to help us pin things down.'

'Okay, make the arrangements,' Alison said. 'See if you can get him in urgently. It doesn't change the fact that, presently, we have nothing. What am I supposed to say to the press?'

Helen met her gaze. 'That we have a new murder and the women of Hampton need to take care. Caution them about going out alone at night. At least until we have a better idea of what we're dealing with.'

CHAPTER 28

Marnie pulled the duvet up to her chin. The room was starting to brighten, a new day dawning. Her days and nights were starting to melt into each other. The curtains remained closed around the clock as she lay in bed and stared into nothingness, breaking only for a few hours when her grandchildren came over, and then returning to her bed after they left. There was a time when she'd loved to cook, when planning and cooking the evening meal became the focus of her day. But there was no inclination to use the kitchen now. Darren reheated cartons from the freezer or coaxed her with a few mouthfuls from the odd takeaway, but she wasn't interested. Not really. It was the same with the television. She never missed her soaps. She made a point of recording them when the children were there, catching up later. Yet she hadn't switched on the telly in days. Hadn't thought about work. Hadn't answered the messages of condolence, or opened the cards spilling through the letter box. Apart from her grandchildren, nothing mattered any more.

Baby house martins twittered outside, waiting for their parents to return with food. Every year, they nested outside her bedroom window and messed down the front of the house. They'd talked about removing the nest when the birds migrated at the end of this summer, but now, in the midst of current events, she found the sound of their calls strangely grounding. A reminder of what was.

Marnie slid out of bed, pulled her robe over her shoulders and tiptoed out of the bedroom so as not to wake Darren.

She was on the stairs when she checked her phone and saw the message from the superintendent. *Could you call me as soon as you get this, please? I need to speak with you about something. Thank you, Helen.*

The message had been sent at 1 am, when her phone was on silent. Her stomach twisted. She lowered herself onto the bottom step and called back, tapping her feet with each ring: one, two, three… When the voicemail kicked in, she left a brief message and clicked off. Had they found Kerry? She hoped so. Because what they really needed right now was some news.

She padded into the front room and switched on the television. A newsreader was talking about trials of a new cancer drug. Marnie moved into the kitchen and made herself a coffee. But the message niggled her. She checked her phone again. Nothing. Perhaps she should call the incident room? It was 8.05 am. Would they even be there at this time? She was searching the noticeboard for the business card the superintendent had left – what had she done with it? – when a voice on the television mentioned a vicious killing. The presenter was talking about Shauna's murder.

Marnie ditched her search and carried her coffee through to the front room. A crime scene filled the screen. Blue and white police tape rustling in the breeze. A reporter's hair flapped about as she spoke into a fluffy microphone. It wasn't Blackwell Wood. No. There was a lake in the background. A shore…

'Only five days since Shauna O'Hennessey was murdered, another young woman's body has been discovered in rural Hamptonshire.'

Marnie jolted forward, wincing as she spilled her drink. The hot coffee seeped through her thin pyjama bottoms. She rubbed her burned thighs. Another murder? She grabbed the remote control, hiked up the volume. And gaped at the television as the reporter talked about a fisherman finding the body of a woman beside the water at Henderson Ley yesterday evening. Louise Carnwell. Twenty-eight. A photo of Shauna flashed up. The one Marnie had given the police. The one Shauna had snapped before she had gone for her interview on Friday afternoon.

'Police have confirmed a woman's body has been found. They believe the two murders are linked.'

A wave of nausea. The message from the superintendent suggested news. She was expecting an update on the investigation. Perhaps news that they'd tracked Kerry down or captured the killer. Never in a million years could she have imagined this.

Her phone rang in her hand, making her jump. It was the superintendent returning her call.

'Mrs O'Hennessey?' The detective's voice was cool, calm. 'I'm sorry I missed your call.'

'I've just seen the news about the new murder,' Marnie cut in.

'I'm sorry, I wanted to speak with you first, before the press release, hence my earlier message, but we couldn't wait any longer. Is Darren there with you?'

'Yes.' She didn't mention he was asleep upstairs. How the hell was she to share this with him? He was already at breaking point.

'Good. As I say, we needed to get the victim's details out as quickly as possible to help with the appeal for witnesses.'

Appeal for witnesses. They'd done that after Shauna died. Several times. And it had yielded nothing. Marnie sank into the sofa. This was worse than she could have imagined. 'Do you think it's the same person? The same killer who took our Shauna?'

'It looks like it. I need to ask you whether Shauna or any of you knew Louise Carnwell?'

'The latest victim? Why would we?'

Just then, a face graced the screen. A young woman. Dark hair, attractive. Quite similar to Shauna. The camera had caught her on centre, her mouth stretched into a wide smile. It looked as though she was staring directly back at Marnie.

Marnie's mouth dried.

'Mrs O'Hennessey? Are you still there?'

'Yes, I'm here.'

'Do you know the name?'

'No, we've never heard of her.'

A beat passed.

'Superintendent?'

'Yes?'

'What does this mean?'

'We're not exactly sure. We are doing everything we can to find out. I'll be in touch again when I know more.'

CHAPTER 29

Helen wove her pen through her fingers. In and out, in and out. The incident room was like a ghost town. It was almost 3 pm on Thursday, a day after the second murder, and most of her staff were out interviewing Louise Carnwell's friends and family, or watching CCTV from the town's cameras, trying to track down her car. So far, they'd established that Louise had followed her normal Wednesday routine. Dropped the kids off at school and gone to work. Colleagues said she seemed fine, bright, normal. She'd spoken to a helper at the after-school club about her son's homework when she picked up the children, then driven straight to Jasmine's, leaving her sister's just after 5 pm. And that's when they drew a blank.

The dress store had no record of a return yesterday evening. And what's more, no one saw Louise in The Royal Oak the evening before.

Something was amiss, and it had been amiss awhile.

Her body was discovered by the fisherman at 9.03 pm. Between 5 pm and 9 pm, Louise had travelled to Henderson Ley. Why? Her sister said she wasn't interested in fishing; she didn't think Louise had ever been there before. What took her there last night?

The victim's house search had yielded nothing of interest,

and with no obvious connection between the two women and no clues from friends and family, the murders were looking more and more like stranger attacks. Why those two women? She desperately needed to find out more about the killer's motivation. Their methodology, their background. The profiler was due at any moment. Hopefully, he could shed some light.

Pemberton put his head around the door frame. 'Looks like we've located the car,' he said. 'At number thirty-three Stephenson Street in the town centre. In the car park at the rear of,' he checked the piece of paper in his hand, 'Ashcombe Bed and Breakfast. The manager has just seen the appeal on the telly and phoned in.'

'Does he know how long it's been there?'

'He can't be sure. He claims he doesn't know Louise. Reckons he's never met her.'

'Okay, let's get over there.'

She pulled her jacket off the back of her chair, lifted a file off her desk and moved into the incident room.

'The profiler, a Richard Hughson, is due here any minute,' she said to Spencer. She passed him a buff file. 'I've put together some details for him to take away and study. Can you give him an overview of the case and take him out to view the murder scenes? We'll need him to brief us first thing in the morning, when he's had a chance to digest everything.'

* * *

Ashcombe Bed and Breakfast was two three-storey terraced houses knocked together, halfway down tree-lined Stephenson Street in Hampton town centre. A rendered building painted cream, it was flanked by red-brick residential terraces. More houses sat opposite, all with the same walled front gardens and steps leading up to the front door. A line of police tape ran along a thin channel at the side of the B&B, which led to the car park behind.

Helen gazed at the horde of onlookers gathering on the pavement opposite the guest house: rubberneckers drawn by the presence of police tape and a sentry guard. It wouldn't be long before the press arrived. 'At least uniform managed to cordon off the car park,' she muttered to Pemberton. It would take several hours to get the car lifted and taken away for forensic examination.

The B&B sign above the door of number 33 resembled a pub sign and swung in the light breeze: *Ashcombe B&B & Bar* written in swirly black writing on a cream background, accompanied by a simple drawing of a fireplace and a man sitting in an armchair reading. Understated, restful. It would have been quite charming if it hadn't been for the line of bird excrement running down the centre.

Bar, Helen thought to herself. That suggested visitors other than residents. Though it didn't look much like a pub from the outside.

A light rain started to fall as they opened the gate. Helen turned up her collar. Two hundred yards away, shoppers bustled through High Street to get their wares, yet it was surprisingly quiet and free from traffic here.

They were just entering the front garden, about to climb the steps to the entrance when a balding man dressed in a lilac polo shirt and beige trousers rushed out to meet them. 'Can I help you?' he said enquiringly. He looked harried.

'Mr Ian Richmond?' Pemberton checked. The man nodded as they held up their warrant cards.

'I'm so glad you're here,' he said. 'I can't believe it. She wasn't one of our guests.'

He motioned for them to follow him to the channel at the side. When he reached the police tape, he turned back quizzically. 'Okay for me to cross?' he asked.

Helen nodded. He'd have been in and out of there already, his DNA all over the place.

They followed him to a tarmacked car park around the rear surrounded by high fencing with enough spaces for eight cars. A large sign – *Private Car Park for Residents Only. Unauthorised vehicles will be clamped* – hung on the back wall.

Only three bays were occupied today. A white Toyota was close to the entrance, a Discovery beside it. Louise's white Polo was next to the fence at the end.

One way in, one way out, Helen noted. They needed to speak with the residents nearby to see if they saw or heard anything.

'Who do they belong to?' Pemberton asked, pointing to the other cars.

'The Toyota belongs to a guest. She's been here all week on a business conference. The Disco is mine. That's how I spotted the Polo. I left my glasses in the car last night. Came out to retrieve them earlier, after I saw the appeal. I couldn't believe it when I checked the number plate.'

Pemberton pulled his notebook out of his pocket. 'When was the last time you were out here, before today?'

'Two-ish yesterday. I had to go to the cash and carry. I was back by three. It wasn't here then.'

Helen clocked a camera on the back wall. 'You have CCTV?'

Ian shook his head. 'That's just a dummy, a front.' He hunched his shoulders against the rain. 'We had problems with shoppers parking here when we first moved in, five years ago. Couldn't afford security cameras. We put that up to deter them.'

'What about residents?'

'They tend to park on the road outside. I think the sign puts them off.'

Helen approached the white Polo and peered in the window. An empty crisp packet sat on the back seat. A scrunched tissue in the front well. Apart from that, it was clear. They needed to get it covered urgently to preserve any fingerprints, DNA. If it was anything like the murder scenes, there would likely be nothing of the killer on it, but it was still worth a try.

The rain was coming down heavier as they retraced their steps back through the opening at the side of the building. Helen climbed over the police tape. She was speaking to the guard, asking him to arrange a forensic cover for the car, when she glanced at the crowd opposite, then did a double take, narrowing her eyes at a familiar figure, standing beneath an umbrella on the edge of the crowd. It was Guy Thorne.

'I'll meet you inside,' she said to Pemberton, indicating for him to follow Ian into the guest house, and crossed the road.

Guy Thorne moved a few steps away from the others as she approached. The convenor of The Alternatives was wearing a denim shirt and jeans, a grey waistcoat over the top. He held a yellow shopping bag in his free hand. 'Detective,' he said. 'It's good to see you again.'

The feeling wasn't mutual. 'What are you doing here, Mr Thorne?' Helen said in a low voice. She noticed a few onlookers watching and motioned for him to move further down the pavement.

He looked taken aback, lifted the carrier bag in his hand. 'A spot of shopping. I always come out on a Thursday, before the weekend rush.' He craned his neck past Helen. 'Something to do with the new murder, I assume?'

Helen ignored the question. His presence, so calm and assured, at the scene where the second murder victim had been, less than twenty-four hours before, needled her.

'Where were you last night?' she asked.

Guy raised an alarmed brow. 'At the Rose and Crown in Boddington discussing budgets with one of the club members.'

At that moment, the police guard crossed the road and started to disperse the onlookers. Guy bowed his head in his usual theatrical manner and made off down the street. But his presence left Helen with an uneasy sense of disquiet.

* * *

A blue *Vacancies* sign on the door wobbled as Helen entered Ashcombe Bed and Breakfast. In the hallway, landscape prints adorned the cream Anaglypta walls. Helen's gaze fell on a small wooden desk, covered in leaflets. Hamptonshire wasn't much of a tourist area, being set in the heart of the Midlands, but Ian Richmond had done his best to highlight areas of interest, with literature about the shoe museum, Blackwell Wood and Jericho Falls, a natural beauty spot on the edge of the county.

He led them through a door on the right and into a surprisingly large room which was bright and airy, and dotted with round tables and chairs. A bar ran along the end. 'Do you get much passing trade?' Pemberton asked.

'Not really. Guests use this room if they want to be sociable. Outside visitors are supposed to attend with guests. We've a dining room too on the other side that's for residents – mainly for breakfasts.'

'How many staff do you have?' Helen asked.

'I live on the premises, on the top floor. This was my retirement project. Supposed to be a joint enterprise for me and my wife. She passed away a year after we moved in, so it's just me now.'

'I'm sorry.'

He shrugged. 'I'm usually around. I cover the desk, do the breakfasts. I have a cleaner that comes in daily to sort the rooms – we have four rooms in total. An accounts lady comes in twice a week and covers if I want to pop out. We all muck in.'

'What about yesterday?'

'Emily, the cleaner, was here. She left about twelve. Then just me. I was here all evening.'

'How many guests do you have staying?'

'Just the one last night, the businesswoman I was telling you about.'

'What about in the bar?'

'Sam, my guest, was in for a while. Other than that, it was empty all evening.'

'Right, we'll need the details of your guest and those of your staff too,' Pemberton said.

Helen looked out of the window and into the road out front. Louise had driven down the side and parked at the back, then left her car there. She'd chosen that car park. Why? Granted, it was only a five-minute walk into town. It was conceivable she'd parked there to pop in and run her errands. But Ian said locals didn't tend to use the car park; it was only for guests. Unless she was meeting someone there…

'Mr Richmond,' Helen said. 'Where were you between five and eleven yesterday evening?'

'Here.'

'And last Friday evening?'

He looked affronted. 'What are you suggesting?'

'I'm not suggesting anything,' Helen said. 'The second victim left her car here. We need to eliminate you from our inquiries.'

* * *

'Guy Thorne was here earlier,' Helen said to Pemberton as they made their way back to the car.

'What?'

'Standing amongst the crowd, watching.' She pointed to the pavement opposite, now empty.

'What was he doing here?'

'Shopping, apparently.' She scratched the back of her neck. It could be a coincidence. But Helen had been in the job long enough to learn that 'coincidences' in police work were always worth exploring. And something about his presence left her uneasy. She glanced across at Pemberton. 'He said he was in the Rose and Crown last night in Boddington, with another group member. Get that checked, would you?'

CHAPTER 30

Richard Hughson, the criminal profiler, was a tall, wiry man with a bush of brown hair, a thick Welsh accent and a wide, toothy smile. Bony wrists poked out the ends of the suit jacket he wore over a white open-necked shirt and a pair of faded olive slacks. 'I've read through the case notes,' he said, peering over his glasses at the detectives and support staff huddled in front of him. 'Let's go through the information we have.'

Helen stood silent at the side of the room. Outside, a storm was brewing and the low-slung clouds glared dark and heavy through the windows. It was Friday morning. A week after the first murder, two days after the second, and every tick of the clock beat inside her.

'This is someone who follows his victims, watches them, has a window into their life. He has a specific type: the victims are female, dark, petite. Both are mothers and both live locally.'

'He?' Spencer piped up.

'Yes,' Richard said. 'Our killer is male.'

'You sound pretty sure.'

The drone of an aeroplane overhead filled the room. Richard waited until it passed before he continued.

'To stand behind someone and garrotte them while they

struggle, then strip them post-mortem, takes an immense amount of strength. We know Shauna O'Hennessey was dragged up the riverbank too.'

'It could have been a strong woman.'

Helen could see where Spencer was coming from. She looked at the photo of Kerry O'Hennessey on their noticeboard, the tall woman who held a grudge against her family. The best lead they'd had for Shauna and, while they hadn't yet found a link with Louise, one the team didn't want to let go.

'It's not just a case of strength,' Richard said. 'The way the women were laid out, bare and raw, suggests a misogynistic motive. He wanted to expose them, humiliate them in death. Few female killers plan so meticulously and when they do, they tend to go for something safer, often closer to home.

'He's not only strong,' Richard continued, 'he's well-built and fit. We know he chased Shauna through the woods. Aged between twenty and sixty years old, I'd suggest he lives alone. There's a lot of planning gone into these scenes: sourcing the right locations, stalking his targets. He's fastidious about cleanliness too, or can be when he wants to be.'

Helen folded her arms across her chest as Ian Richmond's neat kitchen came to mind. House-to-house near the guest house hadn't thrown up any leads. No one saw anything. They'd checked out Ian's alibi for Friday and Wednesday. On Friday, his accountant had been there working late and said he was there, although they weren't in the same room all evening. On Wednesday, the guest confirmed Ian was in the bar and she neither saw nor heard anything. Was it possible he could have slipped out at some stage?

'These weren't chance attacks,' Richard said. 'Timing is important. He selects locations that are reasonably remote but close to pathways – he wants his victims to be found. He has a good local knowledge too. We are looking for someone that either lives nearby or has lived here at some stage.'

The trip to Jenkins's apartment tripped into Helen's mind.

'Both victims were laid out beside water,' she said. 'Is that significant?'

He passed her a knowing glance. 'I was just coming to that. This individual is acting out their own personal ritual. Certain elements are important to them, including the existence of water. They've probably dabbled in Satanism or the occult, read a book or looked online, dipped their toe into it and, in their twisted mind, linked the inversion of the pentagram to evil. That's how he sees his victims – as evil. He's keeping their clothes, their personal belongings, because he's proud of what he's done. He believes he's on some kind of warped mission.'

A loose window rattled in the wind.

'How do we stop him?' Pemberton said.

'There's something in these women's backgrounds that repulses him. Something that makes him target and expose them. A trigger. If you find out what that is, it'll bring you closer to finding him.'

Helen scanned the dejected faces of her team. This wasn't what they'd hoped for. Being specific about their perpetrator being male and working individually turned their investigation upside down. 'Is there anything else you can tell us?' she asked. 'Anything specific?'

'Louise left her car in town. It's likely he met her nearby. He's not concerned about being recognised, which suggests he's quite unremarkable in appearance. Not someone who stands out. He's also charming, beguiling and manipulative. The victims were killed at the scene. He's managed to lure each of them out to remote locations, despite the inherent personal risk. That involves a level of persuasion and trust.'

'Are you suggesting they knew him?' Pemberton asked.

'Not necessarily. But they will have met him previously, he wasn't a complete stranger, and he'll have been watching them, getting to know them from afar. I cannot stress enough, he chooses his victims for a particular reason. He'll have stalked other women too, and dropped them when they didn't meet his criteria.

'He's also a driver. Someone with use of a vehicle. A vehicle he used to transport the victims out to their rural locations.'

'Right,' Helen said. 'Let's go through the CCTV footage from around the crime scenes again. See if we can spot the same vehicle passing through. And we'll renew our public appeal for witnesses near where Louise left her car. Someone must have seen something.'

Helen closed the meeting and was thanking Richard when Pemberton approached.

'We've verified Guy Thorne's movements for Wednesday evening,' he said. 'The landlord confirmed he was in the Rose and Crown all evening.'

'Right.' She couldn't deny that something about Guy Thorne didn't sit right, though clearly he wasn't their killer.

'There's something else.' He excused them both from the profiler, called her aside. 'A man has just called into Cross Keys Station with some information about the recent murder. He said he'll only speak to the person in charge.'

CHAPTER 31

Helen viewed the man in reception through the one-way mirrored glass at Cross Keys Station. Greying hair thinned around a widow's peak. He was lithe, bespectacled, and the navy suit he wore looked tired and creased.

'He came in an hour ago,' the desk officer said. 'Insisted on speaking to whoever was leading Operation Allen. Wouldn't give any details.' Helen thanked the officer and peered out again. Operation Allen, as the investigation had been named, had been featured incessantly in the press. She desperately hoped this wasn't a fantasist, a member of the public fascinated with the macabre details of a murder investigation, feigning information because they wanted to be part of it. They got their fair share of time-wasters in homicide.

The man looked up and stood as she unlatched the door.

'Acting Superintendent Helen Lavery,' she said, proffering a hand. 'I'm heading Operation Allen.'

He viewed her extended hand, hastily shook it. 'Is there somewhere we can talk?'

'Of course, Mr?'

He looked towards the desk wide-eyed.

Helen traded a fleeting glance with the officer behind it, then guided the man down to one of the gentler interview rooms, with a sofa and a coffee table, that they reserved for speaking with vulnerable witnesses. She motioned for him to make himself comfortable and took the armchair opposite. A light flashed intermittently from the small camera above the Monet painting on the wall.

'Can I get you a drink?' she asked.

'No, thank you.'

'What is it you wanted to see me about?' she said, resting her hands in her lap.

He sat tall as if there was a rod of iron down his back. 'I've got some information. Before I give it to you, I need to be assured of complete anonymity. You can take my prints, my DNA, whatever it is you need to do – I'm not personally involved.' He took a breath. 'But I can't afford for my name to come out, not even in the investigation.'

'This is a murder case,' Helen said. 'I'll do what I can, but I can't confirm anything until I hear what you have to say. At the very least, I will have to take your contact details in case I need to speak to you again.' When his face paled, she added, 'I promise, I'll be discreet. I do appreciate you coming forward.'

He gave her his name and address and she jotted them down. 'Now, what is it you have to tell me?'

'The girl,' he said. 'Louise. I knew her. That is to say, I've met her. She used a different name – Lola – but I'm sure it was her.' He spoke quickly, punching the words out as if he was short of time. When he said Lola, his hands trembled.

'Okay,' Helen said calmly. 'How did you know Louise... or Lola?'

'I didn't know her well. I only met her once.' His hands trembled again. He slipped them beneath his thighs.

'Right. Let's go back to the beginning. We're trying to get to know Louise at the moment, to build up a picture of her life. The more you can tell me about how you met her, the more it'll help us.' She gave a gentle smile. 'How were you first introduced?'

'We weren't. Well, not as such.' He swallowed. 'I found her on a website, booked her for the evening before she...' Another swallow.

Booked her. Helen leaned forward. 'Take your time.'

'I don't usually use escorts, but the site was very discreet. None of the tackiness you see on some websites. You contact the girls direct to make the arrangements.'

Helen's insides reeled. Louise was an escort. *How could we not know this?* 'How did you reach her?' she said, doing her best to conceal her surprise.

'There's a phone number on the site. I messaged her, asked if she was free.'

'When was this?'

'On Tuesday afternoon. She messaged back and we arranged to meet at The Royal Oak at 6 pm. She was waiting for me outside. She'd organised the room in advance at Bluebells B&B next door.' He buried his eyes in the table. 'I didn't recognise her at first. I asked her to come without make-up. I don't like it when they're all dolled up.'

Tuesday evening. Louise's sister had said she'd looked after the kids two nights in a row, Tuesday and Wednesday, and Tuesday was the night Louise was supposedly on her date.

'How did she seem?' Helen asked.

'Fine. That's just it. She was fine. Vibrant. Alive.' Tears filled his eyes.

'You had sex?' Helen checked.

'Yes. I was with her just under an hour. Then we parted. I left the room at about ten to eight. I guess she left shortly afterwards.'

'Did you hear from her after that?'

'No. I wasn't expecting to. I couldn't believe it when I saw her picture in the news this morning.'

'Did she talk to you? Tell you anything about her life, her connections, other clients maybe?'

'No.' He shook his head, eyes glistening with tears. 'We weren't exactly there to talk.'

The room quietened.

'You said you found her on a website,' Helen said carefully. 'What was it called?'

156

CHAPTER 32

'Found it. Adult Services For You,' Pemberton said.

Helen and Pemberton were standing beside Spencer's computer in the corner of the incident room. After phoning the details through to the office and requesting urgent checks, she was relieved to arrive back to find they'd dug up a wealth of information about the website.

Spencer pointed the end of his pen at a photo of Louise or 'Lola', as she was called, on the screen. She was barely recognisable. Sandwiched between two blondes, Cherry and Tina, her photo was a head-and-shoulders shot, her face lathered in make-up, the top of a black camisole showing off a generous portion of breast.

'Classy,' Helen said.

'Oh, believe me,' Spencer said. 'I can tell you from my days in vice, this is pretty tame. It could be a whole lot worse.'

The text beneath was limited – *Call now, for a night you won't forget*. A phone number was listed beneath.

Helen recalled a stint she'd done with organised crime. They were monitoring some of the known sex websites to ensure the girls weren't being exploited or abused. She'd been amazed when they had visited a massage parlour, just off High Street, where girls were earning up to two thousand pounds a week for additional services. 'There's not much information listed, is there?' she said.

'Leaves a lot to the imagination, I guess. Clients discuss with the girls what they offer.'

'And no price.'

'They don't want to put people off. Ask too much and it limits interest. These people work on the basis that once a girl speaks with a client, they'll hook them in.'

'We've spoken to the manager at Bluebells. He confirmed a room was booked by a Lola Levison on Tuesday evening. She paid in cash. He never saw the client. And we've discreetly checked out your informant too. He was out of town on Wednesday night, at a business conference in Leeds.'

Helen thanked Spencer. She hadn't suspected the informant. It was unlikely he'd come forward and offer his prints if he was involved, but they needed to account for him, just in case.

'Anyway, that's not all we wanted you to see,' Pemberton said. He nodded to Spencer, who scrolled through numerous other profiles.

Spencer paused at a photo at the bottom of the page. A dark-haired woman, again heavily made-up, with red pouty lips – Sherry.

Helen cast them both a bewildered look.

Spencer clicked on the profile. A photo of Sherry filled the page, an arrow beside indicated further photos. He clicked along. Sherry in a red camisole, crawling towards the camera. Sherry glancing beneath her thick lashes bashfully. Sherry looking over her shoulder. And then Helen spotted it – the edge of a teardrop birthmark at the side of her neck.

'Ah!'

'Exactly,' Spencer said. 'Both our victims were working from the same site. Both potentially sex workers.'

Helen stood back, leaning against the arm of the chair. The profiler said there was something about the women that repulsed the killer… 'How could we not have known this?' she said.

'We can't crack the passwords to either of their iPads and we don't have their phones,' Pemberton said. 'We've been right through their social media history, and there's no hint of anything like this on there. We're still interviewing Louise's friends, family and work colleagues, but so far, no one has mentioned anything about a second job. It seems she kept it secret. Shauna's parents indicated she kept things to herself too. There's a stigma attached to sex work. Clearly, the women didn't want anyone to know.'

Helen recalled the portraits of Shauna in her parents' front room. The naturally pretty girl with the smoky eyes, translucent complexion. They couldn't be more different to these pictures.

'The internet has opened things up,' Spencer said. 'Women can advertise online, arrange meets, rent a room. It means they can keep things private.'

'Surely one of them would tell someone where they were going, or who they were seeing?' Helen said. 'Even just as a safety precaution.' She thought for a second. 'Do we know if Kerry O'Hennessey has ever been involved in the sex industry?' She was struggling to see how this woman fitted into things now, if she did at all.

Spencer shook his head. 'No idea. We've worked our way through the London homeless charities and made inquiries with the Met. No one has any details on Kerry for the time she was away.'

Helen looked back at the website. The average age of the women on this site was twenty-something. Young. In their prime. 'Was there any indication in our victims' finances that they were struggling, enough to take a second job?'

'They were both maxed out on credit cards,' Spencer said. 'But who in their twenties isn't these days?'

'We know Shauna was struggling financially after the relationship break-up,' Pemberton said.

'Okay, how do we find out who runs the website?' Helen asked.

'We've already had the techies working on it. It's registered to a Mr Will Sheridan. Lives at nineteen Riordan Close, the new estate just outside Roxten. He's not known to the police.'

'Right. Good work, Steve. Make sure you screenshot the profiles in case anyone changes or tampers with anything.' Helen glanced sideways at Pemberton. 'Let's pay Mr Sheridan a visit.'

They were interrupted by Dark jumping up from her desk. 'We've a witness who believes they saw Louise yesterday evening in Stephenson Road,' she said.

'Was she with anyone?'

'He says she was alone. It was only a fleeting sighting. He recognised her from the red jacket her sister said she wore. He said it looked like she was waiting for someone.'

'Okay, can you follow that up? We'll head out to see Mr Sheridan.'

CHAPTER 33

Riordan Close was an exclusive development of mock-Tudor detached homes. Helen surveyed the sweeping block-paved driveways, the immaculate black front doors, the double garages and sparkling latticed windows.

'Clearly sex pays,' Pemberton said under his breath as they stood under the wide porch of number 19 and rang the bell.

The door was answered by a woman in black jeans and a loose white T-shirt. Blonde hair swept back from her face in a high ponytail. 'Can I help you?'

Children's voices carried down the stairs. Loud and shrill.

Helen held up her badge. 'We're looking for a Mr Will Sheridan,' she said.

Alarm fluttered across the woman's face. 'Why do you want to speak to him?'

'And you are?'

'Emma. His wife.' A crash sounded from above. She glanced up and frowned.

'It's in connection with a case we're working on,' Helen said. 'Is he home?'

Emma invited them in and they squeezed past a mountain of suitcases piled in the hallway.

'Going somewhere?' Pemberton asked.

'Just got back twenty minutes ago, hence the commotion.' Another glance up. 'We got special permission to take the kids out of school for a family wedding. To be honest, I'll be glad when they go back.'

'Anywhere nice?'

'Sorrento.'

Pemberton pulled a face at Helen as Emma motioned for them to follow her down the hallway, past the stairs to a door on the left.

'Will,' she said, knocking once. A man looked up from a desk as she opened the door. He was short and bespectacled with thinning fair hair spiked on his head and a bird-like face that glowed red from the sun. The grey polo shirt he wore hung off his bony shoulders.

'The police are here to see you.'

Will swivelled in his chair.

Another thud hit the ceiling. 'Excuse me,' Emma said and rushed off.

The room housed a desk and a chair. An aquarium of bright-coloured guppies sat beneath the small window at the end.

'What's this about?' Will said, nudging his glasses up his nose.

'Is there somewhere we can talk?' Helen asked. There was barely enough floor space for them all to stand in there.

He guided them through to a spacious front room and indicated for them to sit on one of the sofas. Another aquarium of cichlids stood in the corner.

Emma reappeared at the door. 'Sorry about that,' she said. 'Can I get you a tea, or a coffee?'

They declined. Helen waited until the door closed before she settled into the sofa. 'Mr Sheridan, we're here to ask you about your website, Adult Services For You,' she said.

Will's face tightened. He immediately looked to the door. *His wife doesn't know*, Helen thought. *Interesting.*

'There's nothing illegal about it,' he said. 'It's all legit.'

'I'm not suggesting otherwise,' Helen said. 'But we are investigating the murders of two women, and we think the killer found them on your website. They both have profiles posted there.'

Will's face drained of colour. 'W-what?'

'You're not suggesting you didn't know?'

'No, I didn't. I'm just back from two weeks in Italy. I haven't seen the news.'

'You don't manage the website while you are away?'

'It pretty much manages itself.' He swiped a hand across his brow, swallowed. 'Who were they?'

'Shauna O'Hennessey was killed last Friday. And Louise Carnwell on Wednesday. You might know them better as Sherry and Lola.'

'Christ! I'm sorry. I had no idea.' He watched warily as Pemberton retrieved a notebook and clicked the end of his pen.

'Do you store the details of people who contact girls on your site?'

Will shook his head. He looked like he was going to be sick. 'No. It's all confidential between the girls and their clients. I don't have any contact with the clients at all.'

Helen's stomach plummeted. No contact meant no registration process. No starting point for tracing an individual's activity. 'How long has the site been running?'

'Err... Must be... almost two years.'

Pemberton looked up from his notes. 'You don't seem sure.'

'I'd need to check my records to be certain.'

Helen sat forward. She wasn't sure what she imagined Will Sheridan would look like, but she was expecting someone more robust. This man seemed to shrivel beneath their eyes. She scanned the room at the stripy curtains, the swags and tails, the elegant scatter cushions to match, the oversized television in the corner. A zebra cichlid moved to the front of the fish tank and stared at her. 'Is this your only job?' she asked.

'No, I'm an accountant. I work for Todds in town. This is just... a sideline.'

Helen recalled investigating a burglary at Todds when she was in uniform. It was a sprawling manufacturing plant located on Cross Keys Trading Estate. 'How many women do you have on your Adult Services website?'

'Twenty-eight.'

'That's quite a sideline. How does it work?'

'The women get in touch with me if they wish to be featured. They supply a short profile and a photo or series of photos. I upload the details and charge them a monthly subscription.'

Helen leaned forward. 'The women pay to be on your site?'

'Yes. I do all the advertising – we target travelling businessmen. The clients contact the women directly, make the arrangements and pay in cash at the meet.'

'The meet for sex.'

He gave her a hard stare. 'I run an introduction agency. To provide company. It's up to the individuals what additional services they supply. I don't take a cut of earnings, I only receive the standard monthly subscription charge.'

'How very gallant of you,' Pemberton said.

'I'm not a pimp.'

'All right,' Helen said, desperate to calm the situation. 'How much is the monthly subscription charge?'

'It depends where they are on the listing – those at the top of the page pay more, those at the bottom less, but it averages about £50 each a month. The girls can double or triple that in a couple of hours if they are savvy.'

'Fourteen hundred pounds a month.' Helen pulled down the corners of her mouth. 'Do you have any other websites or sources of income, other than your day job?' There was always the possibility the people who used his site were involved in other lines of business with him.

'I don't run other sites. I advertise other products on this site to boost the income, if that's what you mean.'

'Oh, yes. I saw those,' Pemberton chipped in. 'Sex toys and the like. But, of course, you are not selling sex.' He struggled to keep the sarcasm from his voice.

Will scrunched his eyes. 'Everything I earn is declared to the Inland Revenue,' he said, indignant. 'Adult Services is a registered business.'

Helen sighed inwardly. Technically, she couldn't arrest him or ask him to take down the site because he wasn't officially doing anything illegal. It was against the law to solicit on a street corner or run a brothel, but in selling the suggestion of sex, he was doing neither. 'Do you meet the women?' Helen asked.

'Once. After the initial contact – usually at a bar in town. Just to make sure they look like their profile, to keep the site legitimate.'

'And how about afterwards. Do you monitor them?'

'How do you mean?'

'Health and safety. They are meeting strangers, after all.'

'Not exactly.'

'Not exactly,' Helen repeated, enunciating every syllable.

'Well, no. They're self-employed, responsible for themselves. They can leave any time they like. Cancel their subscriptions, have their profiles taken down. There's no notice period.'

'What about their personal safety?'

'I give them safeguarding advice when I meet them. Encourage them to meet in a public place, use a separate phone for work, that sort of thing.'

A separate phone. No wonder nothing had been highlighted on either of the women's personal phone records. 'I see.'

He was quiet a moment. 'What happened to them? The women that died.'

'They were strangled.'

Footsteps thudded the stairs, the door crashed open and the

faces of two girls appeared. They were young, no older than ten. 'Daddy—' one of them started.

'Out!' Will said. 'Can't you see I'm busy?'

They glanced at each other, retreated and closed the door.

'We'll need the names and contact details of all the women registered on your site,' Helen said. It galled her that she had no powers to close it down.

'What?' He looked bewildered. 'Why?'

'We have a duty of care to contact them, let them know what's happened and alert them to potential danger. Does anyone else have access to their details?'

'No, only me.'

'Right.' Helen stood. 'I want the phone numbers you have – the alternative numbers – for Shauna and Louise. And take the girls' details down off the site. Now. The families won't want those images floating around the internet.'

* * *

Back in the car, Helen looked across at Will Sheridan's hollow face at the window as she fastened her seat belt.

She pictured him sitting watching television with his wife of an evening, his two girls sleeping upstairs, while the women on his website were out meeting clients and entering potentially dangerous liaisons.

They'd check the flight details, but if Sheridan was telling the truth, he couldn't be responsible for the deaths. The killer had taken their clothes, their bags, their phones. But what bothered her was the bank records. Sheridan said the women paid him a monthly subscription. They were still working through Louise's bank account, but they'd gone through Shauna's with a fine-toothed comb. Why hadn't the transaction flagged up?

Helen's mobile rang as they pulled off down the street. *Dark* flashed up.

She switched it to speakerphone and answered. 'How did you get on with the witness?' she asked.

'Good. It was only a fleeting glance, but the moment was recorded on his dashcam. Louise was standing on the pavement near Ashcombe B&B. I've had him email the footage so we can freeze a still. Her sister said she was wearing a red jacket. It certainly looks like her.'

Ashcombe B&B. Yet the manager hadn't seen her. Helen thanked Rosa and ended the call. 'Let's head back to Ashcombe,' she said to Pemberton. 'I'd like to have another word with our Ian Richmond.'

CHAPTER 34

They arrived at Ashcombe B&B to find Ian Richmond behind the bar chatting with an elderly customer sat on a stool in front. Ian looked up as they approached. 'Hello, officers! Come for a drink?'

'I didn't know you opened at lunchtime,' Pemberton said.

'I open when I have customers.'

'Yeah, sometimes we serve ourselves!' the customer sniggered.

Ian shot him a look, then turned to Pemberton. 'Only when I get called to assist another guest. It's very rare.'

'Can we have a word?' Helen cut in, eyeing the customer, an elderly gentleman dressed in a grey suit, his girth overhanging his trousers. He was leaning forward, eyes shining as he listened in.

Ian made his apologies to the customer and guided them around the bar and into a large kitchen behind, which was surprisingly clean and tidy. Late morning sunlight glinted off the laminate work surfaces.

Helen brought up Louise's profile picture from the website that she'd saved on her phone earlier. 'Have you seen this woman before?'

His eyebrows shot back. 'Lola? Yes. She's been in here. Why?'

Helen ignored the question. 'In what capacity?'

'I'm not sure I'm with you.'

'As a room guest or a customer in the bar?'

Ian's eyes narrowed. 'Both.'

'So, she uses your premises for her work.'

His face hardened. 'It's not my place to ask what guests get up to in their rooms,' he said defensively.

Interesting, Helen thought. He clearly had no compunction about allowing escorts to use his premises. 'Do you keep a note of... friends that guests invite to their rooms?'

'No. We're all consenting adults. As long as they pay the full nightly rate, they can do what they like.'

'So, you turn a blind eye,' Pemberton said.

Ian lifted a single shoulder, then let it drop.

'How many other girls use your premises for this purpose?' Helen asked.

'I have no idea. I'm not a brothel.' He looked away, let out a long breath. 'Most of my customers are business travellers, here for conferences. But there isn't much money in B&Bs, not here, and competition is fierce. People like Lola can make a difference as to whether you survive or fold.'

Helen brought up Shauna's profile on her phone. 'What about this girl?'

He shook his head. 'Never seen her.' His face suddenly paled. 'Oh God. Are you suggesting Lola was one of the women killed?'

'What makes you ask that?' Pemberton said.

'You were here the other day as part of the murder inquiry.' His pallor was almost ghostly now.

Pemberton pulled out a chair, guided him into it, then grabbed a glass from a rack on the side, filled it with water and placed it in front of him.

'I can't believe it,' Ian said. 'Not Lola. She was such a lovely girl. So vibrant. Polite. Wait... Are you saying Lola and Louise, the second victim, are the same person?'

'It's possible,' Pemberton said. 'I'm sorry. But we'd ask

you to keep our discussions confidential at present, until we know more.'

Ian's hand shook as he took a sip of the water.

'Do you have any cameras inside?' Helen said. 'In the bar maybe?'

'No.'

Disappointment caught Helen. No cameras. No records. It was becoming a constant theme. 'Okay, when was Lola last in here?' she asked.

He thought for a moment. 'Last Thursday. She came in alone about 7.30-ish, booked a room. She always pays up front in cash. Sometimes she comes and chats in the bar. Sometimes she meets her… friends there. Sometimes she stays in her room. The front door is left unlocked until 11 pm. After that, paying guests have their own key. Customers come and go.'

'So, she entertained her clients in the room last Thursday,' Pemberton checked.

'Possibly.'

'Did she arrive in a car?'

Helen could see what he was getting at here. Surely Ian would know his guests' cars, especially if they were regulars. Which meant he had known the dead woman was Louise.

'No, I don't think so,' he said. 'I've never seen her with a car before. Unless she parked out on the street. I wouldn't have noticed it there.'

'Right, we'll need details of all your customers,' Helen said.

'No. No way. I don't want people thinking I'm a knocking shop. I'll lose all my trade.'

'Mr Richmond, this is a murder inquiry. Two women are dead. One of them stayed here. We'll be as discreet as we can, but I need your customer list.'

* * *

Helen watched the dashcam footage of the car crawling down Stephenson Street, passing a line of terraces, the guest house and… there she was, Louise standing at the kerb, beside the opening to the car park. The camera only caught her for a couple of seconds. She replayed the footage, then switched to the still of Louise in her red jacket. It was hazy, a little unclear, but she certainly looked like she was waiting for someone.

Helen rubbed the back of her neck. Her team had spent the afternoon scrutinising the dead women's phone records from the second phone they'd used for their Adult Services business. Most numbers were pay as you go, unlisted and unregistered – the owners couldn't be traced – and those they did manage to reach had firm alibis for the nights of the murders. Another bitterly disappointing dead end. There also wasn't an untraced number repeated on both women's records, which meant if the killer had contacted them both, he was using a new number each time.

They were missing something, somewhere. But she couldn't for the life of her see what it was. She combed her hair back from her face with her fingers, tied it with a scrunchie at the nape of her neck and looked back at the still of Louise. Why hadn't she sent her sister a text to say where she was going on Wednesday evening? She clearly hadn't thought she was going to be in any danger.

Helen didn't notice Alison enter the incident room. Eyes still glued to the screen, she didn't see the assistant chief constable nod to colleagues as she weaved through the desks.

'Afternoon,' Alison said.

Helen jumped as Alison pulled out one of the chairs opposite Helen's desk and settled herself into it.

'I thought I'd come and see where we are,' Alison said. She pulled back her sleeve, checked her watch. 'I've a meeting with the chief constable in half an hour. Be good to pass on some news.'

'We've had a bit of a development,' Helen said. She relayed the witness interview, the information about Adult Services.

'They were both sex workers?'

'Escorts. Sheridan calls it an introduction agency aimed

at providing company to travelling businessmen. Though...'
Helen pulled up the website on her laptop and angled it for
Alison to see, '... the profiles suggest more.'

'Hmm. I presume we're thinking the killer could be
someone with a grudge against their line of work.'

'It's possible.' Helen paused, meeting her eyeline. 'I want
to release more details to the press.'

Alison looked sceptical.

'It's hard enough with sex workers walking the streets,'
Helen said. 'But at least they tend to stick together, look out
for one another. It gives us a starting point. This is more
difficult because we have women in their own homes, hiding
behind a profile on a website. To the outside world, they were
parents with mortgages, regular jobs, coping with large credit
card debts and life's usual struggles. But they were living dual
lives, and the nature of the work means they kept it quiet, a
secret from friends and family. We're alerting all the girls
registered on the website, but it isn't enough. Now we know
the link between the two women, we have a duty of care to
other sex workers, to alert them to the risk.'

Alison squinted. 'Go on.'

'I want to release the existence of the pentagram too.
The profiler agrees we are looking for someone with local
knowledge. It might encourage people to examine their
friends, colleagues or acquaintances more closely. Perhaps
they know someone interested in the occult, or maybe
somebody obsessed with witchcraft or devil worshipping.
They might come forward, even anonymously.'

'It's a big risk. The reporters will jump on the bandwagon.
We're inviting sensationalised headlines.'

'The women were killed five days apart. It's already
Friday. If that time span is significant, it doesn't give us long.'

'If... That's the point. We don't know.'

'I'm not suggesting we mention an engraving, just that
a sign has been left with the bodies. If we ask the public for

help, there's a chance we might root out the killer before they have the opportunity to strike again.'

Alison rubbed her forehead a second. 'I'm sorry to have to ask,' she said, changing the subject. 'I know you've got a lot on, but where are we with the audit prep?'

Helen resisted the temptation to roll her eyes. 'I'm working on it. Or I will be when we get this case nailed.'

Alison inhaled loudly and spoke through her exhalation. 'Let's give it a couple more days on the symbol,' she said, rising to her feet.

Helen couldn't believe her ears. 'It needs to come from us, and it needs to come out soon.'

Alison rested a hand on the top of her chair. 'We have a duty to protect the public, to reassure them of their safety, and we make decisions on that basis. We can't afford to go out on a limb. I agree we should release the fact that the victims were working as escorts. It'll alert the sex industry, but also reassure the wider public that the killings are targeted at escorts; they're not random. But releasing the symbol now will likely set off a panic. The media will have a field day and, quite frankly, that's the last thing we need. Plus, if the killer is after notoriety, and from the way they've arranged these women, it looks like they are, then we are playing right into their hands. Let's work the case first. I'll review it in a few days.'

'But—'

'That's my decision. Get a statement out to the press as soon as.'

Helen bit back her anger. 'I need to speak with the families first.' There was no way she was going to let recently bereaved loved ones hear this information in the media.

'All right. But I want that statement out by five.'

CHAPTER 35

'I don't believe you,' Marnie said. Her eyes were as black as coal. 'She might have been private, but something like that… We would have known. *I* would have known.'

Helen eased forward on Marnie O'Hennessey's sofa. They'd been in the driveway, climbing out of their car, when she and Pemberton arrived earlier. It was the first time she'd seen Marnie wearing a dress instead of her usual jeans and T-shirt, and a touch of make-up. Darren looked smart in a shirt and formal trousers, and they seemed brighter, more relaxed. 'We've been to an assembly at Ollie's school,' Darren had said, inviting them inside. Marnie had smiled as she told them how Ollie stood up and said the line of a poem himself.

They were bearing up, focusing on their grandchildren, cherishing those special moments. No idea of the news about to be delivered. Helen felt a pang. It was hard enough telling people a loved one had passed. Delivering more shocking news, only a matter of days later, was downright cruel.

'I'm afraid it's true,' Helen said. 'Shauna used a separate phone for her appointments. We've traced the number and are now going through the calls, tracing the owners.'

Marnie clamped a hand to her mouth, smothering an animal-like yelp.

'How long?' Darren asked. He'd sat rigid and quiet, his

face like stone as Helen talked them through the website, how it worked and Shauna's registration as an escort.

'According to the website, she'd been registered for three months.'

Another cry from Marnie. She pressed the other hand to her face.

Darren stretched his arm around her shoulder. 'Is she still on there?'

'We've requested her profile be removed.'

'I want to see it.'

'I'm not sure that's a good idea.'

'I don't care,' he said through clenched teeth. 'I want to see the photo on there with my own eyes.'

Pemberton pulled the screenshot up on his phone, carefully widening it so that it didn't show her pen-name or tag line, and held it out.

A muscle flexed in Darren's jaw.

'No!' Marnie said, pushing the phone away. Mascara stains streaked her face as the tears started to flow.

'I'm so sorry to have to tell you this,' Helen said. 'Louise, the other girl that was killed, was also registered on the site. We believe the two murders are linked and this is how the killer found them.'

Silence fell upon them. A gust of wind whistled down the side of the house.

Helen switched back to an hour earlier. Sitting in Jasmine Carnwell's front room. Watching Louise's children play tag in the back garden through the patio doors as she relayed the information about the woman's late sister's profile on the website. Jasmine's ghostly face, the realisation dawning that when Louise had asked her to babysit the children, she wasn't going out with someone she'd met on a dating app, it was actually a business meeting. She recalled Jasmine saying that Louise had always been super careful about her dates, meeting them in public places, saying she'd call if there was ever a problem. Louise had kept the truth of what she was doing to herself, but she had made provisions, given herself a safety net if anything went wrong.

'Did Shauna ever talk about meeting someone?' she asked gently. 'Perhaps when you were looking after the children?'

'No,' Marnie said.

'She might have said she was going on a date.'

'Why would she say that?'

'The site is designed for escorts, providing company for travelling business clients,' Helen said. She explained how the other victim told her sister she was meeting people from a relationship app. 'Are you aware of any "dates" she's had over the past few months?'

'She didn't say,' Darren said.

'Is there anyone you think may have known? Perhaps someone she confided in.'

Darren shook his head, stricken.

Helen gave them a moment. If the desperation in their faces was to be believed, they clearly had no idea about their daughter's actions.

'What about Kerry?' Darren asked.

'We're still looking for her.'

'But you don't now think she was involved in Shauna's murder?'

'I can't say. We do believe these profiles on the website might have formed part of the killer's motive though.'

'I want it shut down,' Darren said.

'We're speaking with the owner,' Helen said gently.

'Speaking with him! I'll speak with him. I'll give him a piece of my bloody mind.'

'Don't!' Marnie said. She gripped his forearm.

'Mr O'Hennessey,' Helen said. 'I know how difficult this must be for you, but we have to ask you to leave the investigation to the police.'

Darren glowered at her.

Helen's heart wrenched as she straightened, aware she was about to pour even more fuel on the fire. 'There is something else I need to tell you.' They both looked up as she took a breath. 'We are putting a press statement out this evening. It will mention that both victims were working as escorts.'

'What?' Darren's face clouded as he jumped up. 'No. No way.'

'Mr O'Hennessey.' Helen stood, flat hands raised in an effort to placate him. 'Please—'

'How dare you bring something like this into our home!' he snarled.

Pemberton rose. Quiet and measured. 'Mr O'Hennessey. Calm down. Let the superintendent explain.'

'No,' he said, switching from one to the other. His face was puce now. 'I'm not having you drag the memory of my daughter through the mud.' He took a step closer.

Marnie was behind him, glassy eyes staring into space.

Helen could feel his breath on her.

'Mr O'Hennessey!' Pemberton stepped forward. Darren was tall, but nothing on the sergeant.

'It's okay,' Helen said. 'Mr O'Hennessey, please sit down.'

Darren eyed Pemberton for a couple of seconds then stepped back and sat, eyes still dark. Marnie sunk into the space beside him, zombie-like.

Helen's insides reeled. They'd taken in their nephew, raised him as their own and lost him in the forces. Now to lose a daughter in the most gruesome circumstances, then find out a secret like this, only to discover it was to be revealed in the press... It was excruciating.

'I completely understand your distress.'

'Then don't do it. Don't say anything,' he said.

'I'm afraid I have to. If the killer is targeting' – she almost said sex workers, it was on the tip of her tongue, but changed at the last minute – 'escorts, then we have a duty of care to alert others in the industry and this is the only way we can reach them. I really am very sorry.'

* * *

Darren was at the window, still glowering when Helen and Pemberton climbed into the car and wrestled with their seat belts.

'Do you think he's going to behave himself?' Pemberton asked.

'I don't know. He doesn't know the name of the website, and her profile's been taken down now, so I doubt he'd be able to trace Will Sheridan. Unless he knows something we don't.'

CHAPTER 36

Marnie looked down at the mug she'd been nursing for the past hour. The coffee was cold, a dark gelatinous skin sitting across the top. It was almost 5 am, the front room slowly brightening. Daylight seeped through the folds in the thin curtains.

Her brain was mashed. Ever since the detective had delivered the news yesterday, she'd wandered about in a zombie state, the ghouls of her mind feeding on the new information like it was their last supper. She had wanted to talk about it, to work things through, but Darren refused. Just as he refused to believe the detective. Instead, tiptoeing around their late daughter's actions. Going through the motions of cooking dinner, sitting in front of the television, going up to bed early. He was the same after they lost Tom. He tucked the details away in the vaults of his brain then too, refusing to talk about it.

To those outside their inner circle, Darren was a strong character. At work, he exhibited a formidable exterior his colleagues were afraid to cross. Yet at home, he was a loving husband, a thoughtful father and grandfather. Taking it upon himself to drive to Manchester last December, two days before Christmas, when the roads were clogged, to collect a board game the children really wanted because there weren't any available nearby or online and he didn't want them to miss out. Bringing Marnie flowers when he returned from a long trip because he knew how much she liked them. Cooking her favourite dinner after she'd had a rough day at work.

But when it came to problems at home, he crumbled.

He'd scared her after Tom had died. Fallen into such a deep depression, she'd wondered if she was going to lose him too. Kept to their bedroom. Didn't wash, didn't dress. Eventually, after six months away from work, when Marnie was at the end of her tether, Shauna announced she was pregnant and persuaded him to get help. And now, after losing his girl, she suspected the only thing keeping him going was his grandchildren.

Her daughter, an escort. Selling herself. How could Marnie not have known? Surely there would have been signs. She cast her mind back over the last six months, looking for anomalies in Shauna's behaviour, moments when she wasn't quite herself, little clues that seemed like nothing at the time, but now, put into context, might mean something. Delving far into the filing cabinets of her mind. As she searched, a little voice from within spoke up. Shauna hadn't told her she was seeing Kerry. And Kerry didn't keep the best of company. Did Shauna's aunt introduce her to the world of sex work?

She scrubbed her hand across her forehead, digging her fingers into the creases above her brow. A tear escaped, running down her cheek, landing in the coffee with a plink. They'd lost their daughter in the worst possible way. How much more were they to take? How many more secrets were to be revealed before this was over?

Pain seared Marnie's chest. The detective said the murders were linked – they were looking for the same killer. Both women had secretly moonlighted as escorts. Was that why they died?

Another pain, stronger this time. Marnie placed down her coffee, hugging herself as more tears followed. When did things get so desperate? She'd suspected money was tight but never, not for one second, had she imagined it to be this bad. Especially when Shauna refused her offers of help. 'I'll sell the house, get another job,' her daughter had said when Marnie asked her how she would manage after the break-up.

Never once hinting at what the new job might be.

And now it was to be shared with the world. Thankfully, her grandchildren were too young to understand. Though, once reported, the news would always be out there. She couldn't protect them forever.

Her iPad taunted her from the bookshelf in the corner, the morning news drawing her like a magnet. Darren would tell her to ignore it, to stay away. 'Don't do it to yourself,' he would say. 'It'll only upset you. The police will contact us if there are any developments.' And he would be right. She didn't want to see it. Didn't want to read what the journalists had written about her daughter. But she couldn't ignore it either.

She moved across, grabbed the device. The screen lit as she switched it on. She glanced at the door. All was quiet. Moved back to the sofa and googled *Hampton Murder News*.

An array of listings filled the screen. A Facebook police appeal for anyone close to Henderson Ley on Wednesday evening. Myriad headlines about Shauna's murder. She scrolled down, and her heart skipped a beat. *Detectives Reveal Murder Victims Worked as Escorts*. Her mouth dried. Jagged lines danced in the corner of her vision. Her finger hovered over the article for a split second, her eyes blurring, before Marnie pushed the iPad away. Dropped her head into her hands. And wept.

CHAPTER 37

KILLER ON THE LOOSE. SEX WORKER KILLING SPREE.

The headlines were getting worse. The murders were lead stories of not only Hampton's news sites but also neighbouring counties now. It wouldn't be long before the national media got hold of them. Helen rested back in her chair and rolled her shoulders, listening to the cartilage pop and crackle. It was Saturday morning, and the phone was ringing off the hook after the press statement yesterday. Everyone was watching the case, speculating over when or where the murderer would strike next.

Pemberton put his head around the door to her office, brandishing a file. 'The forensic report is through on the second victim,' he said.

'And?'

'As we thought, another clean scene.'

Helen's stomach dipped to her toes. She didn't relish being proved right, especially when they had little else to go on.

'Where are we with members of The Alternatives?' she asked.

'We've been through the membership list.'

'And Louise's friends, family?'

'Pretty much done. Looks like her sister was her closest confidante. For what good that was.'

'And customers from Ashcombe B&B?' She was reaching now.

'Still working our way through. Nothing of interest yet.'

They were interrupted by Helen's phone buzzing with a text. *Mum* flashed up. *Are you coming home before the match or meeting us there?*

Pemberton looked across, hopeful.

'It's only my mother,' Helen said. 'Robert's got an important cricket match this afternoon against their rival school.'

'Good on him,' Pemberton said.

Her smile was weak, pride tainted with anxiety over work. She tapped a quick message back. *I'll meet you there.*

Another text. *Okay. Match starts at 2 pm. Robert's team are batting first.*

'There's a woman on line three.'

She looked up to find Dark had joined Pemberton in the doorway. 'Says she's got some information that might be of interest, and she wants to speak to the woman off the telly.'

Helen raised her eyes to the roof. 'The woman' was Alison, of course, though there was no way the ACC was going to take her call. Not if she could help it. 'Well, she'll have to make do with me,' she said. 'Put her through.' Helen made a face at Pemberton and picked up the receiver.

A sharp intake of breath winged down the line, almost as if someone was smoking a cigarette, inhaling the nicotine, holding on to it. The caller didn't utter a word.

'Acting Superintendent Helen Lavery speaking. I'm heading the investigation. How can I help you?' A brief hesitation. Helen could hear more breaths. Shorter, swifter now. 'Hello?' she said.

'I've got some information. I need to be assured of confidence.' The words were clipped.

'What do you want to tell me?'

'Not like this.' Another pause. Helen could almost see her checking over her shoulder. 'Can you meet me in an hour?'

It was Helen's turn to wait. She was trying to detect the edge of an accent. 'I can arrange for you to come into a station...'

'I can't do that. Do you know Kempleton's?'

Kempleton's was a café, mostly frequented by truckers, behind the Esso station on Hampton Ring Road. Helen remembered being called out there when she worked on incident response – an argument between two lorry drivers that had got out of hand. 'I do.'

'I'll meet you there in half an hour. Please come alone.'

Helen opened her mouth, about to ask for more information, a description so that she knew who to look out for, when the line went dead.

'Everything all right?' Pemberton asked. He was still standing in the doorway, watching her. Helen placed the receiver down, asked him to close the door and passed on the details.

'Sounds very clandestine,' he said. 'I'm coming with you.'

It was only what she would say to any member of her team. She was meeting a stranger, and without a name, they had no means of checking her out, assessing the risk. But at the same time, this was potentially the first piece of fresh information they'd had in a while and Helen didn't want to do anything to jeopardise it. 'Kempleton's is a popular stop-off. She asked me to come alone.'

'Still, we should do this by the book. Organise backup.'

Helen considered this a second. 'I don't think so,' she said. 'She's not from round here. There was an accent. And she sounded frightened. If she sees anyone else, it might scare her away. There'll be plenty of other people about.'

'Then I'll follow you, stay close, and have backup on standby.'

CHAPTER 38

The morning sun sparkled in a clear sky stretching to the horizon. Helen steered into the petrol station and parked away from the pumps. Kempleton's café shared half of a modern brick building with the petrol station and had its own entrance, separate to the service station shop, around the rear.

The sound of passing traffic from the ring road clattered through Helen's ears as she crossed the car park. Out of the corner of her eye, she could see Pemberton in an unmarked Fiesta. Head bent as if he was texting on his phone. The doors of the café in his eyeline.

A woman at the coffee machine behind the counter gave a nod as Helen entered the café and told her to find herself a table. It wasn't busy. A bearded man in a denim jacket licked his finger and thumb and rubbed them together as he finished the first half of a toasted sandwich at the counter. A woman with a grey ponytail sat with her back to Helen, bony shoulders hunched, nursing a mug of coffee.

A woman at a table in the corner with her head buried in a book caught Helen's eye. An empty glass sat on the table in front of her. She peered up furtively, met Helen's gaze. Wide eyes fixed in anticipation. Anticipation and… what was that? A flash of fear.

The woman stood as Helen approached. Red hair tied up in

a loose knot on top of her head. Black-rimmed glasses perched on a face devoid of make-up. A silver ring glistened in her nose. She looked tiny in a baggy black T-shirt and fitted jeans, barely older than Matthew.

'Acting Detective Superintendent Lavery,' Helen said, keeping her voice low. 'Helen.'

The woman nodded and invited her to take the seat opposite.

'And you are?' Helen asked.

Within a second, the waitress was at her side. 'What can I get you?'

'Oh, erm...' A fleeting glance at the board behind the counter. 'A latte, please,' Helen said. She looked enquiringly at the woman opposite to see if she wanted another drink, but she shook her head.

The waitress disappeared. The chair leg squeaked as Helen sat. She dropped her bag to the floor and folded her hands together in her lap. No notebook. No phone. The witness looked cautious enough. She didn't want to do anything to put her off. 'I didn't catch your name,' Helen said.

'I didn't give it to you.'

Helen raised her brows. She hadn't come all this way to be messed around.

'It's Clare.'

'Clare?' Helen angled her head, waiting for the surname.

'I'd rather not say.' Her eyes darted to the door, the windows outside.

Helen could see the Fiesta in the distance. Pemberton's head still bent over his phone.

Witnesses came in all shapes and sizes, and with their own stories. Many of them had concerns and hang-ups. But Helen knew some of the best leads came from members of the public and police work wouldn't achieve nearly as many results without their assistance. Which meant working with those who came forward, putting them at ease, teasing the information out of them. 'How can I help you?' she asked.

Clare bit her lip. 'I asked you here because… I think I might have met the killer of those women.'

Helen kept her face impassive. 'Okay. What makes you think that?'

The waitress bustled over and delivered the coffee. Clare waited until she'd placed the latte down and retreated to the counter before she answered. 'You see, the thing is...' She chewed the side of her lip. 'I don't quite know how to say this.'

'Take your time.'

'I work a couple of nights a week. That is to say... I...' A heavy sigh. 'I guess you'd call me an escort. A sex worker. Well, I was before these murders.' She looked down at the empty glass.

Helen couldn't imagine Clare's plain, studious face filling the colourful websites like Adult Services, but if experience had taught her anything, it was to be non-judgemental. People harboured secrets. Sometimes small, sometimes irrelevant. And they were usually hidden behind a facade. 'Go on.'

'A client contacted me last week. They wanted to meet at The Lemon Tree.'

Helen narrowed her eyes. The Lemon Tree Hotel was on the Hellidon Industrial Estate, on the outskirts of Hampton. 'How did they contact you?'

'I have a profile on a website. Clients contact me through there.'

'Can I ask the name of the website?'

'I'd rather not say.' She cleared her throat. 'We'd arranged to meet at 7.15 pm. I'd been waiting about ten minutes, was about to give up when he arrived. I thought it was another no-show.'

'Do you get a lot of no-shows?'

'Some.' Clare lifted a shoulder, let it fall. 'Some new customers lose their nerve. It's part and parcel of what we do. I'd had one a couple of nights before and I was convinced someone had tried to follow me. I only lost them at the motorway roundabout when I made a sudden turn-off.' She shuddered. 'Anyway, this one did show. And as soon as he approached me, he remarked on my hair. Said the colour was hideous. I should dye it back.' She met Helen's eyeline. 'It's dark on my profile photo. I only dyed it red recently. He said I looked bloody awful. Told me I was a fake. That he couldn't possibly go ahead with me looking like this. Then he stomped off.'

'Do you always meet your customers outside a...' Helen searched for the right word, 'venue?'

'It depends on the client. Some like to meet in a bar. Others want you to book a room and meet you there. Some treat it more like a date and we meet outside. It varies. But something about that exchange spooked me.' Fine lines appeared down her nose as she wrinkled it. 'He wore sunglasses, big wasp-like sunglasses, even though it was a dull evening. And an overcoat with the collar turned up. And he was shifty. Kept looking around.'

Helen had a feeling there was more to come, so she took a sip of her coffee, said nothing.

'I didn't think much of it afterwards,' Clare said. 'You meet some strange people in this job. Then I was telling a friend of mine – she's in the same line of work – and, blow me, he'd contacted her a few days later.'

'When was this?'

'Last Thursday.'

The evening after the second murder, Helen thought.

'He arranged to meet her outside The Hawthorn Hotel.'

Another hotel on the edge of town. There was a pattern here. Helen was reminded of the profiler's words – he'll have met other women.

'Anyway, he didn't meet her.'

'I don't understand.'

'It was a no-show. He was there though. She saw him watching her. About ten yards away in a car. Same sunglasses, hair slicked back. And he had the collar of his coat turned up. When she approached the car, he sped off. But here's the thing.' She leaned forward, angled her head. 'When she left, she was convinced he'd waited down the road and tried to follow her. Just like my no-show had the week before.'

Helen sat back. The profiler said that the killer learned about his victims. Delved into their lives to see if they fit his criteria. It would make sense for him to follow them, get to know them personally before he committed. 'What sort of car was he driving?' she asked.

'Pardon?'

'When he followed your friend. What car did he drive?'

'A silver Astra.'

'You seem pretty sure he was the same person.'

'He was white, tall, about six foot two. Medium build. Black hair, almost raven-like, greased back from his forehead. And, like I say, he wore a coat with the collar turned up. No one does that these days.'

'Did he speak with an accent?'

'Nothing distinguishable.'

'Let me get this straight,' Helen said. 'If this was the same man and he contacted you both twice, surely you have his phone number?'

'That's just it. He used a different number each time. It's not unusual for us to entertain the same clients,' she said. 'It happens sometimes. But it is strange for them to change their number.'

Helen's ears pricked. They'd worked through the phone records from Shauna and Louise's business phones. Out of the callers they couldn't trace, none of the numbers were repeated. If this was the killer, he was using multiple phones, changing the numbers.

'What happened when he followed your friend?' she asked.

'He tailed her all the way home. She had to drive past the uni, lose him in the backstreets...' Clare stopped short, alarm flickering across her face. She'd said more than she intended.

'You're both students,' Helen said.

A slow nod. 'You mustn't tell anyone.'

Hampton didn't have a university – the closest were those

at Nottingham and Leicester. Far enough away to live a separate life. That explained the hint of an accent. 'And that's why you only work part-time,' Helen said.

'I have three sisters,' Clare said. 'Two of them are at uni. I couldn't ask my parents for money; they've enough to deal with. They think I'm working in a bar a few nights a week.'

'Don't you get a loan?'

Clare straightened. 'I know what I'm doing. I didn't come here for financial advice.' Another glance at the door.

Helen softened. She hated the idea of this young woman selling herself to get through uni. But it was a personal choice; she had no powers to intervene. And she couldn't afford to lose her now. 'Of course. I'm sorry.'

'You mustn't tell anyone,' she repeated. 'My parents would be devastated. I don't know what would happen at the uni...'

'I understand,' Helen said. 'I appreciate you coming forward. Are you sure your friend won't speak with me?'

'No way.' Clare looked scared. 'She doesn't even know I'm here.'

'What about the website you advertise on?'

'We made it ourselves. My friend's a whizz at IT. We didn't want to be beholden to anyone.'

Helen stared at her. This was an intelligent young woman who'd made a choice to supplement her degree this way.

'Please. I can't afford to lose my job. I need to go back to it when you catch this bastard.'

Helen was in a difficult position here. She couldn't promise complete anonymity for a witness – there was always the possibility they might be involved in some way, even on the periphery – but she could treat the information as intelligence and keep her name out of the investigation, unless crucial.

'The best way for me to follow up on this guy is for you to give me everything you know,' she said, pulling her notebook out of her bag. 'Dates, times. Every little detail.' Helen watched the woman bite her lip. If this man was the killer, she'd seen him, described him. There was a possibility she could identify him. 'Would you feel up to working with me to put together a likeness of him?' she asked. 'It's a very straightforward process. I can make the arrangements today.'

Clare looked wary. 'I'm not coming to a police station.'

CHAPTER 39

Helen glanced out of the window at the wide patio outside, the stone steps leading down to a pathway between two perfectly manicured lawns centred with Roman statues. The bridge over the river in the distance. Clare took a sip of coffee and shifted nervously in the chair beside her.

The poor woman looked deathly pale. She'd come forward of her own volition, clearly wanting to assist the investigation and do the right thing. Provided a schedule of dates and times of meetings. Been scrupulous in her description of the man she suspected. But she had drawn the line at meeting other police, concerned about her identity and her job being revealed. Helen had to use all her powers of persuasion to encourage her to work with an officer from the ID suite and it wasn't until she suggested them meeting at Memington Hall, a country house converted to an upmarket hotel on the fringes of the county, that she finally agreed.

Set in its own grounds, Memington Hall was mainly hired for chic events like weddings and conventions. Helen had got to know the team there well when she'd investigated the sudden death of a member of staff earlier that year, relationships she'd nurtured when she'd taken her mother there for afternoon tea after the case was closed, a birthday treat. The manager,

Phillipa Hartwell, had greeted her like an old friend when she'd phoned earlier. Met them herself when they arrived at reception, only too happy to be of service. Smoothing her immaculate shift dress, heels clicking on the stone floor as she ushered them down a wood-panelled corridor and into a small room filled with leather high-backed chairs tucked beneath a shiny, long mahogany table.

'You won't be disturbed here,' Phillipa had said. Only to return a few minutes later with a tray of coffee and biscuits, a jug of water and three glasses.

'What about his mouth?' George Ellwood asked, clicking another button on his laptop. He was a burly PC, twelve months off retirement, with a friendly, calming temperament. In the office, he was known for his abundant patience, a disposition which often meant he was allocated the most nervous clients. If anyone could put a witness at ease, it was George.

Clare took a sip of her coffee and stared at the screen as he moved through a series of options. 'That one.' She pressed a hand to her chin, staring hard. 'No, it was wider.' Clare shifted again and looked towards the door. Even though she'd followed Helen here in her own car and been assured she could leave at any time, she'd never completely relaxed.

'Take your time,' he said.

Helen watched the picture slowly come together. A swarthy man in dark glasses, hair greased back. Could this be their killer?

She thought about how and where they met him. In public places. Public places with cameras.

* * *

An hour later, Helen, Pemberton, Dark and Spencer were standing beside their murder wall, gazing up at the e-fit of their new suspect. Four pairs of eyes scanned the row of images pinned to the board. Before photos: of two attractive young women with smiley faces. After photos: of greying bodies laid out bare, glassy eyes staring skyward. A pinched reddish ring around their throats. The familiar inverted pentagram engraved into their chests.

'The profiler thinks our killer has a set of preferences for his victims. If he was stalking them, it would give him a chance to get to know them,' Helen said. She thought of Shauna and Louise, dropping their children off at school, going about their daily business, oblivious to someone watching, following their every movement.

'Perhaps we're not dealing with one killer,' Spencer said. 'Maybe there's a group, working together.'

Pemberton scratched the back of his neck. 'It's possible.'

Helen sighed. She'd been concerned about Shauna's bank payments to Will Sheridan not showing up on her statements and was beginning to wonder if there was a third party involved herself, but when they'd checked, it transpired that Shauna paid for her profile on Adult Services in cash. Delivering the money each month herself. She didn't want to leave any clues as to what she was doing…

'Anything back from the source handlers?' Helen asked. It was common practice to reach out to informants in the field while working a case, to see if anyone knew of someone acting strangely, or if someone was harbouring somebody.

Dark shook her head. 'No one's talking.'

'Right. Let's see if the hotels Clare mentioned have CCTV. Try the businesses nearby too. At the very least, we might be able to trace his car.' She moved down the line of photos. 'We don't know how many other women he's met or how many he's followed, but he's certainly selective about who he kills. Why these two? The autopsy reports don't show any sexual interference. Let's pick through our victims' lives again, look for any other similarities. Maybe they share the same beautician, or their kids go to the same swim class. There is something in our victims' lives that triggers his interest in them. We need to pinpoint what that is.

'The e-fit has gone out to the press and been circulated

within the force as a person of interest. We need to contact the DVLA, find out how many silver Astras are registered in our area. We'll prioritise Hamptonshire first – we know our killer has local knowledge – then try neighbouring counties in case he lives outside the border.'

Helen turned back to the board as the others moved back to their desks, working her way through the photos again.

'Don't you have a cricket match to go to?'

Pemberton's voice, low and out of earshot of the others, made her jump. She hadn't realised he was still beside her.

The clock on the wall read 1.40 pm. Helen cast an anxious look back at the room. Family came first and this match clearly meant a lot to Robert. All the same, it felt wrong to be lazing in the park with her family when her team were beavering away. 'Are you sure you'll be all right?'

'We're just continuing with background checks. Waiting for calls.' He gave her a reassuring smile. 'I'll ring you if anything comes up.'

CHAPTER 40

Helen reached Oakwall cricket pavilion to find the car park rammed. Vehicles filled every bay, some double-parked to make best use of the space. It was nearly 2.15 pm. She could see the pitch from here, surrounded by a large group of spectators – friends and family sitting in clumps on the grass, come along to support their loved ones – the game already in full swing. Luckily, bowling was Robert's speciality, his batting skills more average, which meant he wouldn't be first in line. But she wasn't sure where he was in the order.

She lowered her window and steered towards the exit. A cheer filled the air as she left the car park. Her stomach twisted. *Don't let that be Robert.* She desperately didn't want to miss his moment. She continued along the road just as – *thank goodness!* – a car exited a place further up. It was a tight squeeze; she had to shuffle back and forth several times. Eventually, she was out of the car and jogging over to the ground, breaths coming hard and fast. By the time she reached the entrance, she could feel sweat trickling down her back.

On the way in, Helen slowed to a walk, taking time to greet Robert's English teacher and nod at a couple of other parents she recognised. She rolled up the sleeves of her shirt, scanned the area for her family. It was Matthew she picked out first, lying on his side, his long lean body resting on the grass, head propped up by a hand on his chin. His grandma beside him, a tartan picnic blanket laid out in front. Robert was sitting on a bench with his teammates across the other side of the pitch, watching the game intently. None of them spotted her.

The ground quietened. The bowler took his run, released the ball, and... another cheer filled the air. He'd hit the wickets' middle stump. The bowler was triumphant, jumping up and down, hugging his teammates. Helen took advantage of the break in play to scoot around the edge.

'Hi, darling,' Helen said to her eldest son as she reached him.

'All right, Mum.' He looked up, smiled and turned back to the match.

'How's it going?' she whispered to her mother.

'You're just in time.' Her mother beamed. 'There are two more then Robert's in to bat.' She wrinkled her nose. 'They've not done too well so far.'

'Thank goodness I haven't missed him.' Helen sunk to the ground beside her.

'Drink?'

'I'd love one.'

She poured her a lemonade, passed it across.

Helen took a sip, her breaths evening as the next batsman took his place. She pulled her sunglasses down to shade her eyes and checked the scoreboard. St Edmund's were twenty-eight for three. Not an impressive achievement. Especially when the three batsmen were the best of their team.

'Help yourself to nibbles,' Jane said.

Helen surveyed the food laid out on the blanket in front and smiled. Her mother's version of nibbles was a full-on picnic with sandwiches, pork pie, crisps and strawberries – a particularly welcome feast to someone who hadn't eaten since breakfast. She shovelled food onto a paper plate, sat back and basked in the sunshine as she ate. The next batsman passed, and the next. Helen cast her plate aside, jumped to her feet and cheered loudly as Robert walked onto the pitch. He looked so smart in his whites, so grown-up, that her heart squeezed with joy, and when he glanced over, gave her a quick smile, it was like he was small again, in the Christmas play at primary school. Helen stayed on her feet, her mother beside her, cheering at every run and boundary struck. When he survived the next over, Matthew got to his feet too. By the time he was caught out, Robert's partnership had almost doubled the score and he left the pitch to roaring applause and pats on the back from his coach.

At the next change of innings, a tall boy with sandy hair and piercing blue eyes approached. 'Hello, Mrs Lavery,' he said to Jane.

'Zac, it's good to see you here. This is Robert's mum,' Jane said, motioning to Helen. 'Helen, this is Robert's new friend. You know, from school.'

Zac tipped his head, flashed a smile.

'You didn't fancy playing?' Helen asked. With those long arms, she imagined he'd make a stonking bowler.

'Got to work on my technique first,' he said. He turned to her mother. 'Those burgers were tops the other night. I told my mum she's got to sharpen her skills!'

Jane Lavery chuckled.

Helen watched Zac wink at her mother and make off to chat with a group of lads behind the wicket. 'Bit of a charmer, isn't he?'

'Who, Zac?' Jane waved her hand in the air. 'Lovely kid. Really nice manners.' She leaned in close and whispered, 'Matthew's got an interview at the newsagent's later.'

'You kept that quiet, Matt,' Helen said, nudging her elder son.

Matthew rolled his eyes. 'It's only an interview.'

'I think we're more excited about it than he is,' Jane said, a smile teasing her lips.

Helen stood and straightened her back. She placed her hands on her hips, inhaling the afternoon air, the tension just starting to trickle out of her shoulders, when she heard a voice behind her.

'Superintendent Lavery. Well, well, well...'

The hairs on Helen's arms upended as she turned on her heels to face Guy Thorne. He was wearing an open-necked plaid shirt, loose denims. A Collie dog stood beside him on a long lead.

'What are you doing here?' she asked quietly. She stepped between him and her family, trying to block their view, but she was too late. Matthew had jumped to his feet and was beside her, stroking the Collie's head. The dog nestled into his hand.

'Just out with Nigel,' Guy said. His usual wide-eyed stare. 'We often come here on a Saturday. He likes to swim in the river.'

The first time they ran into each other, she'd forced herself to put it to the back of her mind. This was now the second time, and within days, and his presence was starting to irk. Was he interested in the investigation, or her? And the fact that she was off duty, with her loved ones, only frayed her nerves further.

'You're such a cutie,' Matthew said to the dog, smoothing his head. Nigel wagged his tail.

A round of applause rippled around the ground. The players were taking their places on the pitch, the game restarting.

'Well, we'd better get going. Nice to see you.' Guy waved at her mother, vexing Helen further, and made off towards the river.

'Who was that?' Jane asked as Helen and Matthew sat back down on the edge of the picnic blanket.

Helen watched him until he disappeared in the distance. 'No one important.'

* * *

The rest of the afternoon passed easily. Robert took two wickets, much to the joy of the supporters, and very soon the game was over with Ryland declaring victory over St Edmund's ninety-two runs, by reaching ninety-four for nine.

Matthew left for his interview amidst a host of good lucks from his mother and grandma. Helen and Jane were gathering up the picnic when Robert's coach arrived, her son at his side. 'You've got yourself a star here,' he said, looking on approvingly.

Robert scrunched his face. 'Didn't win though.'

'We were nipping at their heels,' the coach said. 'That's the closest we've ever come to beating Ryland. You should be proud of yourself.'

Robert gave an embarrassed nod and they moved off to collect their belongings.

Jane shovelled the last of the food into a bag and placed the folded blanket on top. 'Are you coming back with us?' she asked Helen.

'I've got my car down the road,' Helen said. 'I'll meet you there.' She was relieved to find no new messages on her phone from work. Still, it would be good to check in. She'd hate to think of her team giving her a break when they needed assistance. She hugged her mother, grabbed one of the bags, moved off to the edge of the pitch and dialled Pemberton.

'What's the score?' he said without preamble.

Helen laughed and passed over the details. 'Robert played really well,' she said. 'Surprised us all with his batting. Any news there?'

'Not much. None of the hotels your contact mentioned have cameras, sadly. We're checking businesses nearby, but it looks like our killer has been careful about his arrangements. Preliminary forensics and autopsy reports are back on the second body. Nothing we didn't already know. Public appeal's gone out with the photofit of our suspect. Late shift is set up to cover the phones. I'm heading home shortly.'

Helen thanked him, cut the call and glanced skyward. No issues, no surprises. She should be relieved. But any relief was short-lived. Already, the leads were drying up on Louise's murder. Two bodies in less than a week and they couldn't be sure the killer wouldn't strike again. If the appeal on the photofit didn't raise anything, she needed to come up with a new strategy, and fast. She sighed, hauled the bag to her side and made for the exit. The crowds thinned. She spotted her mother twenty yards or so in front, chatting to another parent, Robert at her side. Helen sped up to join them.

They met at the exit. Jane bade farewell to the other parent. Helen congratulated her son again. They were walking through the gates when Robert called out, 'Zac!'

Zac was standing at the edge of the car park, hands in his pockets. He looked over his shoulder, beamed from ear to ear and waved.

Robert waved back.

'Does he have a lift?' Helen said to her son. She was just about to offer to take the boy home when a man approached and nudged his shoulder affectionately. Helen stopped short. She felt her mother's hand grip her wrist. Robert had continued walking ahead.

The man looked at Zac, then across at them. Recognition spreading like a shadow across his face as he hooked their gazes. It was Davy Boyd, Chilli Franks's half-brother.

For a split second, it seemed as though there was only him and the two women there. Then he tore himself away and moved off.

Oblivious, Robert was in the car park now. He turned and frowned. 'What have you stopped for?' he said.

Jane released Helen's wrist. The two women quickly recovered themselves.

'Who was that with Zac?' Helen said, fighting to keep her voice even.

'His dad, why?'

'No reason.'

Helen did her best to keep her face impassive as she piled the bags into her mother's car. She watched Robert climb in, exchanged a loaded glance with her mother and moved off, heart thumping her chest. Her son's new friend was the nephew of Chilli Franks, the man who'd threatened her family for as long as she could remember. What the hell was going on?

CHAPTER 41

The house was quiet when Helen arrived home. Her mother was in the kitchen, unpacking the picnic bag.

'Where's Robert?' Helen whispered.

'Upstairs. In the shower.'

Helen pushed the kitchen door closed and turned to face her mother. 'How could we not know that Zac was Davy Boyd's son?'

Jane's face was flushed, the shock still working its way through. 'I don't know. I mean, you wouldn't expect...' She placed the plates she'd pulled out of the bag on the table, slid into a chair.

'Didn't Robert say anything about where he'd come from?'

'He just said he was new to the area. You know what kids are like. They're all about the here and now.'

Helen thought for a moment. 'Why is he at Robert's school?'

'He lives on Kingsland Avenue. It's the closest school to him, I guess.' She waved a hand in the air. 'I dropped him off last week, after the burger evening.'

Helen baulked. 'Kingsland Avenue?' She scraped her hand down the front of her face. Kingsland Avenue was on the other side of her estate, less than fifteen minutes' walk. The Boyds weren't just living in her home town – they were on her doorstep. 'So, you think it's a coincidence?' Helen said.

'Don't you?'

'I don't know what to think.' She pictured Davy's glare, the same striking eyes he shared with his half-brother. His face frozen in shock when he noticed them. 'If it is a coincidence, it's a bloody unlucky one.'

Jane took a breath. 'Maybe it's time we said something to Robert. They've only known each other a few weeks. Perhaps he could gently distance himself, introduce Zac to some other friends…'

Helen grappled with her thoughts. She remembered Pemberton's comments – Davy was married, raising a family. There was no reason to suggest he was involved in anything criminal. But the way he'd crawled past and surveyed her the Friday before last made her skin crawl. And the look he gave them today didn't help.

'What would we say?' she said. 'That Zac's uncle is one of the most ruthless gang leaders Hampton has ever seen? That doesn't make Zac a criminal, or his father. And haven't we always encouraged Robert to treat people as you find them? It would be like going back on everything we've ever taught him.'

'The Franks are dangerous.'

'Chilli is, yes. I agree. But the rest of the family?' Helen shook her head. 'We don't know that. These people haven't lived in the UK for years. Zac's probably never met his uncle.'

'You're saying we do nothing?'

'I'm not saying anything. We just need to think about this, tread carefully. I don't want to speak to Robert until I'm sure I'm doing the right thing.'

'What if Zac's father says something to him in the meantime?'

'Then we'll deal with it.'

At that moment, Robert pushed open the kitchen door. A fusion of hair gel and soap filled the air. He'd changed into long shorts, a baggy T-shirt. Crafted the curls on his head into spikes. 'What's for tea?' he said. 'I'm starving.'

Helen laid back in the bath, the hot water soothing her weary limbs. Dinner had been an excitable affair. Matthew's interview had gone well and he was offered the job at the newsagent's, starting on Monday. Robert was still on a high from the match. Usually she soaked up these moments, sitting at the table with her family, revelling in their happiness and success. If the job had taught her anything, it was to make the most of the good times and it was rare, in the middle of a high-profile murder inquiry, to get the opportunity. But today, she faked her joy at their achievements, put on a brave face and pushed the food around her plate, her stomach winding into knots as she listened to her sons' random chatter. Sharing occasional sideways glances with her mother. Jane was unusually quiet, clearly struggling too. As soon as dinner was over, her mother declared she was tired and took to her flat for an early night.

It was a relief when the boys finally retreated to their rooms. But Helen couldn't settle. A Lavery associating with the nephew of Chilli Franks. Her father would seethe in his grave.

She closed her eyes, held her breath and slipped down beneath the water.

Robert was a gregarious, affable lad. One of those children who made friends everywhere. Throughout primary school, he had been inundated with invitations to sleepovers and play dates. Unlike his brother, who had to be coaxed to go to birthday parties. There was a genuine warmth to Robert, which was probably why he'd been picked to buddy the new kids in secondary school. Perhaps when he'd had a chance to get to know others in his year group, Zac would find his own crowd and their relationship would peter out. She desperately hoped so.

She lifted her head out of the water and gasped for breath, clearing the water from her eyes. Yes, that was it. This was a fleeting friendship. Zac was new to the school. It would all change when he found his way.

A distant sound caught her attention. She twisted her head. A muffled ringing. It was her phone, tucked in her trouser pocket. Perhaps there was some news on the e-fit.

Helen hauled herself up and stepped out, dripping water across the floor as she tussled with her trouser pocket. Answering the call on the fifth ring, just before the voicemail kicked in.

'Ma'am?' It was Pemberton. He sounded grave.

Helen grabbed a towel with her free hand and pressed it against her. 'Is there some news?'

'A woman's body was discovered at 10.45 pm beside the river at Oakwall Park. Her chest is marked like the others. We've called out the pathologist, CSIs.'

Helen pushed a strand of wet hair out of her eye. Oakwall wasn't a remote location. It was situated in the centre of town. She'd only been there that afternoon to watch her son's cricket match. The back of her neck prickled. She pressed the towel harder to her chest. The killer was changing tactics. Becoming bolder. 'I'll be there in ten minutes,' she said.

CHAPTER 42

The white boards of the cricket pavilion loomed in the distance as Helen arrived at Oakwall car park. She pictured it earlier, the grass littered with families picnicking, basking in the afternoon sunshine, enjoying a school cricket match. Oblivious to the fact that, within a matter of hours, it was to be the scene of yet another gruesome murder.

Helen shivered as a gust of wind caught her hair, still wet from the bath, and looked out into the darkness. The idea of a killer walking the same route as her family, their shoes stroking the same blades of grass, made her stomach curdle.

The car park was a hive of activity. Liveried police cars were parked beside the entrance. Officers moved around. The blue and white police tape marking the cordon flapped in the light breeze. The CSIs would be here soon. She spotted Pemberton talking into his phone at the far side entrance and nodded an acknowledgement.

He crossed the car park to greet her, his face grim. 'The victim was an Eve Porter,' he said. 'Twenty-seven.' He placed his hands on his hips. 'A son under five.'

Another death. Another young family suffering. 'How was she identified?'

'The husband found her.'

Helen grimaced. That was a sight no loved one should see.

'According to Mr Porter, she was visiting a friend at Newport Manor, had taken the dog with her.' He tilted his head towards a complex of apartments, fifty yards or so down the road, flanking the park railings. 'She visits every Saturday evening, but this one was special because it was her friend's birthday. She texted her husband at ten to say she would be late. Half an hour later, the dog arrived home alone. When he couldn't reach her on her mobile, he called her friend, who said she'd left her apartment at ten. He has his mother staying with him, so he left her with the kid and went looking for Eve.'

'Where was home?'

'Streeton Walk, the other side of the park. About a fifteen-minute walk.'

Fifteen minutes. The difference between life and death. The thought made her shudder.

'Why would a woman walk across a desolate area in the dark?' she asked. 'Why not take the streets?'

'It's the shortest route. And she had her dog with her. I guess she believed she was safe. The question is, why didn't she use her car?'

'What?'

'Her Renault is still parked outside the apartment block. She drove to see her friend and walked back.'

'Maybe she'd had a drink.'

Pemberton shrugged.

'What about the husband?' Helen said. They couldn't rule Mr Porter out as a suspect. He wouldn't be the first offender to call in his own kill, pretending he'd found the body. The cynical side of the job left her hollow, but it couldn't be ignored.

'Uniform escorted him to the station after the paramedics cleared him,' Pemberton said.

They'd seize his clothes, take his prints. Given the circumstances, the way the woman was killed and left – the pentagram engraving not released to the public – it was unlikely he was involved. But they wouldn't be doing their job if they didn't rule him out properly. Still, it was gut-wrenching to put someone through that after finding the dead body of a loved one. And in such grisly circumstances. 'Make sure he's placed in one of the vulnerable witness interview suites, will you?' she said. 'I want him questioned as a witness.'

Pemberton nodded.

'Where's the victim's car?' Helen asked.

'Still parked on the road, outside the apartments.'

Pemberton switched on his torch and motioned for her to follow him across the grass. The moon slipped behind the clouds, thickening the darkness. They walked the two hundred metres or so down to the river in silence. The wind, gustier in the open area, caught at Helen's wet hair. But she barely noticed. The route, the location, the timing troubled her. She turned at intervals, checked over her shoulder, working through the victim's last movements. Leaving the apartment block. Walking across the damp grass, her dog at her heel. It was a bold move to attack a woman with a dog.

'I take it her clothes and belongings are missing.'

Pemberton nodded. 'Same as the others.'

'Guy Thorne was here this afternoon,' she said. 'At the cricket. He sauntered over, said hello.'

Pemberton stopped in his tracks, caught her arm. 'What was he doing here?'

'Walking his dog. Apparently, he comes here a lot on a Saturday.'

'I don't like the sound of that.'

'Neither do I.' She couldn't make Guy out. He appeared to have no link with the victims, yet his presence, both here and at the last place Louise Carnwell was seen alive, was disconcerting. 'I'm wondering what he's playing at.'

'The hotel in Oxford had him on camera the night Shauna was killed,' Pemberton said. 'We checked. And he was with a friend the night Louise was killed… I'll get his movements verified for last night anyway.' He lifted his phone to his ear, made a call.

They walked along the riverbank, another fifty yards, and

rounded a corner to face a beacon of police lamps illuminating an area on the other side of the river. Helen placed up a hand to shield her eyes as they crossed the bridge. She could see the body in the distance now, laid beside the water's edge.

'Looks like Charles has nipped off for a loo break,' Pemberton said, looking around as they arrived.

'He's already here?'

'He arrived same time as me. Keen to make a start.'

'Any wounds?' Helen asked.

'The welt on her neck from the garrotte. Cuts and scratches on her fingers where she tried to stop it.' Pemberton sucked in a long breath and looked across at the willow trees lining the bank. 'He's changed his habits,' he said. 'It's risky coming here. Where someone could happen by.'

She looked down at the corpse. The engraving was clean, crafted. Done with a calm hand. Not someone rushing, fearful of being caught. Admittedly, this was the quieter end of the park, away from the play areas and grassy pitches. Frequented by joggers, the odd dog walker in daylight hours. But it was still public and in the middle of town. Right under their noses.

* * *

Gemma Stone was a tall woman with bright blue eyes and a pale complexion. Swathes of blonde hair snaked across the shoulders of a bathrobe hanging loose over tartan pyjamas. Her feet were bare.

'I'm sorry for your loss,' Helen said. They were sitting in Gemma's top-floor apartment in Newport Grange. An open-plan living area with two sofas facing each other at one end and a sizable kitchenette at the other, separated by a breakfast bar and tall stools. Spotlights in the ceiling bounced off the wooden flooring. A row of birthday cards overlapped each other on the mantel.

Gemma dabbed a soggy tissue to her cheek. 'I can't believe it. I mean, she was only here a couple of hours ago.' A sob choked her words. She grabbed another tissue from the box beside her.

'How long have you known Eve?' Helen asked.

'Two years. We worked together at Fleming's call centre on Cross Keys before it closed in January. We've kept in contact since.'

'Would you say you know her well?'

'I suppose so.'

'How did she seem this evening?'

'Fine.'

'What time did she arrive?'

'About nine-ish. She was supposed to have come earlier, but her son, James, has got chickenpox. The spots are at that itchy stage, driving him mad. He's only four, poor little mite. She didn't want to leave until he was asleep.'

Helen nodded. 'How long did she stay?'

'Not long. She didn't want to be away in case James woke. We had a quick coffee.' Her lip quivered. 'She brought me a cake for my birthday.' A tear slipped down her cheek.

'A coffee,' Helen said. 'No alcohol?'

'No, she wanted to keep a clear head. In case James was ill in the night.'

If Eve hadn't left her car there because she'd been drinking, there had to be another reason... 'I'm sorry, I realise this is difficult,' Helen said. 'If you could talk me through the evening, it would really help.'

Gemma gave a juddery nod and blew her nose. 'There isn't much to say. We chatted about what we'd been up to.' She stared into space. 'I'd been out to lunch with my mum to celebrate my birthday. Eve was looking after James. She was excited about a job she'd applied for in some printing firm. School hours. It would...' She hesitated, her face falling. 'It would have really suited her.'

'She was out of work,' Helen said.

'Yes. She's been looking for something since we were

made redundant. It's more difficult when you've got to fit your hours around little ones.'

Interesting, Helen thought. 'What about evening work?'

Gemma looked up, sniffed and narrowed her eyes. 'She was strangled, wasn't she? Like the others.'

'We're still waiting for her to be examined,' Helen said, not wishing to give too much away. 'But it's possible. Yes.'

A sob broke out. Gemma pressed a hand to her mouth. Her eyes filling afresh.

'I'm so sorry.' Helen gave her a moment before she spoke again. 'Gemma, I'm afraid I have to ask you this. Do you know if Eve ever worked as an escort, or—'

'No! She wouldn't.'

'Are you absolutely sure?'

She sat back, eyes darting about the room. 'I think so. I mean, I can't imagine...' She met Helen's gaze. 'If she did, she never mentioned it to me.'

'Okay, thank you. What time did she leave?'

'About ten. She wanted to get back to check on James.'

'Did she call you or text you afterwards?'

'No. I thought she'd driven home. I went to bed. Didn't know anything until Sam, Eve's husband, phoned to say Harvey, her dog, had arrived home alone and he couldn't reach Eve on her mobile. I was beside myself, didn't know what to do.'

'He didn't ask you to help search for her?'

'No, he didn't want me out in the dark on my own.'

She checked the time of the call and waited while Pemberton wrote it down. The apartment was at the back of the building overlooking the park. Gemma wouldn't have been aware of Eve's car still parked on the road out front.

'I was pacing the floor until you knocked,' Gemma said. She pressed the tissue to her eye.

'Sam Porter didn't call you when he found her?'

'No. I suppose he was in shock.' She dabbed her eye again.

'Eve should never have walked through the park, not at that time of night.'

'I understand she had her dog with her,' Helen said.

'Harvey, yes. She got him a few years ago as a rescue. Such a sweetheart, but he's hopeless. Frightened of his own shadow. That's why she takes him everywhere, to try and build his confidence.' She sniffed. 'How is Sam?'

'He's doing the best he can, given the circumstances.'

CHAPTER 43

Sam Porter's large frame spread across the sofa in the interview suite. The shock had finally set in and, blond hair clipped to number two, a line of stubble covering a square jawline, he sat, elbow resting on the arm, staring at the carpet, unspeaking.

Helen watched him on the screen. Having attended the scene, police policy prevented her from interviewing him personally. If he was guilty, she risked inadvertently transferring blood or airborne fibres from the victim to her husband. Though she needn't have worried. They'd found no scratches on the backs of his hands or forearms – something to be expected from someone who had committed a strangulation or garrotting. But policy was policy, and she'd brought in the next best team to interview: Dark and Spencer. Him taking notes, her taking the lead. If anyone could encourage Sam Porter to talk, it was them. But they were ten minutes in and, so far, it was slow going.

Dark angled her head. 'Sam?' She leaned in closer. 'We need to catch whoever did this to Eve,' she said gently. 'And if we're to do that, we need to confirm as many details as possible while it's still fresh in your mind.'

He didn't respond.

'Sam. You do want to help us catch whoever did this to Eve, don't you?'

He snapped his gaze to her. Wet eyes wide. 'Of course I do.'

'I understand she was visiting a friend,' Dark continued softly. Stretching out the silence to encourage a reply.

'Yes.' He shook his head as if trying to order his thoughts. And when he started, he couldn't seem to stop. He talked about Eve visiting Gemma for her birthday, a tear glittering his eyelash as he said how she loved to bake. How she always made a cake for someone's birthday. He went on to talk about their son having chickenpox, her leaving just before nine. Saying she'd only be an hour.

A pen scratched the paper as Spencer scribbled down the times.

'Around ten, she messaged me to check on James. When I said he was comfortable, fast asleep, she replied to say she'd be a bit longer. Back around eleven-ish. I didn't pay a lot of attention. Thought she was having a nice time with Gemma. She deserved a rest.'

'What time did your dog return?' Dark asked.

'About 10.30. I didn't hear him myself. It was my mother. She lives in Newcastle, is down visiting. She heard him at the door, scratching and whining.'

The door clicked open. Helen turned to see Pemberton enter.

Pemberton gave Helen a backwards nod. 'Just been on a call with Charles. He said every indication points towards Eve being dead for at least an hour when he arrived at 11.30 pm. We've spoken to Sam's mother, who confirmed he was at home until 10.30; they were watching a film together on television. A neighbour also saw him leave.'

Helen looked back at Sam Porter. She imagined the poor man sitting at home waiting for his wife. The shock when the dog arrived home alone. The panic when she didn't answer her phone. Coming out to search for her. Finding her car

214

outside the apartment block, empty. Walking across the park, desperately searching. Wondering if she'd fallen, maybe even knocked herself out. The body's coping mechanism holding on to any tiny thread of hope. Hope that was shattered when he happened across her lifeless body.

He'd lost his wife in the worst possible circumstances. Witnessed the cruel sight of her naked, broken body. A sight that would haunt him for weeks, months, years to come.

'Who would do something like that?' Sam said to Dark. 'Cut her, mutilate her?'

Dark pressed her lips together. 'Mr Porter. Has your wife ever worked as an escort?'

He stiffened. Beads of sweat glistened on his upper lip. 'She's like the others.' His face contorted as realisation set in. 'Were their bodies marked too?'

Dark didn't answer. 'If you could answer the question.'

He looked away, aghast. A thick silence filled the room.

'Mr Porter?'

'I didn't want her to do it.' It was a while before he spoke and when he did, his voice was tiny, high-pitched. Fresh tears filled his eyes. 'I pleaded with her not to.' A tear meandered down his cheek. He wiped it away. 'After she was made redundant in January, things were… difficult. We were struggling to pay the bills. We took a three-month mortgage break, thinking that would be long enough for her to find something, but there was just nothing out there. And then I was put on short time…' He shook his head again. 'We considered selling the car. I could get a lift to work. But then she wouldn't be able to get to interviews. It was like a catch-22.'

'How did she start?' Dark asked.

'She brought it up.' He shrugged a single shoulder. 'We talked about it. We didn't have any secrets in our marriage. I thought it was a joke at first. Couldn't believe it when she was serious.' Another headshake. 'I was dead against it. Adamant. But we were struggling to feed the kid. Something had to give. And, as with most things, Eve got her way.'

'How did she go about it?'

'I didn't want her on the streets. I drew the line there. She found a website, registered. The clients contacted her. She worked a couple of evenings a week. Left home after she put James to bed. Came back late. In two months, we'd paid off our debts.' He hung his head, his face lily-white.

'Do you know the name of the website?'

He met Dark's gaze. 'No. We didn't discuss the details. It was easier that way. Easier for me to cope with. And it was only ever temporary.'

'Did she tell you about her clients? Their names, details?'

'No. Like I say, we didn't discuss... details.' He swallowed as if the idea lodged like a fish bone in his throat. 'We've never had any secrets in our marriage, but that was the one area I couldn't talk about. She kept it to herself. Met them in hotels on the other side of town. I was worried she might be recognised by someone we knew, but the make-up, the clothes she wore... It was like she'd taken on a different persona. I watched her get ready. Went to bed. But I never slept. Not until she was home, and I heard the shower go on. Then she was mine again.'

He took a breath, glanced up at the ceiling for a second before meeting Dark's gaze once again. 'I relaxed a bit after she left the website. Not completely though. Not until she gave up.'

Dark angled her head. 'When did she finish?'

'She took her profile down at the end of May. She'd built up a good cushion of savings by then. Started applying for jobs. Things were getting back to normal. And then this happens.' His chin quivered.

'I'm sorry, I have to ask you this.' Dark paused. 'Was Eve interested in alternative sources of religion or spiritualism?'

'No. Never.' Another quiver. 'I don't understand. Everything was improving. Everything was getting better. How could this happen?'

CHAPTER 44

'He's becoming bolder,' Richard said. 'Taunting us. It's all about the message.'

Helen leaned against the side of the room as she listened to the profiler speak. They were in the incident suite at headquarters. Saturday night had stretched into Sunday morning. They hadn't taken Sam Porter home until after 2 am, which only left a couple of hours for sleep before she had to be back in to prepare the press statement with Alison to go out first thing. But she wasn't weary. She was wired.

'He wants to be caught,' Richard said. He scratched his temple. He was looking fresh in a loose white shirt, black trousers with a neat iron line running down the front.

Spencer jolted forward, making those around him jump. 'What?'

'These are mothers with homes, families, mortgages,' the profiler continued. 'Loved ones that cared for them and missed them. People that contacted the police within hours of their disappearance. All working secretly in the sex industry to make ends meet. Shauna and Louise kept it from their families. Eve only shared it with her husband. It was a route they all took, a choice they made.'

He pointed to the map on their murder wall where the latest crime scene at Oakwall Park was circled in yellow.

CSIs were still combing the scene. They'd started questioning Eve's friends and family – though, if this murder mirrored the others, they were unlikely to be able to offer any assistance.

'He's making his message stronger, louder,' Richard said. 'He wants the world to know. I'd suggest his next move is going to be something big, and public.'

'Where are we with silver Astras?' Helen asked.

'Working our way through. There are over two hundred in Hamptonshire alone,' Spencer said, 'and that's without looking at neighbouring counties. Assuming our suspect's is legal and registered, of course.'

A phone rang in the background. Helen turned back to their murder wall as Dark picked up the receiver.

All their usual methods of detection, all their training, was falling short. The questioning, the traces. Picking through victims' lives, searching for clues. This killer was one step ahead, every time. And he gave them nothing. There were no cameras on the apartments where Eve Porter disappeared. And they'd had nothing of any significance back from the photofit appeal. It was almost like he could read them, predict their next move.

It was time to branch out, do something different...

Dark slammed down the receiver and stood. 'You're not going to believe this,' she said.

The eyes of the room landed on her.

'Uniform have just broken up a street fight in Atherton Road. Two men. A guy called Vic Yorke – it was outside his house. The other was Sam Porter.'

Helen checked her watch. It was just after 9.30 am. Sam Porter had been quiet when they'd dropped him home in the early hours. She'd watched him walk up his path, fall into the embrace of his mother at the door. Her heart clenched at what the next few hours had meant for him: breaking the news to his young son; dealing with the grief, the tears... What the hell had happened? 'What do we know about the incident?'

'Not much. That was the officer on scene. Apparently, a

neighbour called the police. When they arrived, Porter was laying into Yorke in the street. They had a job to separate them. He arrested them both with causing an affray. He saw Porter was connected to our Operation Allen when he booked them in.'

'Where are the men now?' Helen asked.

'At Roxten Station. They're waiting for the duty doctor to examine them both before questioning.'

'Okay, what do we know about Yorke?'

Pemberton had already crossed the room to his desk and was busy carrying out the checks. 'That's interesting...' he said. He clicked a few more buttons, sat back and blinked.

'What is it, Sean?'

'Victor James Yorke. Twenty-seven Atherton Road. No previous, no record, but...' he looked up, 'plenty of intelligence.'

Helen could bear the suspense no longer and crossed the room to join him. 'What kind of intelligence?'

'He was arrested and questioned for the rape of a nineteen-year-old woman, outside Coutts bar in town, three years ago. She dropped the allegation. It wasn't pursued. Another arrest last year of sexual touching of a sixteen-year-old in The Crown at Little Hampstead. Again, dropped by the victim.'

'A thoroughly nice chap then,' Spencer said.

Helen scratched the back of her neck. Their victims were all in their late twenties. She couldn't see how this fitted. But she couldn't ignore it either, and she was intrigued by Porter's actions, the morning after his wife's murder. 'Do we have a photo of Mr Yorke?'

Pemberton clicked a key and brought up a picture of a scrawny man with olive skin, hard eyes. A bush of dark hair.

'Okay, let's get over there,' she said. 'See what they've got to say.'

CHAPTER 45

Marnie drew a breath and slid the key in the lock. The door swung open to reveal Shauna's pink carpeted hallway. The line of ducks on the doormat. The row of coats hanging neatly on the wall: Charlotte's pink anorak, Shauna's denim jacket, Ollie's Puffa, the kids' fleece jackets. Shoes, sandals and trainers overlapped each other on the rack beneath.

Her gaze rested on the open door at the end of the hallway, the kitchen beyond. The late morning sunshine bounced off the surfaces. Many a time she'd walked in here to find Shauna in the kitchen, baking or cooking a meal for the family. It was the kitchen that had sold the house to her: plenty of space for her large double cooker, her farmhouse table where they ate their evening meal. There was so much room in this house, yet Shauna spent most of her time in the kitchen. Singing and dancing while she cooked. Chatting with clients as she did their hair. Sitting at the table helping the children with their homework. It was the noisy hub of the house. Though today it was empty, the silence deafening.

Even the smell was odd. Strange, stale. Air that hadn't been disturbed in days. A lump filled her throat.

A rumble of wheels. She turned and watched Darren lift the suitcase over the front step, his face whitening as he stepped inside. He didn't want to come here; neither of them did. It wasn't the same without Shauna jigging about the kitchen, the kids running around. The television babbling away in the front room. But the children needed more clothes. They didn't have enough outfits at Daddy's to sustain them long-term, and they missed their toys.

'I'll get the other bags out of the car,' Darren said, parking the suitcase beside the front door.

Marnie moved into the front room, fighting back tears at the photo of Shauna, flanked by the happy faces of her children on the mantelpiece. The painting of Port Isaac Harbour they'd chosen together while on holiday in Cornwall last year on the wall. So many reminders, so many memories. Yet… A pain seared her chest. There was a side to her daughter, a dark world she inhabited, that Marnie had known nothing about.

She scooped up the Xbox and placed it in the suitcase, along with a pile of games, a handful of books. A pine chest in the corner overflowed with jigsaws and more toys. She sorted through, pulling out a couple of Barbie dolls, a remote-controlled car, the kids' iPads.

Darren was in the hallway when she returned.

She handed him the case and took the bags. 'Just need to get their clothes,' she said.

He nodded. Wet eyes darting about.

'Why don't you wait here, love?' She touched his hand. 'Won't take me a minute.'

Darren didn't argue, vacant eyes staring into space.

Upstairs, Shauna's bedroom door was closed. Marnie moved into Charlotte's room and set about emptying the wardrobe and sliding the contents of the drawers into her bags. In Ollie's room, she gathered up his belongings. In less than five minutes, she was back downstairs, passing the bags to Darren. Lifting jackets and fleeces off the coat hooks as he packed the bags in the car. She was just filling the final bag with shoes and trainers when she heard Darren's voice from the drive. She paused, angling her head. He was talking to someone. That polite tone he used when it was someone he didn't know well.

At the end of the driveway, a young woman she didn't recognise was dressed in Lycra running gear, her hair tied back from her face. She looked up as Marnie approached.

'You must be Shauna's mum,' she said, extending a hand. 'I'm Cecily Thomas.'

Marnie looked quizzically from Darren to Cecily. Was she supposed to know that name?

'I'm the lady that found your daughter. I'm so sorry.'

Marnie opened her mouth and closed it again, a fish out of water.

'I was just saying to your husband,' Cecily said. 'I only live two streets away. I had no idea she lived here until I saw the police cars the other day and put two and two together. I can hardly believe it.'

'You're the jogger.' Marnie's voice was barely a whisper.

'Yes. I haven't been back to the woods since. It's all so awful. I hope you don't mind me stopping to speak to you. I've run past the house several times, watched the police come and go. When I saw your husband, well… I guessed you were family. And I wanted to say how sorry I was.'

'Thank you,' Darren said. He moved away, towards the car. Busied himself with placing the final bags inside. 'We ought to get going,' he called to Marnie.

But Marnie's feet were rooted to the spot. She couldn't take her eyes off the young woman. A sheen of sweat covered her brow. A stray strand of hair stuck to her neck. Tears glazed her eyes. It couldn't have been easy stumbling over a dead body in the middle of the woods.

'I hope they catch them soon,' Cecily said. 'It must be dreadful for you. Especially with that terrible carving on her chest. I mean, why would someone do that?'

Marnie's blood chilled. 'Carving?' Nobody had mentioned anything to her about a carving.

'You didn't know!' Cecily pressed a hand to her mouth. She looked horrified. 'The police told me not to say anything, not to talk about it, and I haven't. I promise.' The words were

coming out like bullets now, breathless, fast. She grabbed hold
of Marnie's hands. 'I assumed they would tell the family. I
mean it's different for you, isn't it? You knew her.'

Acidic bile rose in Marnie's mouth. 'What was the carving?'

Cecily paled. Her hands fell. She looked like she was going
to be sick. 'I'm so sorry. You should talk to the police.'

'No, it's okay,' Marnie said with as much reassurance as
she could muster. Her heart was hammering her chest now.
'We need to know. It… it helps.' The engine roared as Darren
started the car.

'A five-pointed star. I knew what it was as soon as I saw
it. My brother used to be into the occult.'

'What?'

'A pentagram.' Her face fell. She reached out, pressed a
hand on Marnie's forearm. 'I really am so sorry.'

Marnie swallowed. She could barely breathe. Why weren't
they told this?

'I have to go,' she said, looking back at the car.

Cecily watched, wide-eyed as Marnie climbed into the
passenger seat.

'Poor thing,' Darren uttered, fiddling with the gearbox.
'She must be going through hell.'

He doesn't know either. Marnie could tell from his slack
face. Why hadn't the police told them?

She clipped in her seat belt, heart still hammering her chest
as he reversed out of the drive. Marnie rubbed her forearm, the
heat still emanating from Cecily's touch. *A pentagram carved
on her chest.* She was beginning to wonder if she knew her
daughter at all.

CHAPTER 46

Sam Porter clasped his hands together on the Formica table. His knuckles were scuffed and scratched. A bump the size of an egg protruded from the side of his forehead and his left eye was swollen, the surrounding skin purple. It was hard to believe that this was the same man who'd answered their questions about his dead wife less than twelve hours earlier.

'Are you going to tell us what this is about?' Helen asked.

'Why don't you ask Yorke?' Sam said.

'I will. At the moment, Mr Porter, I'm asking you. This is your chance to give your account.'

He looked away, eyes like stone. Helen and Pemberton exchanged a glance. Where had this belligerence come from? They'd arrived at Roxten Station to find Vic Yorke being examined by the doctor and immediately started questioning Sam with a view to releasing him quickly. His wife had just died. He should be at home with his family. This was the last thing they expected.

The officer called to the scene said both men had said they didn't want to press assault charges, which was why they were arrested with causing an affray for fighting in the street. What was this all about?

Helen decided to change tack. 'How is your son doing?' she asked, her voice gentle.

He shot her a wary look. 'He's with my mum.'

'I'm sure you want to get back to him,' she said. 'This is a difficult time for you. Help me to help you.'

He shifted in his chair uncomfortably.

'How do you know Mr Yorke?'

'I didn't know him. Well, not properly. I never met him before this morning.' He took a long breath. 'Eve mentioned his name a few times. He used to work on the website Eve used for her... work.'

Helen sat forward. Vic's name hadn't cropped up in their inquiries. 'What did he do there?'

'He used to do their advertising. Left a couple of months ago, launched his own site.' He cursed. 'If you can call it that.'

Helen let the silence hang in the air.

'Sex In Your Home dot com. He pays women to film themselves in pornographic poses, charges punters to watch them.'

'Okay,' Helen said slowly. 'What gave you cause to visit him this morning?'

He took a breath, exhaled long and hard before he answered. 'He phoned and emailed Eve several times over the past couple of weeks. He wanted her to record footage for his site. Wouldn't take no for an answer. Last time he phoned was three days ago – Thursday. I took the phone off Eve, gave him a piece of my mind. Told him in no uncertain terms to leave her alone, she didn't want to work for him. I thought that was the end of the matter.' His nostrils flared. 'This morning, I logged into her email and found a message from him, sent yesterday. The dirty bastard had also been one of her punters. And he'd set up a secret camera, filmed her on the job.'

'Did she know he'd filmed her?'

'No. No way. Eve would never have allowed that. She hated women posting pornographic pictures online. Was always on about how dangerous it was, how widely they could be shared. How they could ruin lives.' He swiped a hand across his forehead. 'In his email, Yorke said if she didn't supply footage for his new website, he'd put his recording on social media.'

Helen's insides curdled. What an email to receive on the morning after your wife's death. 'So, you went to confront him?'

'Too right. She was my wife!' He clamped his teeth together. 'How dare he?'

* * *

Vic Yorke stared defiantly at Helen across the table. His cheek was bruised and swollen. A graze ran the length of his nose. And his gaze was piercing.

'Mr Yorke,' Helen said, after the initial introductions. 'Tell me what happened in Atherton Road this morning.'

'It's obvious. He attacked me.'

'You're saying Mr Porter attacked you?'

'Yeah. He banged on my door, pulled me out onto the street. Just ask the witnesses. Half the bloody street was watching.'

'And why do you think that was?'

'No idea. I've never met him before.'

'What about his late wife, Eve Porter?' Helen asked. 'You knew her, didn't you?'

A flicker of recognition passed across his face, betraying the fact that he'd seen the early morning news bulletin, heard about the murder. A muscle flexed in his jaw. 'No comment.'

'Have you been in contact with Mrs Porter recently, either by phone or email?'

'No comment.'

'I'm sure you're aware, we can check.'

He rested back in his chair, said nothing.

'Tell me about your website,' she asked.

He met her eyeline. 'No comment.'

'Mr Porter, where were you between nine and eleven last night?'

Yorke's solicitor, a rotund, fifty-something man with a

comb-over of sandy hair, looked up from his notes. 'My client was arrested for causing an affray.'

Helen ignored him. She wasn't interested in a brawl between two men in the street. She was interested in what had happened to Eve Porter and the other women. She returned Yorke's stare, lifted a brow.

Yorke sneered. 'You can't pin that on me,' he said.

'Pin what?'

'I must object—'

Yorke waved away his solicitor. He didn't trust the police and he clearly didn't think much of his solicitor either. 'I saw it on the news this morning.' He curled his lip again. 'I was nowhere near Oakwall Park.'

'Can someone verify that?' Helen asked.

'Yeah.' He sat back. Folded his arms across his chest. 'My girlfriend. I was with her all evening. I'm happy to give you the details.'

* * *

'What do we know about his website?' Helen asked.

She and Pemberton were in the CID offices at the back of Roxten Station.

'It's just gone live. There are a few videos on there. He's clearly set on building his business.'

'Does he have any link with Adult Services?'

'Spencer has been back out to see Will Sheridan. Doesn't look like they know each other. Eve must have worked from a different website to Adult Services; she wasn't registered with them. We can't link Yorke to Shauna or Louise either.'

Helen sighed.

'His girlfriend lives in Bristol,' Pemberton said. 'She confirmed he was there last night. He travelled back early this morning. We'll check the motorway cameras for his car, but if he's telling the truth, it doesn't look like he's our man.'

CHAPTER 47

Marnie slumped into the chair at the kitchen table. Darren's footfalls pounded the landing. A door closed upstairs. Then all was quiet.

They'd barely spoken in the car after they left Shauna's earlier. When they had arrived at Aidan's, they'd turned on their happy faces, scooped up their grandchildren for long hugs, listened to them chatter about their day, and helped them unpack the suitcase and bags until the front room floor was filled with clothes and toys and there was no space to move.

It was bizarre. Surreal. Sitting on Aidan's carpet, surrounded by the children's possessions. Possessions that had once littered Shauna's floors. His girlfriend, Jade, looking on. Marnie hadn't met Jade before Saturday and she had wondered about the impact of another woman on her grandchildren at present, at a time when they needed the undivided attention of those close to them. But, since the murder, Jade and Aidan had both taken time off work to spend with the kids and, Marnie had to concede, the young woman was good with them. She'd watched Jade crouch down today, stroke Ollie's hair as he attempted to steer his remote-control car through the mass of clothes, books and toys on the floor. Later, Charlotte had climbed onto Jade's knee and showed off her favourite

Barbies. The kids seemed to know her well, be comfortable with her. One small blessing.

As soon as they had arrived home, Darren had retreated upstairs. It was like role reversal. For the first few days, she'd barely emerged from their bedroom, and he'd handled everything. Now he'd regressed to lying on the bed with the curtains drawn, wide awake. Moving only to wander along the landing to the bathroom and back. The force of his daughter's murder and the events surrounding it, finally hitting him. No music, no sound. God only knew what was going through his head.

Marnie had laid on the sofa downstairs this afternoon, hour by hour passing as she stared at the ceiling. Dark thoughts crawling around her mind, preventing any chance of rest. Only getting up because she thought she should eat something. Though, now she was in the kitchen, the very idea of food made her queasy.

Her phone caught her eye on the end of the table, its screen blank. They'd turned off their mobiles after the news of Shauna working as an escort broke. The buzz of all the calls and messages had been overwhelming. Friends and family were only being considerate; Marnie knew that. Checking up on them, making sure they were okay. But she couldn't bear to talk about it, or to think about it. Even to dwell on the subject for one second was heartbreaking. No. If anyone needed them urgently, they'd phone on the landline.

Marnie grated her teeth, pressing them against each other. She hadn't told Darren about the tail end of her conversation with Cecily. Hadn't mentioned the carving. He'd only worry, tell her not to get involved, and he was already fragile. But Marnie couldn't get it out of her head. A pentagram. It sat there, picking away at the side of her brain.

What did it mean? And why didn't the police say anything?

She scanned the kitchen, her gaze resting on her iPad on top of a pile of papers on the side. She pulled it down, googled the word *pentagram*.

Pages of listings came up. Companies called Pentagram. A blog. She clicked on a Wikipedia page. It was linked with religion. Wicca. Witchcraft. Paganism. Devil worship.

Marnie's blood ran cold. What the hell was Shauna involved in?

She recalled the detective asking whether Shauna was religious, the inquiries about her hobbies. Questions that seemed odd at the time. Questions she'd shrugged off in her grief. Now they were beginning to make sense.

She'd been told her daughter had been strangled and laid out beside a river. Darren didn't want to talk about the identification and, when she'd probed him, he said she looked like she was sleeping. But he'd only seen her face. Her body was covered.

Should she contact the police? Confront them? Ask them what else she hadn't been told about her daughter's murder? They had been quick enough to share that Shauna was working as an escort. But... they'd already kept information back. Why would they tell her any more now?

Her thoughts unspooled into a messy pile of anger and hurt. Hurt at the grisly, abrupt end to her daughter's life. Anger at being kept in the dark.

She needed a drink.

The chair scraped the floor, like bare chalk on a board, as Marnie stood and moved into the dining room. She opened the door to the cupboard at the bottom of the dresser, glanced inside. They seldom drank alcohol at home. The odd glass of wine with dinner if they had guests, or to celebrate a birthday. Darren had an occasional whisky. They bought spirits at Christmas and rarely finished them, and the bottles sat in the cupboard year after year. She pushed past a half-full bottle of gin, a bottle of Dubonnet, her hand resting on Darren's Scotch.

Marnie didn't drink whisky. She preferred the softer spirits mixed with a dash of lemonade. But today she needed something strong. Something to dull the pain thudding her head, smother the gruesome images crowding her mind. She poured herself a generous measure, took a glug and coughed. The spirit was sour on her tongue and burned her throat. She swallowed, took another glug, and another. Heat filled her cheeks. She refilled and took the glass and the bottle through to the kitchen.

Darkness was closing in now, casting shadows across the work surfaces. She'd avoided the news, avoided everyone, but maybe it was time to take a quick look. She fired up her iPad again and googled *Hampton News*. Immediately, the headline *Woman's Body Discovered in Oakwall Park* flashed up. She dropped her eyes to the accompanying photograph of a young woman smiling at the camera, and her stomach twisted.

Another murder.

Marnie scrolled down, skimmed the article, her heart shrinking with every word. *Eve Porter... Body found beside the river in Oakwall Park... Strangled... Police linking it to the other murders...*

Another swig of whisky. Why hadn't the police told her? She should call them, give them a piece of her mind. She was just thinking this through when she gazed up the hallway and something on the doormat caught her eye. She moved towards it. A card from the acting superintendent, asking her to get in touch urgently. How did she miss this earlier? She crossed to the landline. Two missed calls. They'd tried to reach her, and she'd missed them. And her mobile phone was off.

Tears filled Marnie's eyes as she moved back into the kitchen. More whisky. It was going down easier now.

Three murders. Did the others have engravings too? She finished the whisky, refilled the glass, then reread the article. The words were starting to blur and move around on the screen. She had to focus, concentrate. She sniffed and switched to another piece, a later article, published only an hour earlier. There was no mention of a pentagram on any of the bodies.

Why could they not share this piece of information?

A fireball of anger rose inside her. It needed to be shared. Marnie's head swayed as she switched to Twitter. It was about time the public knew what they were dealing with.

CHAPTER 48

Helen suppressed a yawn as Matthew climbed out of the car. 'Good luck,' she said.

'All right, Mum.' He pulled a face and looked up and down the street to make sure it was empty.

Helen resisted the temptation to laugh. 'See you later,' she said and waited in the car until he disappeared inside the newsagent's. His first job. It felt like a seminal moment.

Another yawn. Not a good start to a Monday morning. She let this one out and accelerated down the road, her mind turning to yesterday at work. Another long day, another late night, another dead end. She'd persuaded the custody sergeant to drop the charge against Sam Porter. He was dealing with the horrific loss of his wife – an affray charge was the last thing he needed. Unfortunately, dropping it against him meant dropping it against Vic Yorke too. And what galled her was that they couldn't pursue the blackmail against Eve Porter because the complainant was dead. CID had promised to visit the other girls featured on Yorke's website to ensure their videos were consensual, but Helen's heart burned to watch Vic Yorke's smug face leave the station. Her victims weren't girls walking the streets. They weren't alcohol dependent or feeding a drug habit – they were just trying to pay their bills. Yet even at this clinical level, it struck her how easy it was to fall into the world of selling sex. And how difficult the industry made it to escape.

She slipped down a gear and pulled out onto the main road. They were no closer to catching their killer. He'd branched out with his third victim, become more confident. A tiny part of her harboured the vague hope that maybe he'd also slipped up, forgotten something, or left a trace behind. Yet after a late night waiting on forensics results – only to be told the scene was, once again, clean – her hopes were dashed. And no witnesses had come forward.

They were looking at this the wrong way. They needed to find a way to bring the killer to them.

The car in front braked as the traffic lights ahead turned red. It was 7.28 am. Helen switched on the local radio. The news would be on shortly. Hopefully, they'd mention the appeal again, direct people to the e-fit photo on the Hamptonshire Police website. She had a meeting with Alison this morning to discuss the current media brief. It would be useful to know what reporters were saying.

Robbie Williams's voice filled the car – a song she didn't recognise. The car in front edged forward as the lights changed. She joined a line of vehicles waiting to enter Cross Keys roundabout. The tune faded and the DJ handed over to the newsroom for the 7.30 bulletin.

Helen hiked up the volume and glanced around. A man in a bus shelter – wrapped in a roll of cardboard, fast asleep – caught her eye. She watched him a moment. Unmoving. Unflinching amidst the early-morning traffic.

'And our headline story is "The Pentagram Killer".'

Helen jolted forward. *What?*

'Twenty-seven-year-old Eve Porter's body was discovered in Oakwall Park on Saturday night,' the newsreader continued. 'She'd been strangled. Police are linking the incident to the recent murders of Shauna O'Hennessey and Louise Carnwell. People online have dubbed the murderer "The Pentagram Killer" following a tweet from the mother of the first victim, Shauna O'Hennessey, yesterday evening, claiming a pentagram had been carved into her dead daughter's chest when she was found.'

Shit. Shit. Shit.

'The tweet has gone viral with over a thousand shares. The assistant chief constable will be making a statement at 10 am, but it does beg the question why police didn't release this information earlier.'

How the hell did Marnie find out?

Helen grabbed her phone and googled *The Pentagram Killer*. Her heart sinking at the numerous posts that came up. Word couldn't have spread quicker. And then she found it, the tweet from Marnie O'Hennessey:

My beautiful daughter was murdered a week ago. Her killer carved a pentagram on her chest & went on to kill 2 more women. Do you know anything? Please help. #stopthekilling

It was accompanied by a photograph of Shauna, a headshot of her standing on a beach, creamy sand reaching to the blue sea beyond. She was smiling, sunglasses perched on her head, tendrils of hair lifting in the wind.

Helen closed her eyes and rested her head on the steering wheel. This was the last thing they needed.

She was interrupted by the buzz of her mobile. Simultaneously, a car horn beeped behind her. The vehicle in front had moved. She raised a hand in apology, inched forward, took the next turning into a side street and parked in the first available space. It was Pemberton on the phone.

'Morning.' He sounded fraught. 'Have you heard the news?'

'Just caught the 7.30 am bulletin.'

'Ah...'

'How did she find out?'

'No idea. The ACC is here already and has phoned down twice. She wants you in her office the minute you arrive.'

'I'm sure she does,' Helen said. If only Alison had agreed to release the information earlier! Yes, they'd have faced a surge of interest and perhaps some unwelcome speculation.

But they could have controlled it, turned it on its head and used the coverage to appeal for information. Now they were on the back foot. She checked the clock. 'I'll be there in fifteen minutes.' She paused a second, her mind working on overdrive. 'Can you contact Dark and get her to go straight out to Marnie's address? We need to get to the bottom of this and find out where she got the details.' They needed to check on her welfare too. The press would be likely camped outside, having a field day. Then they needed to start the process of damage limitation and visit the other families. This wasn't going to be an easy one to play down.

'Will do.'

'And Sean?'

'Yes?'

'Thanks for the heads-up.'

CHAPTER 49

Marnie was awoken by a knock at the front door. Her head pounded, her mouth felt like sandpaper, and she was bone cold. She opened her eyes and peeled her cheek from the kitchen table. The smell of whisky made her heave. She gripped her nose. Dashed to the sink. Just in time to fill it with the contents of her stomach.

Sweat coursed down her back. The door knocker sounded again. She lifted her head, inhaled the aroma of acid bile and whisky floating up into the air and vomited again. And again. Every time she lifted her head, more came.

The letter box sprang open. A voice called out. But she couldn't move from the sink.

Seconds passed. She swilled the bowl, patted her mouth with kitchen roll. She was about to answer the door when feet thundered the stairs.

Darren reached the bottom, grappling with the straps of his dressing gown. He pulled open the door to a cacophony of voices. A camera flashed. 'What's going on?' he said.

Marnie couldn't move, her feet rooted to the spot, the kitchen roll still pressed to her mouth. Voices shouted. Another camera flashed. She heard the name 'Pentagram Killer', and her heart shrank in her chest. *Oh no. Oh no. No. No. No.*

Darren was arguing with people on the doorstep. Warning

them to move back, to get off his driveway. But she couldn't move, her limbs frozen. Her thoughts brushed over the conversation with Cecily, the jogger, yesterday. Surely Cecily wouldn't have said anything. She didn't seem the type.

Then a pain hit her, so sudden and sharp it blurred her vision. She grabbed the glass of water, popped a couple of paracetamols.

The front door slammed. Darren stomped into the kitchen. 'Have you heard what they're—' He stopped mid-sentence, looking from the sink to Marnie. His face contorting at the smell of vomit hanging in the air. Marnie still in yesterday's clothes.

'I had a bit of a drink last night,' she said, turning away.

'More than a bit, by the looks of it.'

He swilled the bowl again, opened a window. Cool morning air flooded the kitchen. Darren's feet were bare. His calves, coated with a carpet of black hair, sat proud beneath the robe that only reached to his knees. Thick muscular calves. Strong. He'd always been a stocky man, a tower of strength, yet inside he was sensitive and soft like putty. That contrast was what had attracted her to him all those years ago. And now it made her sad. They'd been through so much.

He looked across at her, his face turning sombre. 'Come on, love.'

He pulled her to him, rubbed her back, kissed the top of her head. It was the first time he'd shown any affection in days and the gesture brought a lump to her throat. She nuzzled into the comfort of his shoulder.

'We need to stick together, you and me,' he said. 'It's the only way we're going to get through this.'

Marnie wasn't sure how long they stood there, entwined in each other's arms, with the dull sound of voices outside.

Finally, he released her. 'I need to ring the police,' he said. 'I don't know what's been said, but they're coming out with some weird shit out there.'

Marnie closed her eyes. She wasn't even sure where to

start, how to explain, but she needed to say something. At the very least, she needed to tell him what Cecily had told her yesterday. It wasn't fair for him to be kept in the dark. Before she had a chance, the door knocker sounded again.

'Right, that's it,' Darren said, moving past her and out into the hallway. 'If that's another bloody reporter, I'll have their head on a plate.' He pulled open the front door and stepped back. 'Oh, it's you.'

Marnie looked past him. It was the young detective with the short, spiky hair. And what's more, she'd moved the reporters to the end of their driveway.

'I was just about to call you,' he said to DC Dark as he led her through to the kitchen. 'Has something happened?'

'I'm afraid so,' the young woman said. She indicated for them to sit at the table, opposite her. Clasped her hands together.

Marnie could feel the tremble start in her fingers. Darren grabbed them. 'What is it?' he said to the detective.

The evening was coming back to her now. The rage, the anger. The tweet... She recoiled. Darren would have told her to contact the police. To have done things properly. But she couldn't turn the clock back now.

'It's me,' she said, her voice barely a whisper. 'The reporters outside. They're there because of me.'

CHAPTER 50

Alison was standing at the window, looking across the field beyond. She turned as Helen and Pemberton entered, her hand resting on her hip, lifting the edge of the jacket of the charcoal trouser suit she wore, the purple shirt beneath. No greeting. No welcome. Instead, she walked back to her desk and pushed a newspaper across the surface. 'They're calling him "The Pentagram Killer".'

'Original,' Pemberton said.

Alison ignored him. 'National news,' she said to Helen. 'It seems Marnie's tweet has gone viral. Even the BBC were covering it this morning.'

Helen looked down at the headline. *Where Will He Strike Next?* She resisted the temptation to say they should have shared the details earlier. The more an investigation grew, the more people were involved – police and public – and the more difficult it was to keep everyone quiet. Still... No point in exacerbating the situation.

'Right.' Alison exhaled loudly. 'You'd better tell me what we're doing about it.'

'Damage limitation,' Helen said. 'Dark is going out to see the O'Hennesseys this morning to explain the situation and placate them. Spencer will speak with the other families.'

'It's a bit late for that now,' Alison snapped. 'The chief

is going bananas, talking about bringing someone else in. He wanted this wrapped up, the heat off, before the auditors arrive. They'll be here in less than three weeks. Instead, we've got the national media on our doorstep.' She cursed. 'So, where are we with the case?'

'Nothing from forensics on the latest victim,' Helen said. 'Which is pretty much expected. And nothing from victimology. Her husband knew what she was up to. Eve assured him she mostly met regulars. We're doing all the usual checks on Eve Porter, and we're still working through owners registered with a silver Astra.'

'What are we going to say to the press? And the chief, for that matter.'

Helen ignored the question. 'I've been thinking,' she said, almost to herself. 'We should set up a decoy.'

'What do you mean?'

'We know he has a type. Long dark hair. Pretty. Slight build. Let's create a phoney website and a set of fake profiles. I'm sure our techies can put something together and advertise it in the right places. See if *we* can attract our killer.'

Alison scratched the back of her neck. 'It's a reach.'

'It's got to be worth a try,' Pemberton said. 'We're not getting anywhere through the normal channels.'

'What are the chances of us getting a covert surveillance officer that fits the bill?' Helen asked.

Alison looked uncertain. 'I can make some inquiries, but it'll take time.'

Helen sighed inwardly. Time was something they didn't have.

'Wouldn't we be playing into the killer's hands?' Alison said.

Pemberton nodded. 'Absolutely. The difference is we'll be set up with surveillance. We can follow them from the first point of contact. If nothing else, if we suspect something, it'll give us the opportunity to search the vehicle for hair samples, particles, DNA. Could be a game changer.'

Alison stared at them both a moment, computing this. 'I'll make some calls,' she said. 'Give me an hour to get this bloody press conference out of the way. That'll give you time to draw up a plan of how you think it'll work.'

CHAPTER 51

'How could we not have known about this?' Darren said to the detective. He'd stayed silent, frozen, while Marnie had relayed her discussion with Cecily, the jogger. His face darkening in disbelief as she talked about her drunken evening spent on internet searches. Her tweet.

She'd let him down. Gone behind his back. Her breath caught in her throat. She should have told him. She pressed a hand to his thigh. Unsure of what to say, of how to repair things between them.

He surprised her by snaking an arm around her, his thick hand resting protectively on her shoulder. Disbelief turning to indignation.

'You should have told us,' he said to Dark.

The detective opened her mouth to speak, but he wasn't finished.

'We should never have found out from a jogger. Can you imagine how that makes you feel? Your own daughter, your own flesh and blood mutilated – and you hear about it in the street, from a stranger.'

'I appreciate this is difficult—'

'No, you don't appreciate anything. You don't have the right,' he said, his voice raising a decibel. 'She was our girl.'

'Mr O'Hennessey. You are grieving.'

'This has nothing to do with grief. This is about facts!'
Spittle flew out of his mouth.

The detective remained calm. 'We are on the same side here.'

'Then why not tell us?'

'There are often details kept back in a murder investigation, from the family and the public, and for good reason. We have many lines of inquiry which could be jeopardised by sharing certain pieces of information.'

'That's bullshit!'

Marnie grabbed his knee. 'Darren, please.'

'Well, it is.' He didn't take his eyes off the detective. 'Were the other women marked with a pentagram too?'

The detective gave a single nod.

'Then surely sharing it can only help. I mean, people might have information about what it means…'

'We've already taken advice from experts on the pentagram. We know what it means.'

'And?'

The detective's face twisted. 'It's thought the killer is targeting women working in the… sex industry. Singling them out. He marks them with an inverted pentagram because he believes it represents evil.' Her voice was soft, gentle. 'I'm so sorry.'

Marnie's chest ached. She was killed because of her job. A job none of them knew about. None of them approved of. The reality was like a spear to her soul.

'Why didn't you tell us?' Darren said. There were tears in his eyes now. 'You didn't hesitate to tell us or the press that she was working as an escort.'

'We only release information that can assist the investigation. We told you about Shauna working as an escort because we needed to reach out to the public. To alert others to the danger. And we also wanted to encourage other sex workers to come forward. It's a job shrouded in secrecy. We needed other women to open up, share their experiences. It's possible they might have met the killer.'

'And did they?'

'Yes. We're currently following up on their information.'

'I still don't see how sharing the pentagram would compromise you.' Darren's face had turned tomato red.

The detective hesitated a minute. 'We think the killer is making a point, selecting his victims because of their jobs. We didn't want to give him a public voice.'

Marnie shrank back. Was that what her tweet was doing? Giving her daughter's murderer notoriety.

'It's all about a balance,' the detective continued gently.

'You mean we're feeding his ego?' Darren's voice squawked.

'As I say, it's a balance. We all want to catch Shauna's killer. And quickly.'

* * *

Later, Marnie lay on the sofa, hugging her knees to her chest, staring at the blank television screen. The bed springs squeaked as Darren turned in the room above. He'd retreated upstairs after the detective had left, a shadow of his former self. Every ounce of energy he'd found in the kitchen earlier, all the fight, all the indignation, once again drained from him.

The curtains were closed, the room a khaki grey, even though it was only mid-morning. But despite closing the curtains and windows, shutting out the world, she could still hear the babble of reporters outside through her double glazing. What had she done?

Her tweet had been shared over twelve hundred times before it was taken down. Her words repeated all over the internet and across the news channels. There was no escape.

She thought about the families of the other victims. Mothers, fathers, sisters, brothers. Grandparents. Extended family. Children. People like her who'd discovered their loved ones had not only been brutally murdered; they'd also been mutilated. Did they have reporters on their doorsteps too?

The phone rang, making her jump. She curled up tighter, listened to it ring out. She didn't want to answer it. She didn't want to talk to anyone. Aidan had already phoned and chewed off her ears. The children had only just returned to school, for Christ's sake.

Everyone was talking about The Pentagram Killer. What he would do, where he would strike next.

She'd done what she'd intended, raised the profile of the case, made it viral.

She only hoped she hadn't made things worse.

CHAPTER 52

'There isn't anyone available,' Alison said. 'Not that fits the profile of dark hair, slim build. I've tried West Midlands and the Met.'

They were back in Alison's room, the mood solemn. Helen had watched her press conference live and she had to admit the ACC had done a reasonable job of placating a packed conference suite of journalists. Talking about how the leak might compromise existing leads. Saying that they were investigating several lines of inquiry. Finishing up by renewing their plea for witnesses: 'Help us to catch this killer and make the streets safe once again.' Uniting the people of Hampton in a joint aim. But it had taken a lot out of her, and for the first time since the beginning of the investigation, Alison looked tired, wilted.

'Could they wear a wig?' Helen said.

'Possibly. I'm pretty much drawing a blank though. The undercover officers they have are all tied up on operations. They don't have anyone who could assist urgently.'

The air in the room thickened. They were running out of answers.

Helen noticed Pemberton's eyes on her and raised a brow. 'What?'

'Excuse me, I'm being presumptuous. But… petite, long dark hair.'

Helen held his gaze. 'You're not serious?'

'You did do a stint in covert crime.'

'Three months! And most of that was training. Anyway, I'm a good six years older than Louise. Even more so than the others.'

He wrinkled his nose. 'You could pass for younger, with a bit of make-up.'

She snorted. 'Thanks for the vote of confidence.'

'I'm not having my acting superintendent working as an undercover officer,' Alison said. 'That's a ridiculous notion.'

'Is it?' Pemberton looked affronted.

'Yes, sergeant. It is! What about Dark?' Alison said. 'She's got the right build and features. We could get her a wig.'

'No,' Helen cut in. 'She's recovering from an incident on duty on the last investigation.'

Alison frowned. 'She looks pretty well to me.'

'I won't have her put in the firing line again, not so soon.'

The tension in the room tightened. The case was slipping through their fingers.

Helen sighed. 'Just suppose, for one moment, I do it.' She was working it through in her mind as she spoke. 'Isn't there a chance I'll be recognised? Admittedly, I haven't faced the media on this case, but I've interviewed witnesses and I've done press conferences in the past. That's why we usually get undercover officers from other forces, because they aren't known in our area.'

'I said no,' Alison repeated.

'I'm just talking it through.'

Alison's eyes were on fire, but she looked away. They had nothing else. They'd come to the end of the line. Even she had to admit something needed to be done, and fast. The chief constable hadn't accompanied her to the press conference. A sure sign he was losing confidence in them and the investigation. It was only a matter of time before he brought in a review team. A fresh pair of eyes to look over the case. And Helen wasn't one to admit defeat easily.

'We'd have to be extra careful,' she said. 'If I am recognised, it'll blow the whole thing.'

Pemberton brandished a smile. 'When I worked in undercover, we had a job where they used proper make-up artists, theatrical experts. It's always a risk, of course. Though, I'd say, by the time an expert has finished, no one's going to recognise you.'

* * *

'Right,' Alison said. Half an hour later, Helen and Pemberton were back in Alison's room and this time they were joined by Spencer and Dark – the core of their new special op team. 'I've spoken to Sergeant Kelly Evans in technical. She's going to lend us Mick Steadwell – he's one of her best techies. He used to design and build websites for a living. Mick will put together a website to feature our decoy profile on. He'll then advertise it to the same people as Adult Services and do some clever stuff with Google's algorithms to get it to the top of the search engines.' She waved a hand in the air. 'Don't ask me what it is. I haven't a clue.'

A knock at the door interrupted them.

A bald, wiry man entered. He was wearing an open-necked blue shirt. Navy trousers hung off his skinny hips. 'Mick Steadwell,' he said. 'Technical support.'

'Ah, yes,' Alison said. She beckoned him in, introduced the others. 'I take it you've been briefed on the remit?'

'I have.' His eyes shone like a kid at Christmas. 'It's an interesting one.'

'Yes, and an operation that needs complete discretion,' Alison said sourly. She turned to the others. 'I don't want this shared with anyone outside these four walls. Is that clear?'

The message was for everyone, though it was Mick who answered, his face grave. 'Of course.'

'Good. The acting superintendent has kindly volunteered to be our decoy.'

Mick surveyed Helen, his eyes widening to bowls. 'I see.' A pronounced nod.

'We're chasing the clock here,' Alison continued. 'How long is this going to take to put together?'

'The site?' He shook his head. 'I can do that in a couple of hours, as long as I have everything I need.'

'Which is?'

'Well, apart from the obvious computer, I'll need a profile for...' He turned to Helen. 'Sorry, what should I call you?'

'That's still to be decided,' Alison chipped in.

'Okay, I'll need to take a high-pixel photo of you... in costume,' he said to Helen, looking her up and down. He turned back to Alison. 'I take it you're using a make-up artist?'

Alison nodded.

'It'd be cheaper to use someone we know,' Pemberton said. He looked at Spencer. 'Isn't your daughter studying beauty at college?'

It was clearly a joke, but Alison wasn't in the mood for joviality. 'Absolutely not.' She turned to Helen. 'We've booked a room for you at the Travelodge down the road. A make-up artist will meet you there in half an hour. Dark is picking out an outfit for you based on the other victims' profiles.'

'So soon,' Spencer said.

'We haven't got time to hang around. Right.' She stood, indicating an end to the meeting. 'I can't reiterate enough how important it is that the status of this operation stays in this room,' she said. 'We'll use CST for backup, our own covert surveillance team. Mick, can you get started on the site?'

Mick nodded.

'Good.' She looked at Pemberton and Spencer. 'Find us a location, a hotel to work from. We'll need the manager's support and plans of the building if we're to do this properly. We'll meet back here at 6 pm to see where we are and iron out the finer details.'

CHAPTER 53

Jenna James was an unassuming woman in her forties, with dark hair tied in a long plait that lay over one shoulder and a trolley of vanity cases that rattled with make-up pallets, pots and creams.

Helen fidgeted in her chair. A shard of sunlight reached into the room, casting a line down the navy shirt of Rosa Dark, sitting on the edge of the bed, beside them.

Jenna furiously backcombed Helen's hair. 'I'm told you don't want to be recognised,' she said.

'That's right.' Helen winced as she pulled and tugged.

'And I can't touch your hair colour, or length.'

'You got it.'

Helen closed her eyes as the woman worked: brushing, fluffing, spraying. Her thoughts turned to Marnie and Darren O'Hennessey, and the other families. It must have been shocking to discover the mutilation of their loved ones' bodies from someone in the street, or online through social media or a news bulletin. Dark had been round and spoken with them, but she made a mental note to contact the families herself later.

'I hear you're a theatrical make-up artist,' Dark said to Jenna.

'Yup.' A sweet perfumed aroma wafted through the air as the woman moved about.

'Will I know anything you've worked on?'

'Um... *Joseph and the Amazing Technicolor Dreamcoat. The Lion King.* I travelled with *Cats* for a while – that was interesting.'

'Oh, I love *Cats,*' Dark said. 'I bet that was challenging.'

'Challenging, yes, and great fun. I like the unusual, the transformations, best of all.'

Transformation. That's an interesting word, Helen thought.

Jenna pranced around her, spraying, adjusting, tugging, applying make-up. Time passed. Eventually, she stood back, looked at Helen square on and smiled, exposing a line of perfectly straight white teeth. 'Pretty good,' she said, 'even though I do say it myself.' She handed Helen a round mirror.

Helen took one look at her reflection and gasped. She looked like a celebrity auditioning for the Eurovision Song Contest. Her hair was backcombed and pulled away from her face like a mane. Thick black kohl circling her eyes gave her a feline appearance. False lashes covered her own beneath heavy arched brows. Her lips were wine-red and glossy.

'What do you think?' Jenna said.

'It's interesting.'

'Good. That'll do for the site photos. We can tone it down a bit for every day if you like?'

Helen's shoulders slumped. Spending almost an hour to look like this 'every day' was akin to her worst nightmare. She grabbed her phone and messaged Pemberton, who was waiting in the lobby. *All done.*

'You'll need this,' Jenna said, handing over a bottle of cleanser and another of cream. 'Just make sure you get it all off afterwards, give your skin a chance to breathe.'

Helen took the bottles, thanked her and watched her pack the pallets and brushes and creams away. Dark was letting Jenna out when Pemberton arrived, Mick on his tail.

'Well, well, well,' Mick said. 'Don't you scrub up nicely?'

'Yeah, right.' Thoughts of a photo shoot hadn't exactly filled her mind when she'd agreed to become the decoy.

'I'm serious. Think I fancy you myself.'

'Cut it out,' she said as he chuckled.

'You certainly look *done*,' Pemberton said, scrunching his eyes.

'Telling me. I feel like I've been iced like a cake.'

The room erupted in laughter.

'All right, that's enough of the frivolity,' Helen said. 'What are we doing for this picture?'

'Well, that depends on what you want to do, Madam,' Mick said, giving a bow.

Helen shot him a stern look.

'Okay, okay.' He placed his hands in the air. 'I'm thinking you don't want anything too suggestive?'

'You're thinking right. It's going to take me long enough to live this down as it is.'

Pemberton snorted.

'So, let's go for the sultry look. Did you wear the black bra we talked about?'

Helen nodded.

'Good. Slip the top of your robe down a bit and I'll get a head-and-shoulders shot with just the straps showing.' He turned to Pemberton. 'Close the curtains and turn on the lamps. We could do with soft lighting.'

'He thinks he's bloody Patrick Lichfield,' Dark whispered, helping Helen move the robe so that she exposed just enough bra strap without showing any cleavage.

'Okay,' Mick said, holding up his camera. 'Ready to pout?'

She pulled a face. 'Forget it.'

'I was kidding.' He couldn't help himself from sniggering. 'I think we'll call you Cassie, the princess of darkness.'

Helen rolled her eyes as Pemberton laughed again. 'You've got five minutes,' she said. 'Then I'm getting dressed.'

CHAPTER 54

An hour later, Helen was back at headquarters, freshly showered, wet hair tied back in a loose ponytail. She sat around the table with Pemberton, Spencer, Dark and Alison. Mick stood at the front. The blinds were closed, shutting out the early evening sun.

'Right, this is the mock-up I've put together so far,' Mick said.

A website graced the screen beside it, the layout of profiles astonishingly similar to that of Adult Services. Helen's picture appeared on the top line, sandwiched between peroxide-blonde Sandy and a redhead called Fiona.

Spencer spat out his tea. 'Cassie!' he said, reading Helen's name aloud. 'Who came up with that?'

'That was the brainchild of Mick.' Pemberton laughed, then clocked Helen's deadpan face and turned it into a cough. 'Well, we needed something.'

'Operation Cassie it is,' Alison said.

Helen read the profile – *Interested in the dark side of life* – and cringed. She was beginning to wonder if this was such a good idea after all.

'We've kept the description deliberately short,' Alison said, 'to leave it ambiguous. We've got you a pay-as-you-go phone. You'll use text only, for interested parties. No phone calls. We don't want you getting drawn into conversations that could potentially put you on the spot. Keep it short and to business: price and arrangements.'

'What about the other profiles and telephone numbers on the page?' Dark asked.

'They're all dummies,' Mick said. 'Clients will get an automatic pingback message to say they are not available this week and offer Cassie as an alternative.'

'What about the location?' Alison asked.

Pemberton pressed a button, and the plan of a three-storey hotel filled the screen. 'I've spoken to the night manager at The Lemon Tree,' he said. 'He's an ex-cop, used to work in the Met. He'll be discreet.' He pointed to the second floor of the plan. 'You'll have use of room 221. It's at the end of the corridor, furthest away from the lift.' He pointed at a door next to the room. 'You'll arrive in a hire car and park in the staff car park at the rear. Then access the building via the staff entrance at the back and use the staff stairs to reach your room. Once you are in costume and become Cassie, you can use the lift and go down to the lobby, the bar, the entrance. At the end of the evening, you'll go back upstairs, shower, change and leave by the staff stairs, once again.'

'So, all meetings are to be held at The Lemon Tree,' Helen checked. She knew the hotel, on the Hellidon Industrial Estate, close to the motorway. It was one Clare had mentioned using. She wondered how many other escorts used it for their work.

'Yes. You tell the clients you book the rooms and they come to you. Spencer, Dark and I will have a plain clothes officer from CST with us. We'll spread out, cover front and rear. You only meet clients outside, where we can see you. What we're really after are the no-shows – where our killer arranges a meet, then watches his target and follows them. There'll be another hire car at the front of the building for you to use after a no-show. You will then take a drive, doing this route.' He clicked a button, and a map of the industrial estate filled the screen, a circular route around the estate highlighted in yellow. 'We'll be on your tail.'

Helen nodded.

'If anyone approaches you that doesn't fit the killer's photo e-fit, you say you've just had an emergency call from family and can't go ahead. Then tell them to contact you to rearrange. That's your exit strategy.' He passed her an A4 envelope. 'All the details, Cassie's history or *legend*,' he smirked at the word, 'are in there.'

'Okay, so how are we going to run this?' Alison said.

'The website is called Adults For You,' Mick said. 'Amazingly, that domain name was still available. It will go live this evening. I'll test it to make sure it's working. Then we wait for messages.'

'From tomorrow evening, we'll have make-up, the room, and support teams on standby,' Pemberton said.

'How confident are you that we're going to attract clients?' Spencer said to Mick. 'There must be hundreds of sites like this out there.'

'As confident as I can be. We know the killer is local or has local knowledge. This is a site aimed at people from Hampton. It'll take a while for the search engines to recognise it, so I'll be pushing the advertising to draw in traffic.'

'Will Sheridan has also agreed to put the profile on Adult Services too,' Pemberton said. 'The more we can get you out there, the more you are likely to get noticed. He'll also put a link on his site advertising us.'

Spencer baulked. 'He agreed to that?'

Pemberton snorted. 'With a bit of gentle persuasion. He needs the killer out of the picture as much as we do.'

'Okay,' Alison said. 'Let's call it a day. Get a good night's sleep, everyone. We'll be up and running tomorrow.'

CHAPTER 55

The house was unusually quiet when Helen arrived home that evening. She wandered through to the kitchen to find her mother sitting at the table, flicking through a magazine.

'Hey,' Helen said. 'Where is everyone?'

Jane Lavery looked up, her face stern. 'Matthew's at Air Cadets. Robert's got cricket practice – I'm picking him up in half an hour.'

'They don't usually practise on a Monday.'

'He's having an extra lesson. To work on his bowling.'

'Right.'

'Why don't you sit down?' Her mother pointed to the chair opposite. 'We need to talk.'

'If it's about Davy Boyd—'

'Please, darling. Just sit down.'

Helen narrowed her eyes. It wasn't like her mother to be so demanding. 'What is it?'

'I need to tell you something. And I need you to listen to it all and think carefully before you respond.'

'You're scaring me now, Mum.'

'I went to see Davy Boyd this afternoon.'

'You did what?'

Jane arched her forehead. 'I haven't finished.' She licked her lips, rubbed them together as if she was searching for the right words. 'I needed to do something. I was going insane. So, I decided to call round. Speak with him. Confront the issue.'

Helen was astounded. 'Do you realise how dangerous that could have been? With the Franks' history and Chilli's upcoming court case.'

'I went to his house. His wife was there. There was nothing to worry about.'

Helen's pulse quickened. 'And?'

'He didn't know about your father and Chilli.'

Helen recalled Davy's beady eyes surveying her the other Friday evening. 'I don't believe you.'

'He was in Spain when Chilli was arrested.'

'He knows who I am.'

'Davy knows you were the officer in charge of the case that put his half-brother away, yes. He didn't know the link with Robert. He wasn't aware of Robert's surname. But, here's the thing. As far as he's concerned, Chilli is getting his just deserts. Apparently, he's always been a handful, even when they were growing up. "Should have happened years ago", that's what he said.'

Helen thought about him realising Chilli's assets. *What sort of assets?* she wondered. 'So, what is he doing back here then?'

'He has shares in some of his half-brother's businesses. He wants to see what is worth saving. He's been wanting to bring his family back here for a while. He wants his kids to do their GCSEs, A levels, maybe even go to university here. But he didn't want to bring them back while Chilli was running his operation because he didn't want to get involved with his half-brother. Now seemed a good opportunity.'

'Sounds like you played happy families.'

'I wouldn't exactly say that. I did have a cup of tea with them both. His wife is really nice. You'd like her.'

Helen cursed.

'Look, they both agreed we should keep the boys out of it. Zac has a sister, two years younger. She's struggling to settle and make friends. They were both relieved at how easily Zac made the transition; they don't want to do anything to rock the boat.'

Helen felt her shoulders ease. 'That sounds reasonable.'

'I know. I think it's the best outcome we could have hoped for. They really do seem like a nice family. Not at all what I expected.'

'How much do they know about what went on between Chilli and me?'

Her mother's gaze softened. Suddenly, they were back in the hospital room. Her mother anxiously scrutinising her daughter's bruised face. 'They know you were the officer in charge of the case. They don't know about the injuries you sustained. I can't imagine they'd approve of what went on.' She reached out, touched Helen's hand. 'Let's put this behind us now, eh? For a while anyway. At least we don't have to walk around on tenterhooks, worrying about Robert.' She grabbed the edge of the table and pushed back her chair. 'Talking of whom, I'd better go and collect him. Are you coming?'

'No. I think I'll wait here, get something to eat.'

Jane rested a hand on her daughter's shoulder then headed out, leaving Helen sitting at the table.

She should be relieved. Chilli's half-brother's intentions, if they were to be believed, were honourable. Her family weren't in danger. But there was something else bothering her, something that sent her insides reeling.

Whichever way she looked at it, Robert, her son, was associating with the family of a known criminal. And not just any criminal, her worst nemesis.

She placed her head in her hands. Before her mother's visit to Chilli's half-brother, she could have shrugged it off as a fleeting acquaintance. A short passing friendship between the two boys. Lots of cops had children who attended schools with kids from criminal families – hers wouldn't be the first. By introducing herself to Zac's parents and declaring her knowledge of their family links, her mother had acknowledged

259

a relationship. Which meant Helen couldn't leave it. She had a professional obligation to report her son's association, however tenuous or mild it seemed. She could only imagine what her superiors would make of that, especially with intelligence indicating Kerry O'Hennessey had a past link with Chilli... The question was, when?

CHAPTER 56

The following evening, Helen approached the lift and pressed the down button, flinching as the microphone wire attached to her bra strap scratched at her skin. She checked her reflection in the mirrored doors. A black fitted shirt, short leather skirt that shone in the bright hotel lighting, heels. Make-up and hair like an eighties popstar. It was like preparing for a part in a movie.

A voice in her ear. 'Ready for a soundcheck?'

'Sure.' Helen checked over her shoulder to ensure the corridor was empty before she spoke in a low tone. 'Testing. Testing.' A crackle. She pressed her earpiece.

'Are you now?' Pemberton's voice.

'Okay, sergeant. That'll do.'

He laughed. 'Hearing you loud and clear.'

The lift pinged to signal its arrival. Helen took one last look at her reflection in the doors before they opened. It was so much work. The make-up, the hotel room, the cost of overtime, backup on standby. She only hoped it was all worth it. She stepped inside and became Cassie.

* * *

It was a grey evening, the iron-grey sky heralding an early dusk. Helen shifted on the bar stool, swirled the water in her

261

glass and glanced around. A man in a suit sat in the corner staring at the screen of a laptop, top button undone, tie loosened, a glass of whisky beside him. A couple of women were settled in the window, consumed in their own company, their table littered with empty wine glasses and crisp packets. The barman was restocking the spirits, lifting bottles and slotting them into place, humming to an old Take That tune playing in the background.

Her mind drifted to the office. It had been another frustrating day. They'd traced almost fifty silver Astras so far with no luck, and she'd spent almost an hour on the phone with the victims' families, grief-stricken and despondent over an investigation that was leading nowhere.

She swivelled on her stool. As Cassie, she needed to settle into her environment. Take a drink in the bar before she went out to meet her clients, so as not to arouse suspicion. Jenna had toned down her make-up to help her fade into the background but, sitting here, all dressed up on a Tuesday night, she couldn't help feeling out of place. Had Shauna and Louise and Eve sat in bars, waiting for their clients to arrive? She recalled Clare saying different clients had different requirements. Sometimes, they met in the room. Other clients asked them to meet outside in the cold. Like the killer…

She checked her watch. It was two minutes to eight. She finished her drink and moved outside. Two men stood near the entrance vaping as she exited. Both in casual shirts and chinos. One wore a golf jumper over his shoulder and nodded to her. Helen snapped her gaze away. Golf Jumper whispered in his friend's ear. He must have said something funny because the other man laughed as they stood there and vaped. Helen stepped away from them to beside the bushes at the corner of the building.

The clock clicked to eight. Then five past. Helen felt a buzz of excitement. Was she facing her first no-show? She was beginning to think so, when a man emerged from a car out front and stopped near the door, glancing around, before striding over to her.

He was fair, middle-aged. And he spoke with a strong Liverpudlian twang. 'Cassie?'

This wasn't their man. The likelihood of reeling in the killer on their first catch was remote but, still, she felt a twinge of disappointment. Helen turned to face him, neither confirming nor denying his statement.

'I take it the room's booked?' He checked his watch. No warmth, and enough arrogance to fill a football stadium.

She rolled out the family emergency story. Clutching her phone, lifting it as if she'd only just heard.

'I'm not here to play games,' he said. Fiery eyes glued to her. She could smell nicotine on his breath.

'Neither am I,' she said. 'Let me know if you want to rearrange.'

He didn't move, nostrils flaring. Clearly angry at having made a wasted journey.

'Everything okay?' It was Golf Jumper, calling over from the other side of the entrance.

Helen looked at Golf Jumper and then back at the man.

'Right.' He held up a hand, stepped back. 'I guess that's it then.' And with that, he stalked off.

Helen moved to the side of the hotel and let out a breath.

'It's a no-go,' she said into her microphone. 'Stand down, everyone.' She moved back into the bar and waited for client number two.

CHAPTER 57

By the time Helen arrived home, the house was shrouded in darkness. It was almost 11 pm and her family were already tucked up in their beds. She let herself in quietly, made her way through to the kitchen and closed the door.

A no-show for her 9 pm appointment had initially created a flurry of excitement. This was part of the killer's MO, to hang back at some meetings, stalk his targets. Pemberton, Dark and Spencer were watching like hawks from their positions close by. But when they saw nothing, and Helen drove around the industrial estate alone, disappointment rained down. Clare talked about no-shows being part of the job. It appeared they were experiencing a tiny insight into the world she faced regularly.

She opened the fridge, rubbing her lips together at the half-full bottle of Chablis in the door. She poured herself a glass and took a mouthful. The wine was sharp and tart on her tongue.

Scents of honeysuckle and phlox rushed to meet her as she unlocked the back door and stepped out into the garden. It was still mild, the air warm and balmy.

Helen wandered down to the patio, pulled out a chair and lowered herself into it, then dragged another across with her foot and rested her feet on it. Sinking back, staring up at the dark sky. The stars like tiny eyes, looking down. The plump full moon. The same moon she'd stared at the other night when she'd visited the scene of Eve Porter's murder.

This case was testing her like no other. Most people were killed by somebody close to them, somebody they knew. This was someone who sought out his victims, seemingly a stranger to them beforehand. Yet he got to know them, rooted out their secret and punished them for it. Then revealed them to the world. Why?

Helen finished the last of the wine and placed her glass on the table beside her. Her limbs tired and weary, she sunk down further in the chair, eyelids growing heavy. A long breath. She allowed her eyes to close, enjoying the comforting heat as the lids touched. Just a few more minutes, then she'd go inside, get a shower. A rustle in the bushes nearby. Helen stirred. All was quiet. She settled again, just drifting off when a voice made her jump.

'Mum?'

Helen jolted forward. It was Robert. He was walking down the garden wearing just a T-shirt and his boxers, his feet bare.

'Oh, sorry, love,' she said. 'Did I wake you?'

'I was already awake. What are you doing out here?'

'Just taking a few minutes. Enjoying the peace.' She patted the chair beside her. 'Come and sit with me.'

He moved closer, slid into the chair beside her. And jumped. 'Mum?' His face contorted. 'What's that on your face?'

Shit. She'd changed, brushed out and tied back her hair, but it was late when she left the hotel. She was bone-tired from the long day and hadn't yet cleaned her face. Poor kid. He'd only ever seen her with a touch of mascara, a brush of blusher, and that was when she could be bothered to dress up. Nothing like this.

'Oh,' she said, waving her arm in the air as if it was

nothing. 'Spencer's daughter's training to be a make-up artist. She wanted someone to practise on.'

His face twisted disapprovingly.

'Anyway, how was your day?' she said, desperate to move the conversation on.

'Okay. The cricket club are offering extra batting sessions. They're bringing in Pete Osborne from the county team to give us some tips.'

Helen knew little about cricket, but enough to know that Pete Osborne, Hamptonshire born and bred, was a local hero. 'That's great news,' she said.

He bit his lip. 'It's sixty pounds for six sessions. Gran said I need to ask you.'

'Do you think it'll help?'

His eyes lit. 'Oh, it really would, Mum. Mr Hall said I need to improve my grip and stance. And Zac's doing it. His dad's already paid.'

Zac. Helen's chest tightened, any thoughts of their friendship petering out fading. She fought to keep her voice light. 'I didn't think Zac played much.'

'He didn't before he came here. He's really getting into it now though. He's got a pretty good eye.'

Helen surveyed her youngest son. His soft brown curls, his skinny frame. The mole beside his right eye that scrunched when he laughed. At fourteen, he was entering the awkward transition between boyhood and young man. The year before he started secondary school, he'd started gently shrugging off her hugs when they were out together. When she dropped him off at school or at a friend's house these days, she resisted the temptation to kiss his cheek, however much she wanted to. But there were still occasional moments when he cuddled up beside her on the sofa and she relished those.

'I think we should give it a go then,' she said.

He leapt out of his chair. His embrace was so tight it

squeezed the air out of her. 'Thanks, Mum. I can't wait to tell Zac!'

She watched him head back up the garden and into the house.

Zac. That was one situation she was going to have to deal with, one way or another. She just needed to get to the bottom of this investigation first.

CHAPTER 58

'How are things on Op Cassie?' Alison asked.

'Okay,' Helen said. Although it wasn't okay. It was Thursday morning, and they were standing in Alison's office. They'd run the operation for two nights and they were still no closer to catching their killer than they were on the night of Shauna's murder.

'Nothing new then. I take it last night was another false alarm?'

Helen exhaled heavily with a nod. Yesterday evening, she'd met two more clients, neither of whom fitted the killer's profile. The team had become excited at her third when it was a no-show, but she'd driven the route around the industrial estate and once again hadn't been followed.

'Then I think we should consider wrapping this one up.'

Helen felt her frustration. She'd actually only met three clients in total now, out of five calls, and none of them remotely matched the killer's description. She was already sick of sitting still for an hour while Jenna pranced about doing her face, her hair. Bone-tired of having to go through the motions clearing up afterwards, keeping it secret from her wider team who walked in and out of the office each day, putting in the hours, desperately trying to work the case organically. But they had to do something and to axe the operation at this early stage seemed crazy. 'He's killed three women, close together,' she said. 'He's got to surface soon.'

'Doesn't guarantee he'll get in contact with our profile,' Alison said. 'We've had four days now with no new cases.'

'Because the women aren't working. They're scared, staying away.'

'Maybe. Or perhaps there's another reason. But the cost of surveillance is soaring through the roof. I can't sanction this operation continuing indefinitely. The chief's already expressing concern over results. I haven't told him we're using our own acting super as the decoy.' She raised her eyes skyward. 'Goodness knows what he'd make of that!'

'We must be getting close.' Helen could hear the desperation in her voice. Who was she trying to kid? The killer could always use a different site, source different girls. The women wouldn't stay away forever.

'I can give you another twenty-four hours,' Alison said. 'That's it. If there are no leads by then, we close down the website and Operation Cassie is mothballed.'

* * *

Helen's phone rang the minute she was out of the ACC's office. It was Pemberton.

'I think we might have our killer on camera.'

'What?' A phone rang in the distance. She pressed her hand to her free ear to cut out the noise.

'One of the terraced houses opposite the apartments where Eve Porter left her car... The woman's been away a couple of days, visiting a sick relative. She got back this morning and heard the news. She's just emailed the footage through.'

A rush of adrenalin. This was the first piece of good news they'd had in days. 'Brilliant. Call an impromptu briefing in ten minutes. We all need to see this.'

CHAPTER 59

Pemberton met Helen at the incident room door. 'The woman had a few problems with an ex-partner,' he said, walking her inside to where detectives and support staff were huddled together, eyes glued to the screen at the front of the room. 'She had a camera installed as security in case he continued to bother her. It was tucked down beside the alarm box, hidden from the road.'

Helen felt a frisson of excitement as she paused at the side of the room. The killer staked out his locations carefully. A hidden camera was something he wouldn't have bargained on.

Pemberton crossed to his desk and clicked his keyboard.

A road at night appeared. Eve Porter's friend's apartment block opposite. Eve's black Renault, lit in a puddle of light from the nearby streetlamp. The railings of Oakwall Park to the side. The time in the corner of the screen read 10.02 pm. A black cat darted across the road. Several seconds passed. A woman stepped out of the apartments. Helen squinted: Eve. She was wearing a blue tea dress cut to her knees. No jacket. Sandals on her feet. A small dog to her side. She checked her watch and hurried towards the car, stopping as she reached it to rummage around in her pocket.

A figure appeared at the side of the screen. Tall. Broad. Dark. Wearing an overcoat with the collar turned up. Helen peered closer. He walked fast. A wide gait. As if he was short of time. The dog must have made a sound, alerted her to the man's presence, because Eve suddenly looked up. She pressed a hand to her chest as if he'd startled her. Then tilted her head and touched his forearm. A tender, familiar gesture in the manner of a close acquaintance. Helen watched carefully. They spoke for several seconds before he pointed back at the park. Eve checked her watch again and looked at the car. She seemed unsure. Another exchange. He must have said something funny because her shoulders shook as she laughed. Then she nodded. One last cursory glance at the car, and then she followed him towards the park, the dog trailing behind. A beat passed. They disappeared from view.

He knew her. He'd met her before.

The room quietened, a dozen minds ruminating.

'Play it again, will you?'

Helen followed the voice to Graham, their analyst, at the back of the room. 'What is it?' she asked.

His face was scrunched tight. 'I'm not sure.'

Pemberton pressed the button, and the same image graced the screen. They all watched the black cat again, the woman approach.

When the figure joined them, Graham gasped. 'Can you play that part again in slow motion?' he asked.

Helen nodded at Pemberton. He wound it back, slowed it down.

Graham watched intently, his face rigid. 'I think I know who that is.'

The room's eyes turned to the analyst.

'What do you mean?' Helen said.

'Before I came here, one of the last cases I worked on in Cambridgeshire was of a woman beaten half to death at the side of the road by what appeared to be a stranger passing by. There were numerous witnesses. Camera footage of him walking down the street towards her. I was working on the analytics. It took us a few days to catch him. Anyway, he had this…' He wrinkled his nose as if he was searching for the right words. 'Unique walk. Every now and then, he did a funny step, a bit like half a goose-step. It was one of the things they caught him on, a distinguishing feature. The detective on the case nicknamed him Goose.'

'Nice,' Pemberton said.

Graham snorted. 'Apparently, he'd broken one of the bones in his leg as a kid. The odd step isn't always obvious. Only when he's in a hurry.'

'When was this?' Helen cut in.

'About six years ago. He was charged with GBH. Last I heard, he was locked up.'

Six years was a long time. If he'd behaved himself, he could be out now. 'Do you know his name, or the details of the case?' Helen asked.

'Steven something…' Graham looked away, eyes darting from side to side. 'I can make some calls, get the information. I've still got mates on the team.'

'Please do,' Helen said. 'Use my office. We need to trace this person as a matter of urgency.'

* * *

Half an hour later, they reconvened. Graham was now at the front of the room, a notepad in his hand. 'Steven William Kidson,' he said. 'He was charged with grievous bodily harm.'

'Hold on,' Helen said. 'The woman he attacked, was she a sex worker?'

'Not as far as I'm aware.' He pressed a button on his laptop and a woman's face graced the screen. Her lip was split, a half-moon cut into her chin. A bruise covered her forehead and a swelling the size of a golf ball filled her cheek. What struck Helen, what tugged the air from her lungs, were the features behind the injuries. She was much older, but still small, petite. Long dark hair. Just like their victims…

'He was remorseful afterwards,' Graham said. 'Admitted

272

the crime, pleaded guilty. He said he didn't know the victim. When the detectives asked him why he'd attacked her, he told them it was a mistake. He thought she was his mother.' Graham shook his head. 'He had a rough upbringing, by all accounts. Mother was a heroin addict. Father an alcoholic. By the time he was eight, his mother had abandoned them and was living in a squat in the town centre, selling herself for the next fix. Apparently, his father used to beat him. It wasn't until he broke the kid's leg that he was taken into care. That's where the goose-step comes from.'

The wind whistled down the side of the building.

'What sentence did he get?' Pemberton asked.

'That's the thing. My mate, Rinkers, was the officer in the case. Kidson had a list of previous offences as long as your arm. Shoplifting, burglary, ABH. He'd already served two years for beating some guy to a pulp outside a nightclub. The judge sentenced him to six years for this crime. He was a model prisoner, served four. Took anger management courses in prison, came out a reformed character eighteen months ago, on licence. Then went AWOL. His probation officer only met him once before he disappeared.'

'Have you got a photo?' Helen asked.

'Only the mugshot taken when he was arrested.' He crossed to his laptop, pressed a button. A photo of a man graced the screen. Short dark hair. Steely black eyes. A dusting of stubble across his pasty white skin.

'Oh, shit!' Spencer dragged a hand down the front of his face. 'If I'm not mistaken, that's Bradley Jones.'

'What?' Helen felt as though she'd been plunged into an ice pool. 'We are talking about *the* Bradley Jones? Kerry O'Hennessey's ex-partner?'

'It looks the spit of him.'

'I thought Bradley had an alibi?'

Spencer reached for his pocketbook. The room hushed as he flicked through the pages. 'Yes, here it is. He was in The

Red Lion the night Shauna was killed. I checked with the landlord and one of the bar staff.'

'Check again,' Helen said. 'I want confirmation he was in there all night.'

The room cascaded into a cacophony of babble as Spencer moved off to use the phone, everyone discussing what this meant. Was Kerry still involved? Were they working on the murders together? If so, what was their motive?

Pemberton moved to Helen's side. She thanked Graham and met the sergeant's gaze. 'So, Steven Kidson moved across here and changed his name for a new start,' she said.

Pemberton nodded. 'Sounds about right. That would explain why our systems didn't throw up anything when we did the checks on him.'

Helen stood quietly a moment, anchoring her thoughts. It would also explain why the scenes were so sanitised. Kidson's DNA and fingerprints would be on record. No wonder he went to great lengths to clean up.

The door to her office flapped open. All eyes turned to Spencer. He looked ghostly pale.

'I don't believe this,' he said, shaking his head. 'The landlord at The Red Lion served him at seven. He said Bradley was always in there, a regular on a Friday. They had a stag party in on the night of Shauna's murder. The bar woman I spoke to originally, who confirmed he was there all evening, now can't be sure of the times... She was certain she served him at midnight, just before they closed. But she can't be positive she saw him in between.'

'Which means he could have snuck out and returned later,' Pemberton said.

Spencer closed his eyes, gave a nod.

'Bloody unreliable witnesses.' Dark swore under her breath. 'It's not your fault, Steve.'

'Does Bradley Jones own a car?' Helen asked.

Blank faces stared back at her.

'Right.' Helen placed her hands on her hips. 'He should be

at work now. I want a team out to his work. Another, out to his home. We'll get a fresh warrant to search his house. He thinks we've searched it once for Kerry. He might have relaxed and stored stuff there now. We've appealed for witnesses of the car – if it's his, I doubt he'll have parked it near his home. The houses on Beaumont Street don't have garages. Let's check with the council to see if he rents a garage nearby.'

CHAPTER 60

Beaumont Street was busy when they arrived. By the time they'd secured the warrant, it was late afternoon, rush hour just starting to kick in. Pedestrians and motorists taking a shortcut through the backstreets to avoid the town centre. Splinters of wood and chipped paint marked the front door of number 46, a legacy of them breaking down the door a week before. Helen didn't bother to knock. She nodded to the officer with the battering ram. Five seconds, two rams, and they were in.

She stood back, waiting for the team of officers to scurry through the house. Within minutes, the officer with the battering ram was out, shaking his head. 'It's empty.'

'Okay, do a thorough search,' Helen said. 'Floorboards, drainage pipes. This time, I want everything examined. He's got to have disposed of those women's clothes somewhere.'

As he disappeared, the door to the next house opened. An elderly woman poked out her head, alarmed.

Helen lifted her warrant card, about to speak, when Spencer cut in. 'Hello again,' he said, holding up his ID. 'You remember me from the Monday before last. We just wanted to have another word with your neighbour.'

'Brad?' She looked blankly from one detective to another. 'Such a sweet lad. A proper charmer. Always helping me out with jobs around the house.'

'Do you know where he is?' Helen asked.

'He's gone. I had to put my own bins out this week.'

'What do you mean gone?'

'He left on Sunday evening. Didn't say where he was going. I haven't seen or heard from him since.'

They were interrupted by the trill of Helen's mobile. 'Excuse me,' she said to the woman and raised it to her ear.

Pemberton didn't bother with preamble. 'He's not at work. Hasn't turned up this week at all. No phone calls, nothing. His boss is quite pissed off. They had a big job on.'

Helen ended the call and turned to the neighbour. 'Do you know if Mr Jones has a car?' she asked.

'No idea. If he does, he doesn't keep it here. You can never park down this road. It's probably in his garage.'

'His garage?'

'Yeah, he rents one around the corner, at the back of Richardson Street,' she said. 'The one at the far end.'

* * *

The garages behind Richardson Street were a bank of eight with scuffed navy up-and-over doors. Various bright graffitied pictures were painted on the concrete edges. Helen stood back, watching an officer pick the lock when she heard the screech of brakes. She turned to find Pemberton arrive, another unmarked car behind him. He unfurled himself from the car just as the officer flung open the door. Helen's heart sank. It was empty. No Bradley, no car.

'Where the hell is he?' Pemberton said.

'I don't know but I want a full CSI team down here. Let's see if we can find anything linking him to our victims.'

* * *

A sober mood filled the car as they made their way back to the station. They had a suspect with a clear motive. Someone with form for violence. They knew his name, the list of his previous convictions, his vital statistics. The only thing they didn't know was the most crucial piece of information: his location.

Hampton rush hour was in full flow now.

'It's almost 5.30 pm,' Pemberton said, braking for yet another red traffic light. 'Are you sure you still want to do the operation tonight?'

It hardly seemed worth it. But then… There was always the possibility they could lure him in. And if the ACC had anything to do with it, they weren't going to get many more chances.

'Might as well,' she said. 'It's not like I've got anything better on.'

Pemberton laughed, then flicked down the indicator. 'I think we'd better head straight there then. Give you time to get ready.'

'Okay, I'll order pizza.'

He glanced at her askance.

'What?' she said. 'We've got to eat. Might as well make the most of the expenses.'

CHAPTER 61

Helen looked out across the car park and shivered. After the warm temperatures of the last few days, the air was icy cool tonight. More like November than June.

Spaced lights lit lines of cars in little pools of light. It was quiet. No one had passed through the entrance in the last ten minutes. No one had accessed the car park. Quiet but charged. After their failed operation this afternoon, Helen could sense the restlessness of her team out there. Watching. Waiting. The rapid beat of their hearts.

She checked her watch. 10.15 pm. Disappointment gripped her. Just typical that the final appointment of the evening was a natural no-show, with no target to follow.

'Might as well call it a night,' she said into the mic at her lapel.

'You don't want to do a drive around?' It was Pemberton.

Helen surveyed the car park. They were going through the motions. They had a suspect. Every officer on duty was searching, every police car on hyper alert. Perhaps the appeals had spooked him, sent him underground. Or maybe he'd seen her profile and she just wasn't his type. Either way, this was pointless. 'I don't think it's worth it. I think we'll wrap things up.'

'Okay.'

She was turning on her heel, ready to go back inside, when she noticed a movement. It was beneath the line of sycamore trees that separated the car park from the road. Helen froze. Nothing. The inquisitive cop inside her pushed her to explore. 'Wait up,' she said to Pemberton.

'You got a live one?'

'I'm not sure. Keep your position for now.' She weaved through the cars, her breath loud in her ears. 'Who's there?' she called out. All was silent. But she knew what she'd seen.

Someone was out there.

She was two cars away from the trees now. Another flash of movement. A definite figure caught in the traces of light.

'Hey!' she said. 'Police!' She was blowing her cover. Though the operation was over anyway. What did it matter? What was important now was that someone was trying to hide.

She could see the figure through the windows of a parked Audi. Veiled in the shadows, she couldn't see them enough to identify whether they were male or female. 'Stop, police!' she said. Loudly this time, and into her microphone. She rushed forward.

It was enough to spook the figure. They jumped up, ran.

Helen gave chase. Gnarled tree branches catching at her, snagging her bare arms as she raced along the edge of the trees. They were dressed in black. Shoulders hunched as they ran.

She sped up, her chest burning as she followed. *Come on!* She dug deep. Shutting out the commotion in the background. Sirens, car engines, the screeches of brakes. She couldn't afford to take her eyes off her target. She followed them into the next car park. And the next.

You only run if you have something to hide.

And then there it was, her saviour. The high fence, running the perimeter of the industrial estate. The figure turned, alarmed. And she was on them. Grabbing their jacket. Her stockings ripped as she tussled them to the ground. She felt a steely hand push her aside. They tried to haul themselves up.

Lashed out. Wriggled and writhed against her hold. But she wasn't about to let them go now.

A car engine. The slam of doors. Bodies surrounded her. Restraining the target. Pushing them back down on the floor.

'You okay?' Pemberton said to Helen, breathless. He helped her up out of the mud.

Helen nodded. She looked up as they lifted the target from the ground. And gasped.

It was Guy Thorne.

'What the hell?'

Pemberton grabbed the shoulder of his jacket. Spencer fastened the cuffs behind his back. Helen returned the bewildered look Pemberton gave her. They'd discounted Guy as a suspect. Even if his friends were covering for him on the nights of Louise's and Eve's murders, hotel cameras placed him in Oxford when Shauna was killed. It didn't make sense. 'I think you'd better start telling us what's going on,' Pemberton said to him, his face like thunder.

'Is there anyone else here with you?' Helen asked Guy. The only way she could fathom it was that he wasn't working alone.

'No, just me.' Mud smeared his face and caked his hair. 'But it isn't what it seems.'

'Yeah, right,' Pemberton said.

The van's brakes screeched across the tarmac as it joined them. More officers piled out, running towards them. Pemberton read Guy his rights.

'No, no,' Guy said. 'You don't understand.'

'You'll have plenty of time to explain back at the station,' Pemberton said. And with that, he pushed him into the prisoner cage at the back of the van and slammed the door.

'Take him to the custody suite at Cross Keys,' Helen said. 'I'll get changed and join you.' She brushed a smudge of mud from her knee, caught a graze and winced. 'Don't start questioning until I get there.'

The clouds had moved in, covering the moon and making for a gloomy night as Helen stepped back into the hotel. She was a sight. Her stockings were torn, her clothes muddy from the tussle with Thorne. Blood trickled down her arm from numerous scratches.

The night manager looked up from the front desk, face tightening in alarm as she entered the lobby. The jaw of the receptionist beside him dropped.

'Are you okay?' he said, rushing towards her.

'I'm fine,' Helen said in a low voice. 'Just need to get cleaned up.'

He paused a second as if he wasn't quite sure what to say. 'I take it the operation has been successful?'

'Possibly.' She gave a weak smile, motioned to the lift, and he moved aside for her to cross the lobby. Her mind reeled as she waited for the lift. The night manager had promised discretion; he'd think of something to say to his staff until she could update them all later. Right now, her mind was filled with the angular face of Guy Thorne.

The lift arrived. Flashbacks of their recent exchanges skipped into her mind as she stepped in. Outside the bed and breakfast. At the cricket ground with her family. Supposedly chance meetings. But were they, really? Though he'd been helpful, provided a list of group members for The Alternatives. Surely he wouldn't do that. Surely he wouldn't do anything to attract attention to himself, if he was involved in the murders? They'd found nothing in his background to arouse suspicion. And his ethos... He'd told them The Alternatives was more about networking, celebrating achievements, individualism. Exploring carnal desires... The profiler said the murderer wanted to be caught... Did he bear a grudge against sex workers?

Something about this felt too easy. But she couldn't deny he was out there. Watching. Waiting. And why run if he wasn't guilty?

The lift pinged at floor two. Helen moved into the corridor and retrieved her key from her pocket, her thoughts still spinning like a fairground ride as she placed the key in the lock of room 221 and clicked the door open.

Helen didn't hear the soft footfalls behind her. Didn't feel the presence nearby. She was so wrapped up in Thorne she didn't notice anyone approaching.

She felt a hard shove to the back of her head. Stumbled. Lost her balance. Fell forwards. Slap bang into the room.

CHAPTER 62

Back at Cross Keys Station, Pemberton was riled. Was it possible Guy Thorne could be involved in the murders in some way? A man he'd spoken with. A man they'd discounted.

He leaned up against the side of the police car and lit a cigarette, taking a long drag. As soon as the van arrived, he would escort Mr Thorne into custody himself. Make sure he was processed properly. Now that they had him in their sights, he wasn't about to let anything go wrong.

A bat swooped overhead. He watched it flit by, then nodded to a couple of officers who walked out and climbed into a car. He took another drag. Several seconds passed. Finally, the van entered the car park. He waited for the officers to climb out and unlock the cage at the back. Guy Thorne's face was deathly pale. He looked pitiful as he was led out: his denims and trainers slathered in mud, the elbow of his jacket ripped.

'Sergeant,' Thorne said as his feet touched the tarmac. 'I need to speak to you.'

'Not now,' Pemberton said. He'd been here before. Listened to offenders give a confession in the car park, where there were no recording devices, no statements, no official witnesses, then watched them deny everything inside. No. If Guy was to make a confession, it would be in an interview room, in a formal setting. Something that couldn't be questioned in court.

'No, you don't understand,' Thorne said. 'There was someone else. Someone else watching her.'

Pemberton stopped in his tracks. 'What?'

'I saw him in the car park. He's been there all evening. I thought he was watching the hotel at first, and then I realised it was her. Every time she stepped outside, he perked up.'

Pemberton stared at him a moment, his mind oscillating between suspicion and belief. 'What do you mean, him?'

'A man. Tall. Dark. Long coat, collar flipped up.'

Of course, he could be lying. Someone in his position would do anything to plant the blame elsewhere. But if he was right, if there was an ounce of truth in what he said, the boss could be in danger. 'Take him inside,' he said to the officer. He put out his cigarette, shoved the stub into his pocket and then called Helen. The phone rang out one, two, three, four times. By the time the voicemail cut in, Pemberton was starting to feel uneasy.

He selected another number. Spencer answered on the third ring. 'What is it, sarge?'

'Are you still at the hotel?'

'Yeah, I'm out front. We're just finishing up.'

'Can you check in with the boss? She's not answering her mobile.'

'Sure. Give me a couple of minutes to run upstairs.'

* * *

The lights in the hotel room flashed on. Helen blinked, momentarily dazed. She was lying on the floor, cheek pressed against the carpet. One foot bare. She was about to turn, to search for the shoe, when she heard a zip-like sound. Then pain. She squealed as it shot through her wrists. Someone had tied her hands behind her back. She recognised the feel of cable ties pinching her skin. Glimpsed her phone, scattered to her side. She must have dropped it when she fell.

'Up!' a gruff voice called behind her. Rough hands on her arms. She tried to wriggle, wrestle them off, but they were hefty, strong. She was dragged to standing, then pushed forward again. She crashed onto the bed. The hotel room slowly came into view as she turned herself over. A man stood over her. Dark hair greased back. Eyes like coal.

It was Bradley Jones.

'What are you doing?' she asked.

'I could say the same to you,' he said. 'I don't like people who play games.'

Neither did she, though if she'd learned anything from her years in the police, it was to keep a suspect calm. Keep them calm and play for time. The door to the room sat ajar. Sooner or later, someone would pass in the corridor outside.

'Why?' she said. 'Why are you doing this?'

He didn't answer. Instead, he bent down, switched off her mobile phone, slipped it in his pocket, then reached forward and grabbed her hair. Despite herself, Helen screamed in pain as he pulled her off the bed and towards the door. The other shoe toppled off.

'Where are we going?'

'There's something you need to see.'

As they passed the mirror, an idea snuck in. She stuck out an elbow. And with one sudden movement, slammed herself into it with all her might. A loud crack filled the room as it connected, splintering the glass.

'Idiot!' he said, tightening his grip. He pulled a knife from his pocket, pointed the tip at the side of her ribcage. 'One more word, one little scream, and you're finished.'

Helen swallowed.

He pulled the door further open, took a second to check the corridor, then led her out. Away from the lifts. Her stockinged feet scraping across the carpet.

'I don't understand. Where are we going?'

'We're using the staff entrance. That'll be no stranger to you, will it?'

Dread hitched Helen's breaths. He'd been watching her. Scrutinising the operation. A draft of cold air rushed out to meet them as they entered the back stairs. And, as usual, he was one step ahead.

* * *

Spencer exited the lifts and made his way to room 221. The boss probably hadn't answered the phone because she was in the shower. He was keen to get everything wrapped up here so they could get back to Cross Keys and watch Thorne squirm in his interview. There was nothing Spencer liked better than to watch an offender be confronted with their crimes, and these offences were particularly brutal.

He passed the lines of hardwood doors, checking the numbers – 219, 220 – surprised to find the door of 221 ajar. 'Ma'am?' he called out.

No answer.

He pushed the door open with his elbow, stepped inside. And froze. A shoe was discarded in the middle of the floor, another beside the dressing table. A plethora of cracks ran through the mirror.

He checked the bathroom, then raised his phone to his ear, fear clutching at his chest. He didn't like the look of this at all.

CHAPTER 63

Blood rushed through Helen's ears. She was in the boot of a car, coiled up like a snake. He'd guided her across the staff car park, through a gap in the bushes and into the next car park. And then the next. Her bare feet stinging as they navigated the asphalt. The knife pressed to her side. And then she had seen it – the silver Astra. Parked far enough away from the hotel to go unspotted.

The boot was small, the space narrowed by a hard box – a suitcase? – behind her. She tugged at the straps securing her hands, pushed her tongue against the cloth he'd pushed into her mouth before he'd closed the lid. *There's something you need to see.* Where the hell was he taking her?

The engine ignited. The car pulled off. Lumps and bumps in the road jolted every internal organ.

They were expecting her at the station. It would only be a matter of time before her presence was missed and they sent someone to the room to check on her. The mirror would alert them that something was wrong. Thank goodness she'd thought of doing that. But they wouldn't know where she was now…

Helen's stomach lurched. The hotel was surrounded by covert surveillance. How the hell had Bradley got into the hotel without being seen? But then she thought about the chase after Thorne, drawing in the officers watching. It would have created a diversion. Was Thorne involved? Was that his part in the plan?

Her thoughts raced into overdrive. She needed to do something… The back lights! The fittings there were weaker. If she was lucky, she could boot one out, attract attention. But she could barely move… She was inching around when the car suddenly sped up, tugging her back. A pain spiked her coccyx.

She rocked her body, banged her feet against the side of the boot instead, and screeched and hollered. Her efforts muffled by the gag in her mouth and the tight space restricting her movement.

Stop panicking. Stay calm. Track his movements.

She fought to quell the panic within, the primal urge to do something constructive concentrating her senses. A turn left. A busy road, the sound of other vehicles. The blast of a passing motorcycle. Another turn, right this time. He was heading through town.

The next bump in the road was so strong it winded her. She jerked her knees up to her chest, flinched as she caught her nose on the lock mechanism. Pain coursed through her. Blood trickled down her throat.

The car turned again. She'd lost orientation now.

Rivulets of sweat oozed down her back when another thought grabbed her. The microphone! It was still sitting just inside her lapel, switched off. Would they still hear her? Helen wasn't a techie; she had no idea of the range of these things, but she had to try. If only she could get her chin to it, to turn it back on. She curled her head, jutted her chin. It missed by millimetres. Another bump sent her reeling. Again, she tried. It was almost within touching. A sudden brake jolted her. The switch connected with her skin. Was it on? It was difficult to say. There was no noise. No feedback. Was that because they'd finished the operation, turned off the machines, and nobody was listening, or because she couldn't hear them?

'Sean?' Her voice was sharp, breathless. 'Anyone? If you're there, please answer... I'm in the boot of a car. Bradley Jones has abducted me. He's driving me out somewhere. He said there's something I need to see. He's armed with a knife.'

A sudden acceleration shunted her against the cold metal. The car rounded one corner, then another. Terror stretched to every sensory receptor. She was running out of ideas. 'Please, help. This is a 10/0.' The emergency call. If any cop picked up that signal, they'd know someone was in trouble.

The car slowed. Stopped. The engine cut.

The click of a lock. Pressure alleviated as someone climbed out. The tremors began in her fingers, her feet, gathering momentum, surging through her body.

The boot opened. A blinding light forced her eyes shut.

As she opened them slowly, the silhouette in front of her came into focus. Jet-black eyes, thickset jaw. Face taut with anger.

He stared down at her. 'Right, let's get this over with, shall we?'

* * *

Spencer and Pemberton raced through the narrow country lanes.

'Are you sure about this, sarge?' Spencer said.

'As sure as I can be.' Having raced back to the hotel and organised an urgent search, Pemberton was taking no chances. They needed to find the boss, and fast. 'He takes his victims to water. The river in Oakwall Park. Henderson Ley. The flow through Blackwell Wood. The profiler said he was building up to something big. And the most dramatic water source in Hampton is Jericho Falls. It's got to be worth a try.' Pemberton flattened the accelerator. 'Call for backup to meet us there urgently!'

CHAPTER 64

Helen's breaths hitched as she was pulled out of the boot. She cracked her knee on the bumper, cried out. Her screech disappeared into the darkness. An explosion of pain ran down her leg.

'Come on!' He picked up a holdall, hauled it over his shoulder. Shoved her forward. The knife was back at her side. She winced as it nicked the skin through her thin shirt.

The ground was cold and unforgiving. She jumped and hopped as stones in the mud picked at her feet.

It was disorientating in the dark. She stumbled along, glancing about, trying to work out where they were. A dirt track. Rural, desolate. Rolling countryside around them. No landmarks to hold on to. She couldn't have been in the car for more than twenty minutes. Which meant they weren't too far out of Hampton. *Think!*

The wind had picked up, whistling through the trees. It was so loud she could barely hear her own breaths.

A clod of earth came from nowhere. She toppled sideways. Snagged her heel on a bramble and cried out.

He yanked her back up.

They entered a copse of aged oaks. Where had she seen them before? More stumbles. More pain. Her feet were wet now. She could feel blood between her toes.

It was darker in amongst the trees. 'Where are we going?' she asked.

'You'll see.'

Fingers of moonlight reached in as the branches thinned. The wind grew stronger, the noise louder. It wasn't until they were out the other side, the gnarly branches behind them, that she realised... It wasn't the trees she could hear at all. It was the crashing sound of tumbling water.

* * *

Pemberton's brakes screeched on the asphalt. Jericho Falls's car park was empty, the main entrance closed off by a five-bar metal gate. Instinctively, he placed a hand in his pocket for his torch. Then changed his mind. No sense in drawing attention to themselves.

They climbed over the gate and jogged along the path, the sound of the waterfall building in their ears. Past the wooden café building, encased in darkness. Pausing briefly at the red-brick visitor's centre. The path divided there. One route went down to the base of the water. The other, up to the bridge over the top of the falls.

'Up.' He gestured for Spencer to follow him to the lookout point on the bridge. Water cascaded down in front of them as they jogged along the steep gravelled pathway. By the time they reached the bridge, their hearts pounded their chests, their breaths coming hard and fast.

It was empty.

The water crashed down, smothering every other surrounding sound. Pemberton's heart sank. He'd been so sure Bradley would take her to the falls. He couldn't think of another place like it in Hampton. How could he have been so wrong?

He peered over the railings of the bridge, towards the northern lookout, the quieter end, where people ventured for photographs, or to watch wildlife from the shelters. And then he saw it. A movement. He squinted, trying to discern the dark shapes in the distance. Yes, there were two people there.

'We've got it wrong,' he shouted to Spencer. 'Call backup, get them to redirect. They're at the other end!'

Pemberton sped up as he retraced his steps back to the car. He only hoped he wasn't too late.

CHAPTER 65

Helen could see the copse behind them. The trail to the lookout point. He'd parked on a dirt track at the northern end of the falls, avoiding the main entrance. He'd done the same at Blackwell Wood, parked away from the main entrance, on the night he'd killed Shauna...

He pushed her along to a wooden platform that ran over the river – the northern lookout point – then manoeuvred her into one of the wooden shelters used by wildlife enthusiasts and birdwatchers. It was quieter in there, the Perspex screen muffling the sounds of the water. A million thoughts rushed through Helen's head. She'd been here with her boys when they were little. Stood in this very shelter. Walked along the platform. Admired the vista. Gripped their little hands hard as she viewed the drop to the river below. But this was the first time she'd been here at night.

A series of falls rushed down the rocks in the distance. They looked majestic, glistening in the moonlight. Almost ethereal.

'Please, Bradley, let's talk. Just you and me. I can help.'

He shoved her towards the window. 'Down there.'

Helen turned on her heel. 'What?'

'Down there. That's where Kerry went when I found out what a dirty cow she was.'

Helen followed his eyeline and swallowed. It was a fifty-foot drop. The water swirled and gushed over boulders below. She wouldn't have stood a chance. 'Why?'

He coughed a laugh, his eyes glazing. 'She had no idea. She thought I was being romantic, bringing her out here in the dead of night.' His face hardened. 'Until I chucked her over.'

A shiver skittered down Helen's spine.

He swivelled her round to face him. The knife was at her neck now.

'I suppose you think you're funny, don't you? Taunting me. Dressing up like her.'

He edged forward.

'Kerry?' Helen said, stumbling backwards. She couldn't figure out what he meant. She certainly didn't look like Kerry.

'No, not Kerry.' He clenched his teeth. 'My mother.'

'I don't know what you mean.' But she did. She knew exactly what he meant. His mother was dark, petite, a sex worker. Just like his other victims…

'I think you do.'

He was so close now she could smell his oniony breath. She pressed her back against the Perspex, pulled on her training. *Keep the lines of communication open.* The only chance she had to stay alive was to keep him talking. 'I thought you loved Kerry,' she said.

'So did I.' His eyes were unnaturally wide and menacing. 'She deceived me. Oh, she was clever.' He nodded. 'She sucked me in, good and proper. I believed her tales about running off to London to get away from her family. Coming home to Hampton to rebuild her life years later. I thought we were the same, her and me. We'd both had a difficult life, a difficult childhood. But she wasn't like me at all.' He gnashed his teeth. 'She duped me!'

'How?'

He glared at Helen. 'She never told me she'd had a kid. A kid she gave away. Almost a year we were together, and she never mentioned him, not once. What kind of mother does that?'

Helen thought of Tom, dying in action. Of Marnie and Darren's grief-stricken faces.

'Then her niece comes back into her life.' His lip curled as he continued. 'Out of the blue. Her relationship had broken down. She was struggling. I could understand that. But when Kerry said Shauna was selling herself for cash… No, that was too far. Shauna had kids. It wasn't right.'

He paused to inhale a long, ragged breath. 'And then it all came out. That's where Kerry's child came from: a punter. That's why she couldn't keep him.' He shook his head, wild eyes staring at Helen. 'No shame. No responsibility. No consideration for the children they brought into this world. Just like my mother.'

So that was it. In his deranged mind, he was reliving his childhood. Killing these women so that their children didn't suffer like he did.

'It's strange, you know. When you start to look, you realise there are loads of women at it. Hiding behind a computer screen by day, selling their bodies by night while their kids sleep in their beds. The filthy bitches.'

He yanked Helen's arm. A bolt of pain shot through her shoulder as he shoved her out of the shelter, towards the waterfall. She was penned between the wooden structure and the railings. 'Turn around.'

Helen's heart was in her mouth. She glanced down at the knife. It was pointed at her stomach now. She shuffled round so that she was facing the falls. A tugging sensation at her wrists. She started to struggle.

'Stop!' he commanded. The tip of the knife nicked her back.

Helen froze. More tugging. A rip. What was he doing? She peered over the edge. It was a long way down.

Suddenly, her hands were free. She stumbled as he whizzed her back to face him, the knife back at her stomach, blade glinting in the moonlight. 'Don't do anything stupid,' he said.

She stared back at him, her mouth bone dry.

'Undress!' he said.

'No, you've got this wrong.' Her hands and feet were free. Her eyes darted from side to side. If only she could slip out, run… But he'd cornered her.

'I said undress!'

Her hands shot to the buttons on her shirt. Her chest quaking as she undid the top button, gently tucking the wire between the folds of material, out of sight.

He stepped back a couple of inches, shrugged off the holdall. It crashed to the floor, the canvas flap rolling back. Inside she could see cotton wool, make-up remover, a hairbrush. Helen gulped. He was planning to remove her make-up, style her hair. Just like he had done with his other victims. Before he carved into their chests…

In his warped mind, he was cleaning them up, sacrificing them. To whom? The devil?

A flash of movement in the copse. Helen jolted.

Bradley looked towards the trees then back at her. And laughed. 'No one knows we are here,' he said. 'No one's coming to save you.'

Her shirt was undone now, her bra exposed. The cold air seeped into her chest.

Keep him talking, play for time. 'I'm not a sex worker,' she said. 'I don't fit your criteria.'

'You've dressed like one.'

'For my job. I dressed like this to catch you. To help you.'

He threw his head back. The cackle that emitted was pure evil. 'Only I caught you first. Skirt,' he commanded.

Helen bent forward, made to unbuckle her belt, tugging at it as if she was struggling. Then she pulled it out of the stays in one quick movement and whipped it in his face.

He screamed, stepped back. A short movement, just enough for her to escape. And she ran. She ran towards the trees.

At that moment, the whole place lit like a circus ground.

Helen turned, just in time to see a host of officers run

towards Bradley. He lifted his hand to shield his face. Turned to run. But he was too late.

Helen didn't hear the officers shouting. The Taser warning smothered by the sounds of crashing water. All she saw was the silhouette of Bradley's body jolting under the current. Before he fell to the floor.

CHAPTER 66

Bradley Jones sat bolt upright, face like granite, contempt seeping from his pores. The light bulb whirred in the windowless room.

Two hours had passed. Two hours in which they'd both been assessed by a doctor. Helen's feet were dressed. She had a bruise on the bridge of her nose, cuts and grazes on her arms and legs.

The worst thing about it was that her abduction now made her a part of the case against Bradley, which meant she couldn't interview him. She could only watch in real time through the downstream monitor video link. She sat forward, arms resting on her thighs, wet hair clumped on her shoulders as she watched Bradley punch out the answers to Pemberton's questions.

'Tell us how you met Shauna,' Pemberton said.

Bradley sat tall. 'The first time I met her was at the petrol station on the night I killed her.'

Pemberton flipped over a photo: the still of the figure that met Shauna in Bushwell's Services. 'Are you saying that this was you?' he checked.

Bradley took a long breath. Eyes shining as if he was pleased with himself. 'That fooled you, didn't it? Me dressing up in Kerry's gear.' He let out a quick breath with a laugh. 'It was so easy to persuade Shauna to come out to the woods. I only had to introduce myself, tell her Kerry needed to meet her there urgently. She never said a word when I picked her up. It wasn't until we got there that she started to get rattled and ran.' He looked away at the whitewashed wall. 'I quite enjoyed the chase actually.'

Pemberton sat as still as a statue while Bradley talked about catching up with Shauna. Placing the wire around her neck. Tugging it tight.

'What about Louise Carnwell and Eve Porter?' Pemberton said quietly.

'As soon as Kerry told me about Shauna, I did some research online. That's when I realised how many women were out there, duping everyone. I couldn't bear it. They needed to be taught a lesson. The public needed to be alerted to what they were doing.'

When Pemberton asked how he met each of the women, Bradley offered a detailed account of how he'd found them online. Met them several times, built a 'relationship' with them. And he'd also followed them. When he contacted Louise at the last minute and offered her extra money for rural sex, she was only too happy to be picked up in town and taken out to Henderson Ley.

'Eve was the same,' he said. 'Her eyes were agog when I met her outside her friend's apartment and offered her double for impromptu sex in the park.' He sneered. 'She had no idea what was coming.'

Helen recalled Bradley's neighbour calling him charming. Saying how helpful he'd been, bringing in her wheelie bin, doing jobs in the house. He'd manipulated his victims just like he manipulated everyone, playing with them until they were putty in his hands.

The more Bradley talked, the more his chest puffed out. He was proud of himself. He'd refused the offer of a solicitor, was happy to be interviewed. He wanted to tell his story. His story – there was no one else involved. He wanted it on record. As far as he was concerned, he'd completed his mission. Raised awareness about the forgotten and neglected children of sex workers and made the world a better place.

'What about the women's clothes, their belongings?' Pemberton asked.

Bradley smiled. 'You'll find them soon enough.'

Spencer looked up from his notes. What did that mean? But Pemberton wasn't about to be rattled.

'Why these locations?' he said, moving on.

'Isn't it obvious?' Bradley's face stretched as if the detective had gone crazy. 'Water cleanses. And their souls needed to be washed inside out. Dirty cows.'

'And the carving on their chests?' The million-dollar question.

'Because they're evil.' His voice notched up a decibel. 'That's why I stripped them. They needed to be exposed. For the whole world to see them as they really were.'

Helen sat back in her chair in the dark side room, aghast. She should be elated. They'd caught the serial killer, stopped him in his tracks. But all she felt was numb. Because the children of his victims weren't forgotten and neglected. They weren't like him. They were loved, cherished. And the warped pride he took in his actions, in shattering the lives of so many, was monstrous.

Bradley was talking about Kerry now, how he'd thrown her over the bridge.

'Why didn't you kill her like the others?' Pemberton asked.

He snorted. 'I couldn't. Once I'd decided what needed to be done, what *I* had to do, I needed time. Killing Kerry like the others would have led you to me, attracting your attention too early. I'd never have got a chance to draw attention to what these other women were doing.'

The door juddered open behind her.

Dark's impish face appeared around the frame. 'How's it going?' she said in a low voice.

Helen placed her hands behind her head and stretched her

shoulders back, flinching as the jogging suit she'd borrowed from the custody suite caught on her grazes. 'He's coughed to everything,' she said. 'All four. We'll start the search for Kerry's body at first light.'

Dark closed her eyes and exhaled.

'How did you get on with Guy Thorne?' Helen asked, aware that the young detective was interviewing him in a separate room.

'He's pathetic,' she said. 'We couldn't find any connection between him and Bradley. He's just a sad old man who'd developed a macabre interest in the investigation and latched himself to you. Shame we can't charge him with wasting police time.'

Helen pressed her lips together. She pictured Guy at the guest house in his turquoise waistcoat. At the cricket ground with his dog. Tonight, at the hotel. He could have jeopardised their operation. Maybe he did inadvertently draw the killer's attention to it. Though if he hadn't been watching the police operation play out and alerted them to the killer's presence, would they have caught Bradley? Would her colleagues have noticed her disappearance and arrived in time to save her? It was difficult to say. She was sure of one thing though. Whilst shadowing detectives wasn't to be encouraged, the police relied heavily on witness statements. And charging a member of the public, however annoying they were, for what amounted to nosiness wasn't a line she wanted to take.

She rolled her shoulders. 'Give him a warning and take him home,' she said.

'Okay, that's enough.' Pemberton's voice snapped her back to the screen. He was terminating the interview. Bradley sneered as he hauled himself to his feet and Pemberton guided him towards the exit. They were almost at the door when Bradley paused and looked up at the camera. It was almost as if he knew she was there, watching him, and the icy glare he gave her sent a fresh shiver down her spine.

Dark shuddered. 'I'll be glad to see the back of him,' she said.

Minutes later, Pemberton joined them. 'He's back in his cell. We'll charge him in the morning when we get the nod from the CPS.' He looked across at Helen. 'Come on, I'll drop you home.'

'No need,' she said. 'I'm going back to headquarters. I'll get a lift with one of the others.'

'At this hour?' He made a play of checking his watch. It was almost 2 am.

'I want to take another shower, get into my own clothes.' She forced a smile. 'You go on home. I'll see you tomorrow.'

* * *

The gym at headquarters was eerily quiet in the middle of the night. Helen dried herself off and changed into the clean shirt and trousers she kept in her locker. Tomorrow, she'd collect her belongings from the hotel. Tonight, there was something else she needed to do.

Her footsteps echoed as she climbed the stairs. Back in her office, she stared out into the incident room and the line of lights illuminating a thin channel to her door.

Finally, she was alone. Alone with a mishmash of colliding thoughts.

The thrum of a car engine. The sound of her pulse thudding her eardrums as she was thrust around in the boot. The water crashing on the rocks at Jericho Falls. Bradley Jones's twisted face, the shrill sound of his laughter. The buzz of the Taser. Her desperate words into the microphone, only to later discover they'd fallen on deaf ears – she was out of range. She sunk into her chair, her vision blurring as the tears came with gusto.

She could have died… If her officers hadn't reached her in time, God knows what would have happened and where she'd be now. A tear trickled to her chin, her boys' faces filling her mind. So young. So much growing up yet to do. A wave of nausea. She bowed her head, waited for it to pass. Hardly daring to imagine what could have been.

Another wave of nausea, stronger this time. She wiped the tears from her cheeks, swallowed back the bile in her throat. Was her mother right? The finite details of Bradley Jones's capture wouldn't be recorded in the press. Her family wouldn't realise the danger she'd been in, wouldn't see the scratches and bruises beneath her clothes. But was her job placing her life, her children's future, in jeopardy? She'd taken every precaution, assessed the risks of the operation and yet still ended up in a life-threatening situation. Though the nature of police work was inherently dangerous, officers put their lives on the line every day, and at her end of the scale...

She dropped her head into her hands. It was the shock. It had to be. The shock working its way through the tears and sobs. She concentrated on her breathing. Long and deep. Long and deep. Time ticked past. Slowly, her mind settled enough to lift her head. She swivelled in her chair and looked out into the darkness. The case was over. There were no more distractions. Whatever she decided, whatever the future held, it was finally time to declare her son's association with the Boyds.

Helen opened her laptop and logged in. This was one form she wasn't looking forward to completing.

CHAPTER 67

The following day, Helen arrived at Alison's office to find the assistant chief constable's door open. Trepidation prickled the back of her neck. It had been an emotional morning, visiting each of the families. Watching yet more soggy tissues pressed to cheeks as she explained the arrest. Impotent as her words were inadequate, unable to alleviate their pain. All she could do was to impart the information as subtly as possible. Give her condolences and provide assurances about admissions and justice. It was heart-wrenching witnessing the carnage of three families, wrecked in the course of two short weeks. Trying to make plans for the future while the trauma of the past continued to torture them. Jasmine preparing to move her late sister's children in with her. Sam talking about moving away, starting a new life with his son beside the sea. Marnie and Darren – numbed in grief and the realisation that their lives would never be the same again. And the afternoon wasn't promising to be any lighter.

Alison was sitting behind her desk, sunshine seeping through the window behind her and casting a glow across the side of her face. She beckoned Helen in. 'I think congratulations are in order,' she said, lacing her hands together and resting them on the desk. She looked bright and fresh in full dress uniform. Keen eyes glinting, elated. 'The chief's thrilled.'

'Thank you.' Helen had watched the morning press

conference live with her team. The chief constable and the assistant chief constable, standing side by side on the podium, declaring the streets of Hampton safe once again. Thanking their officers for working around the clock, putting their own lives on hold in their quest to apprehend a dangerous killer. The police got enough bad press. It was good to see them deliver a positive message, and they certainly made the most of it.

Alison motioned for Helen to take one of the leather chairs surrounding the low table in the corner. No formality today then.

'Can I get you a tea or a coffee?' she asked.

'No, thank you,' Helen said, settling herself.

'Any more news?'

'CSIs are still working on Bradley's garage and his Astra. They've recovered the victims' clothes and bags – looks like he was keeping them in an old suitcase in his car.' Helen thought of the tiny boot space she had been thrust into last night. Little did she know at the time that the case behind her held the personal possessions of three dead women.

'Good. What about Kerry O'Hennessey's body?'

'Specialist divers have been working on the area since first light,' Helen said. 'They think, with the speed of the currents, she could have travelled several miles downstream. It might be weeks before we find her.'

'Okay.' Alison crossed one leg over another. 'There is something I need to talk to you about,' she said, changing the subject. 'I don't want it repeated outside these four walls. I've been offered a position as chief constable for a neighbouring force.'

Helen felt her mouth drop. This, she hadn't been expecting. 'Which one?'

'That I can't say, I'm afraid, not until the announcement is made. It's been a long, gruelling process, but I found out yesterday. I'll be leaving in a couple of months when Superintendent Jenkins returns.'

'Congratulations,' Helen said. She considered Alison's recent roles. Being the face for the press strategy on a serial murder inquiry. Heading the forthcoming audit. Impressive positions, setting her up for the next notch on the ladder. 'That's wonderful news.' And she meant every word. Alison worked hard; she genuinely deserved the success.

'Thank you. I'm delighted, as you can imagine.' She looked down at her hands a second, her expression turning grave. 'Now, I see you've declared a personal association with Chilli Franks.'

'His nephew is in the same class as my son,' Helen said, trying to make light of it. 'They share friends. It's precautionary, really.'

Alison narrowed her eyes. 'Are you sure it's a good idea?'

'To report an association with Franks's extended family? I don't see I have any choice. He led an organised crime gang in Hampton for years, had fingers in lots of pies.'

'All right. I won't lie to you, Helen, this does muddy the waters somewhat with Chilli's upcoming trial. I should advise you to tread carefully, especially with the history your families share.'

'It's an acquaintance,' Helen said. 'I'm following protocol.'

Alison unfolded her hands and sat tall. 'Well, naturally, I'll do everything I can to play this down to the chief. Make it something and nothing. Luckily, he's still revelling in the result on Operation Allen. That'll distract him awhile. Though I'm sure I don't need to tell you that anything you can do to deter this…' she cleared her throat, '… this friendship, would be greatly appreciated.'

Helen levelled her gaze. She wasn't thrilled about the association either, but unless she saw a hint of danger or a detrimental effect on her son, she wasn't about to intervene.

'Right,' Alison said, piling up the papers on her desk to indicate an end to the conversation. 'If there's nothing else, I think I'll head off. My partner's booked a table at Sacks for eight.'

Helen raised a brow. Sacks was a classy restaurant, off Hampton High Street. Very exclusive. 'Looks like we're celebrating,' Alison said.

CHAPTER 68

'Higher!' Ollie shouted.

Marnie helped Charlotte jump down from the climbing frame and looked across at their grandson.

'Push forward with your feet like I showed you,' Darren said, 'and the swing will pick up speed.'

'You push too, Grandad.'

Charlotte climbed on the roundabout with another little girl. Marnie leaned against the railings. It was a clear day, the sky a cornflower blue. Friday – their day to do the school pickup. She'd toyed with cancelling after the news this morning, but Darren refused. 'We need to keep things normal for the kids,' he had said. 'They're our priority.' And he was right.

The visit from the superintendent, the revelation about the arrest, followed her around like a shadow. So much grief. So much heartache. Any relief that the murderer had been apprehended was tempered by the fact that he had once been connected to a member of their own family.

A lump climbed into Marnie's throat as she pictured Tom, the little boy with the blue eyes and fair curls. When social services had contacted her, all those years ago, she'd had reservations about taking him in and raising him as their own. He was only a few months old. What had he been through? She'd read about babies of addicts inheriting their addiction, sometimes having learning difficulties or developing behavioural problems. But she couldn't bring herself to turn her back on him, and he wasn't with them for long before he'd captured her heart. After a few weeks, he'd settled into such a restful baby. Later, a sweet-natured, kind child.

She swallowed, fighting back tears as she thought of Shauna. Her complex, secretive daughter. So independent. So headstrong. She imagined her, all those years later, striking up a relationship with Kerry. Did Kerry introduce Shauna to sex work? They'd never know now. But one thing was for sure. Shauna wasn't to know that Kerry had hooked up with a felon who'd suffered an abusive upbringing. An upbringing that had damaged him and coloured his outlook on the world. A toxic relationship that would result in Kerry's death, and the death of her own daughter and others like her. Even Kerry, for all her faults, could never have known the danger she'd placed herself in.

At least her tweet about the pentagram hadn't caused any more deaths…

She watched her granddaughter sitting with the other little girl in the middle of the roundabout, chatting while it slowed.

That morning, Aidan had told the children that the bad man who killed their mum was behind bars and couldn't hurt anyone else. Yet they'd still gone to school, still come out to play, their resilience astonishing. The grief would come out eventually. It had to. The school had offered counselling. Their teachers were keeping an eye on them. Marnie just needed to make sure she was there for them. She wouldn't allow their lives to be tainted by the past. She couldn't.

'Grandma, watch me!' Charlotte said. She'd left the roundabout and was on the climbing frame now, swinging upside down from a rail like a monkey.

Marnie's heart was in her mouth. Her instincts screamed at her to run over, catch her, pull her down. But a tiny voice inside held her back. Her grandchildren needed space to grow, to spread their wings. Despite what had happened, Shauna would never have wrapped up her children in cotton wool. And now she was gone, it was Marnie's job to make sure that didn't happen.

'Get a photo!' Charlotte shouted.

Marnie reined in her nerves, retrieved her phone from her pocket and approached her granddaughter. 'Well done, you!' she exclaimed. 'Clever girl.' She switched her phone to camera and clicked.

CHAPTER 69

Alison's words rang in Helen's ears as she peeled the photos of the women off the incident room noticeboard and placed them in the box beside her. She didn't see any reason why Davy Boyd's family should suffer for his half-brother's actions. It did leave her with a dilemma though. If she was called as a witness at Chilli's trial, her name would be reported in the press. And if they linked her father's case, the full details would come out. Sooner or later, she'd have to speak with Robert, and finally share the family history.

She pushed the thoughts aside and looked down at the pictures in her hands. Four women. Four corpses. Ordinarily, her team would be celebrating now. Sharing a pizza, raising a glass. But, today, she'd sent them home early, the usual frivolities suspended.

Police work was all about tragedy; Helen knew that. Tragedy and agony. Dealing with difficult people. Sometimes psychopathic, occasionally evil, and every incident left its scar. Most cops were proficient at tucking the tragedy away in the backs of their minds, making jokes between themselves to push through. But they weren't inured, and every now and then, a case came along that took its toll and drained them of all defences. Worming its way inside, dredging up emotions. And this investigation, with its multiple deaths of

311

innocent women, leaving a string of young children to grow up motherless, was one of them.

They needed time away. To be with friends and families. Roll about the floor with their children in mock combat. Walk their dogs across open fields, suck the fresh air into their lungs and be at one with nature.

Helen pulled down the maps, folded them and placed them in the box. There was so much work to be done. Evidence to record, files to build. The divers were still out searching for Kerry's body. The ghosts of this investigation would linger for a while. But at least when her staff returned on Monday, it would be to a fresh and clean incident room.

She folded the flaps over the top of the box, carried it into her office and placed it down. As she hauled herself up, her elbow inadvertently caught a file on the edge of her desk. Helen cursed as it slipped off, the papers spilling out and splashing to the floor. The audit file.

She dropped to her knees, looked at the reports and spreadsheets. Another project that needed sorting. But not today. She shoved the papers back into the file and placed it on her desk. The audit could wait. Right now, there was somewhere else she needed to be. She grabbed her jacket off the back of the chair and headed out of the office, closing the door behind her.

* * *

The late afternoon sun bounced off Helen's windscreen as she pulled into Leddington School car park. It was just after 4 pm and, with most children and teachers left for the day, spaces were available in abundance. As she climbed out of the car, a distant cheer filled the air. Helen smiled. Another evening. Another cricket match for her son, this time a friendly with a local school.

Robert wasn't expecting her. She was supposed to be at work. He wasn't expecting anyone to be there; her mother had a routine dental appointment.

A round of applause sounded. Helen made her way around the school building, to the sports field behind, and found the match in full flow. She squinted through the sunshine and recognised the batsman as one of Robert's teammates from last Saturday. St Edmund's were batting. Leddington kids were scattered about the field like a series of statues in their cricket whites. A couple of wooden gym benches lined the side of the pitch, filled with families and friends, bags strewn haphazardly at their feet.

A bronzed woman in shorts and T-shirt, who looked like she was just back from holiday, slid up to make space for Helen on the end of a bench.

Helen thanked her and sat. 'Where are we?' she asked. There was no scoreboard.

'St Edmund's second batsman was just bowled out,' the woman whispered. 'By my son!' She glanced sideways at Helen, her eyes shining. 'Ouch, what happened to your nose?'

Helen had almost forgotten the bruise which had now turned a fetching shade of purple. She waved it away. 'Walked into a door.' *How many times had she heard that in the line of duty?* She chuckled to herself, ignoring the woman's disbelieving stare as she placed her bag at her feet and searched for Robert. She spotted him, dazzling in his cricket whites, sitting amongst a crowd of others on the grass opposite. He hadn't noticed her. He was focused on the match.

The next over passed by. Helen folded back her cuffs and revelled in the warmth of the sun, soaking into her forearms. The tension in her neck eased a notch. She was looking around absently when a boy leaning against the school wall caught her eye and waved. Sandy hair. The same glistening smile. Zac. Still in his St Edmund's school uniform. Here to cheer on his friends. Alison's earlier comments tripped into her mind. She ignored them, waved back, gave a half-smile. Searched for his father, shoulders easing when she couldn't spot him. She wasn't quite ready to face Davy Boyd yet.

A cheer brought her back to the present. The game. The batsman had been caught out. Another round of applause.

A glance at Zac. He'd moved across to the St Edmund's crowd. Was talking to Robert, waving his hands animatedly. They both laughed. An intimate moment of close friendship.

Robert stood and made his way to the pitch amidst cheers from his teammates. Helen watched him, pride filling her chest. In that moment, he suddenly looked grown-up, older than his fourteen years. She was just marvelling at this when he turned, spotted her and beamed from ear to ear. He lifted the bat, gave her a nod and her heart filled to bursting.

If the job had taught her anything, it was to hold on to these moments. Hold on to them and cherish them. Whatever the future brought.

Helen stood and gave a whoop. 'Go, Robert!' she yelled.

ACKNOWLEDGEMENTS

First, I'd like to thank my website manager, Richard Bland at Bhambrabland, for giving me an insight into how websites are built and put into action. As always, any errors or discrepancies are my own.

Also, to my dear friend Philip Bouch for his insight and knowledge on cricket. You'll be pleased to hear, I'm keen to go to a match now!

To my agent, Caroline Montgomery at Rupert Crew – I love working with you!

Gratitude to Cari Rosen and Ross Dickinson for their keen editing eyes, and also to Lauren Parsons, Tom Chalmers, Lucy Chamberlain and all the gang at Legend Press for believing in this novel, the fourth in the DCI Helen Lavery series, and championing it.

One of the nicest things about writing books is the wonderful ongoing support from the writing and reading community online. (I've said this many times because it means so much!) The authors who keep me sane – you know who you are! The wonderfully supportive book clubs: Anne Cater and all at Book Connectors; Shell Baker and Lainy Swanson at Crime Book Club; Tracy Fenton, Helen Boyce and all at The Book Club (TBC); David Gilchrist and Caroline Maston at UK Crime Book Club; Susan Hunter and the guys at Crime

Fiction Addict; Wendy Clarke and the gang at The Fiction Café Book Club. Also, to the reviewers and book bloggers – far too many to mention individually – who work tirelessly to spread the word about new books. I'm truly privileged to be part of such a lovely world.

So many friends have listened to my musings and generally offered a shoulder to lean on. Most notably, Colin Williams, Ian Robinson, Rebecca Bradley and Abi Bouch. And my dear local author friends Nicky Peacock and Sue Bentley who fill me with tea and cake and joviality regularly.

To David and Ella. I often say that living with a writer is never easy. You listen to ideas, discuss characters and humour me daily, and I'll always be grateful for your support.

Finally, to you, the reader. This marks my tenth year in publishing, and I'm honoured that you continue to support me on this crazy journey. Thank you from the bottom of my heart.

IF YOU ENJOYED WHAT YOU READ,
DON'T KEEP IT A SECRET.

REVIEW THE BOOK ONLINE AND TELL
ANYONE WHO WILL LISTEN.

THANKS FOR YOUR SUPPORT SPREADING
THE WORD ABOUT LEGEND PRESS.

FOLLOW US ON TWITTER
@LEGEND_TIMES_

FOLLOW US ON INSTAGRAM
@LEGEND_TIMES